Tūla

Jurgis Kunčinas

Tūla

Translated by
Elizabeth Novickas

PICA PICA PRESS

Sections of this translation have been previously published in *The Dedalus Book of Lithuanian Literature,* on www.kuncinas.com and on www.vilnius-review.com.

The translation of this book was funded by a grant from the Lithuanian Culture Institute.

www.picapica.press
Flossmoor, Illinois

As spring comes to life
so I sprang away
God sent you here for me,
Just not me for you!

JONAS AISTIS

I

Speak to me, Tūla, whisper to me, when the illuminated high wall of the Bernardine, as red as it already is, glows redder still; when the Vilnelė boils like lava under all of its little bridges, and most furiously of all right here, next to the Bernardine; when the scarce passersby, spotting the heavy rain cloud, hasten their steps, and, looking around fearfully, scurry off to their urban burrows; when the cloud hangs now right nearby—above Bekešo and Panoniečio Hill, above the dark red folds of the escarpment—speak, and tell me: Who now will remind us of the love that clung to us like an infectious disease, never, as it was, bellowed out in the midwinter courtyards, and so never splattered with the city's dirt—so belated and so useless it was to anyone, useless even to this street prepared for a downpour, to the clump of old trees on the shore, even to the glow lighting up the Bernardine, or that ever approaching cloud, which has stopped now above the drab Bekešo tower—who, come on, say it, who?

Tell me, Tūla, tell me, because only you can answer these questions hanging like those clouds—only you, because nature in the city is always a bit unreal; too grand or what?—and mute. Not quite decoration, not moulage, not a theater prop, but not nature, either. I'm telling you. Look, Tūla, I'm coming to your humble abode over the uncovered Vilnelė bridge, under which the blackish-green water with its barely lighter foam constantly boils; I'm coming to your windows, to your eyes, which reflect nothing but the low sky and the steeples of the Bernardine; I'm coming to your tissues, to the clarity of your bones, to your primeval nerves, which, when touched, tremble and sound of the murmur of the wind, the tinkling of water, the rustling of grass. Bumped a bit harder, they stiffen, and the sounds strengthen—I hear the squeal of a small, unexpectedly frightened animal, the voice of a nocturnal bird stubbornly explaining something; I hear the fluttering of wings above my head and I see eyes—the mysterious eyes of a bird of twilight in your face as white as a sheet; your eyes, Tūla, the eyes of a bird and the eyes of a cloud: I'm coming in the light of the moon, throwing a heavy shadow on the day that has passed, on the day to come and the night of ours to come, on this city, which has sucked us into its dark womb and spat us out together with the silt, the clay, all sorts of shards and old tools, and old coins, too, which have no power in either this world or the next—did we ever really live in it? And I throw a broken, twisted shadow on the hill of Békés and his commander Vadas of Pannonia, where that menacing cloud full of storm dust goes on hanging...

Your dwelling, Tūla, hung with faded pictures where bread molds and flocks of gentle animals graze; it's crammed with boxes and books, albums of art reproductions, all sorts of notes, clothes, boxes with voices and memories; an abode where the plumbing frequently chokes and hardened wine in the old goblets of the pictures subsides into reddish crystals. I come to your barely open dry lips, beyond which yawns the black space of the mouth—there where your words, the ones uttered slowly, almost by the syllable, are hiding themselves—they're all important to me, to me alone; speak, Tūla: They rise, after all, from the very depths, from all of the places inside your flat, patient body, worn out by lethargy, suffering, illnesses, and indifference...

Speak to me, Tūla, tell me, remind me; whisper when I come in the middle of the night, with the Old Town dogs whining trustfully as I cut across the ghostly Olandų Street thruway and through the damp little yards of Filaretų Street, emerging like a ghost on the Polocko straightaway across from the Bernardine graveyard—this

entire disagreeable little world is linked only to you, Tūla, and the
Bernardines, although they've been gone a long time now... Who
says they're gone? With my footsteps in the slushy snow seemingly
drafting a topographic map of this quarter, past the mutt market, the
pharmacy, the fish and shoe stores, I descend to you, I descend and
emerge on the icy shore of the Vilnelė, and the entire old part of
the city, lit up by the moon, really does look like an old city plan,
meticulously drawn and colored by some sort of higher being. I'm
here now, here, while above Bekešo Hill that broad cloud goes on
hanging, surely frozen already into the sole of a shoe and hardened
like a gray slab of cement—it has now, out of what was once pure
drops of rain, turned into a prophet of corporeal disaster, while I go
on to you, ignoring not just the cold, but the despair, the late hour,
the blind man with dark glasses standing by the bridge's railing; by
now no longer making out the bridges, I step into the foaming, rag-
ing water and, slipping on the polished stones, I clamber up to your
shore, Tūla, and it seems to me that a huge lilac bush gleams blue
above my head—I pick the blossoms, and in each hand hold a lilac
bouquet as fluffy as a spotless white cloud—intoxicating, curly, overflowing with life, dripping in silver streams—and, swaying from
exhaustion, I go in the white double door, on which hangs a modest,
bullet-ridden blue mail box, and now I am, Tūla, barely a few steps
away from you, from your husky voice, the fibers of your body, your
most secret little corners...

Whisper softly, breathe so quietly I can barely hear it as I fly
in through the air vent, opened just a crack for the night, clasping
both enormous bouquets of lilac, as I now swoop under the vault—
a soundless bat—without a sound, without a rustle; all the words of
love and despair hermetically sealed within the skull of a tiny, flying,
nocturnal creature, careful not to scare off the other spirits waiting to
seize your soul, body, mind, your most secret thoughts, your dignity
and your tears, your small breasts trembling like a ripple in a stream,
all of you, Tūla; I fly in, and with my little feet clinging to the slanting

vault of your room I listen to you breathe, to the hoarfrost melting on your alveoli, to the blood turning one more cycle of circulation inside your sleepy body, to you, not realizing it yourself, speaking to the bread molding in the picture, to the boxes full of memories; in the moonlight I see your long bones, your pelvic bones, the pearly skull under the short hair: I see how some kind of small, brightly shining bug walks over your stomach, falls into the hollow of your belly button and can't crawl out of it—that's how small it is...

My sensitive nostrils, overstrained by the city, quiver, but I no longer have any spare exits, I have no spare feelings, no spare parts in my imperfect little bat body; perhaps that's why my love is so short—so intoxicating and so unalloyed—a love that can neither lose anything anymore, nor overcome anything; so that's why I watch over you, together with the lilacs, on the ceiling above your shallow cot: I see you, in your dreary sleep, throw your arm aside, uncover the trembling expanse of the heart, and then, then, entirely unexpectedly, a bluish cluster of lilac with two green leaves falls on your chest. I wave my little leathery wings, and now the lilacs fall like rain—in clusters, tufts, little twigs: violet, greenish, hardened into clots of blossoms; soft lilacs, you know, the kind that bloom and wilt in the overgrown garden plots outside the city where farmsteads used to stand, next to the woods, on foundations that have already crumbled...

The lilacs fall, spinning around in the cold air, spreading blossoms over your hair, falling into your unwept tears, sticking to your barely open mouth, winding in strands around your slender neck, darkening on your belly, falling over your bed, the floor, the boxes with dusty albums and memories, descending into the pitcher with water left for the night, while other clusters, bouquets, blooms, failing to find a place to settle, spin a bit longer, and then disintegrate into tiny stars, so much like the fantastic creatures in the depths of the sea. And I dive into the darkness and crash painfully into the window—that would never happen to a real bat! I smile and curl my lip, while black blood oozes from the tiny mouse snout. No one sees where it drips… And where is that? The black blood drips on your bed, unwillingly soaks through the fabric, and now it's dripping onto the black clinker tiles under your eternal cot, Tūla, Tūla…

Lying on my back on the grayish window sill, I see the cloud lying on Bekešo Hill suddenly stir and descend, whistling, at an impossible speed, straight at the house with an apse on the bank of the Vilnelė, straight at us, at you, Tūla, at me…

II

Back then Tūla lived between two little bridges—a covered modern one, leading to the door of Tūla's former Institute, and a utilitarian concrete one across from the old Bernardine monastery. Tūla used to walk to her rented abode and to the foggy city on that one—she no longer had any business with the Art Institute. And I headed into the dark womb of Užupis only on the concrete one—for a long time I didn't even suspect that in the only building with an apse sticking out between those two sturdy, relatively new bridges she, Tūla, took shelter, flitting by there mornings and evenings, leading her guests: painters with shaved heads and sideburns, or girlfriends, fellow art lovers, who resembled peeling frescoes.

From a distance the covered bridge looked downright smart; in bad weather I would see young couples, dressed in wide cloaks and narrow pants barely coming to their ankles, pause on it. Professors with Basque berets or hunter's hats, small and wrinkled but aware of their worth, trotted across it, too; frequently my acquaintance would fly past too, the tall graphics lecturer with a mustache so lush it covered nearly half his long face—only the Germans accurately call foliage like that *Schnauzbart*, snout-hair.

Poverty, despair, drunken songs, spring thaws, fog as purple as spilled ink, and the pale blooming of the gone-to-wild lilacs flowed out of Užupis only via the second, cement bridge. In those days, massive dump-trucks still splashed across it too; the government didn't plan the little bridge for the comfort of plebeians and den-keepers, but so it'd be closer for ferrying bricks, framework, and slabs while constructing the art buildings. Everything an island of art in a sea of poverty needed. But the construction dust settled down and the smell of new settlements faded too; once more it gave off whiffs of soot, soap suds, cat shit, and just a tiny bit of Užupis's lilacs. Burdock doesn't smell, does it, Tūla will say to me after a string of years; we'll be lying in the burdock beyond the Institute, spitting at the water and the stars, everything will be drunk up, and I don't drink blood and tears! I'm the one who will say that. And furthermore—I won't grind my teeth anymore, I'll have you know! Or maybe not like that. Maybe I'll just put my muddy hand on her frog-like, cat-like, or lizard-like stomach, and those five fingers of mine—all that emaciated palm—will soak in, will remain impressed into her flat body until death itself, and after death… You might see that kind of impression in ice age rocks, after you've torn off the moss and lichens. Or maybe not there anymore, either. Maybe not anymore.

It's terribly difficult for me to unwind this caked-on bandage from the trees, the bushes, the hills, from the swarms of people of that time. To scrape the bloody plaster and whitewash the vault above the tower of Bekešo. It's not the kind of work I'm up for, and it isn't my business either, because time, caught between Tūla's ribs, hanging onto the cobwebs of those days, wound into her boxes of threads and needles, into the pleats of her dresses and jackets, covered with dust in her boxes of naive drawings and carefully recorded notebook of dreams, is no longer mine now; nor the convulsively wracked faces of her sophisticated shaved-head and fresco-faced friends, artificially spiritual would-be officials and suicides, not even that impostor lithographer with the colorless eyelashes and hair as white as boiled salt. Malicious Poles have an accurate word for that purpose, they call them *swinski blond*, something like "blond swine," but no… not like that…

Something inside me always stirs—today too—as soon as I see those two bridges again, the long Bernadine monastery, the narrow gap in the enfilade of little yards, and the little gateway, beyond which spread the real intestines and cloacae of Užupis—how much of it's been walked over with stumbling feet, not with Tūla, without Tūla, still not knowing Tūla, and then afterwards... how much this place has been staggered over, and in the mornings, grimly plodded along. It's doubtful whether I have even so much as a theoretical right of spiritual inheritance to this riverbank with its dreary buildings, to the nettles, the burdock, the artemisia, and the inedible mushrooms—the crumbly, flaccid kind—overgrowing the slope to Tūla's house, which, of course, never belonged to her either, just as the long monastery building never belonged to my combative aunt Lydija, her gentle husband the policeman, and my American cousins Florijonas and Zigmas—all of them lived there in poverty during the years of the German occupation. Did they really live in poverty? Aunt sewed, the policeman uncle built stools, and the cousins attended the preparatory school next to Saint Casimir's Church. Nowadays they're both still lively old men (gray or bald?) but only Florijonas, the Chicagoan, when he flew into Vilnius, rushed down to the long building at dawn with a movie camera, circled around it several times, ran over both new bridges as well, and took off headlong back to the hotel—he was expected on an excursion specified by Intourist's carefully calculated plans.

Ma'am, one blindingly golden fall—maybe last year?—I asked a woman with an eagle face hanging out laundry, ma'am, excuse me... didn't you live here during the war? As I said this, I waved at the long monastery beyond her hunched shoulders. I did, I sure did, the Lithuanian woman answered unexpectedly, and what of it? Then did you... I began, and shut my mouth: it wasn't the fumes of Tokay that came out of my hungry mouth, but the stench of Izabella, ordinary, quintessential rotgut—nineteen proof and five percent sugar, a classic! She continued to gaze after me for a long time from the covered gallery: an old, tired eagle.

You see, I'm not talking about Tūla anymore, not about the brown fur jacket she was wearing the first time I saw her, not about

her phlegmatic brother and that brother's arrogant buddies, but
about an eagle, rotgut, a New York cousin who married a real German, Lotta, and his small children in Albany, New York, who probably used to thank him after getting a treat by saying "*Danke, Vati*—
Thank you, father!" Now those children have children themselves,
and Zigmas I saw only once, twenty-one years ago; he wasn't an old
man yet. Apparently, he did well in his studies, cut pulpwood in
Germany, worked hard when he got himself to America—at first,
of course, like all the displaced persons. But Zigmas didn't come to
heave a sigh next to the monastery.

So, Florijonas and Zigmas, my real, true cousins—they still
remember my grandfather Aleksandras whom I never saw, who collapsed by the well in 1944 and never got up again—they'd hurry
to their high school, steeped in dusk, over the other little bridge; it
stands there yet today—serious and solid, with cast iron railings from
the time of the Tsar and ageless embankments of rough-hewn stone
on both sides. If, on occasion, you're in a hurry coming from the
direction of Old Town, then, running over that bridge, you immediately end up in Malūnų Street; dash under the arch, and you're
home already. On the way, a nearly round electrical transformer
from Pilsudski's days still juts out—or maybe that's a Pilsudskian
telephone substation?—but if, finding yourself there, you should go
looking for a foreign spirit, there it is: a little island of Russia in Vilnius's liver, begun by Grand Duchess Uliana, ceaselessly perfected
by the Orthodox community through decades and centuries—*Pre-
chistenska Sobor,* the Orthodox Church of the Holy Mother of God. It
is a pretty church, even if it's as stocky as a country market wrestler;
I've stood next to its great iconostasis and pulled its bitter incense
into my nostrils while Tūla pulled at my sleeve and whispered: Let's
get out of here, let's go, look, the old women are muttering already,
they're glaring at us, let's go… No one was glaring at us, not in the
least; then we went out and headed down along the river. I kept leaning on the metal railings—not the bridge's, the bank's: you can still
see some like that next to the Arsenal and across from the covered

bridge—nice, dear railings, when your feet slide and tangle themselves, how good it feels to put your hot palms on them and instead of smelling cold air soaked in incense, a blast of wind takes your breath away. The same kind of dark railings, but on the other side of the Vilnelė, were visible outside Tūla's windows; she was living at Petryla's then, in the house with an apse, it was just that we so rarely looked out through those windows. But when we did glance out, the first thing we would see was the Bernardine Church, as massive as a blast furnace, melting in the glow—at that time, it was some five years after my distant friend, the black-bearded Jurgis, covered its roof with tiles as bright as the red flag above the Party headquarters. Jurgis wasn't a roofer, no, he was the work supervisor; he would stand below, his thick head set on a stocky body turned upward, and shout: Hey! It's not lunch time yet, why are you climbing down!? Jurgis, I'd say, when, together with him and his drudges, we'd snack on vodka with canned sprats in tomato sauce in the narrow office under a cut-glass vault, Jurgis, what do you mean, playing the idiot that way? Jurgis, dark, bearded, and as grim as Gáspár Békés, wouldn't even smile, wouldn't start whining that there wasn't money, or that the craftsmen were worthless, and these—he'd point to the young roofers—winos! Have a drink, have a drink, it's your turn now, was all he would mutter, let's go, guys! Jurgis was already marked with the waxy sign of death, don't tell me he didn't realize it himself? That cold wax in his reddish face was so obvious. Maybe he didn't want to know? But Jurgis managed to cover the roof anyway—it was the first thing I would see on leaving one of those "soviet" hospitals by the Missionary Church, where I used to visit Uncle Hans after his first stroke; that time he got well quickly, the prognosis was excellent. I'd pause there every time, in the little square next to the old corpus of another former monastery: on a sunny day all of the barely visible city would glimmer, but your eyes would instantly find the red Bernardine roof of their own accord—it was my and Tūla's close neighbor, and the late bearded Jurgis roofed it. Jurgis died, and eight years later his drudges so tore up the church's walls, scraped them so badly—they call that work probing!—that another time, when I stopped by to see Dionyzas, Jurgis's successor (also a great guy, a slow-talking debauchee, apparently a distinguished economist), I just couldn't find my inscription from those days anymore... and after all, at the time I had used green oil paint to write—drunk, of course—her name, in letters nearly a meter high, supposedly translated into some foreign language—THULLA! Yes, with an exclamation point and two l's. Who was it who grabbed the paintbrush out of my hands and started yelling at me? Maybe Jurgis himself? I don't remember anymore.

Tūla's poor house beyond the little "freight" bridge: the Orthodox churches and abbeys surround it today as they did a century ago—all of them much smaller than our Bernardine blast furnace, all of them more graceful—with glittering little steeples, spikes, and brick drapery—St. Anne's most of all, of course; not at all long ago, going up to it, I rubbed the devil on its door handle—his blunt, wide forehead—with my thumb. Maybe you know, O devil, what Tūla is doing now? An inhabitant of the chthonic world, an old idiot, but in other respects, a very dear creature on the door's metal ring... Do you know anything?

In the old days, when I awoke in the night and slurped some flat beer, all I would see out Aurelita Bonopartovna's window was the calm and gentle silhouette of the Blessed Virgin Mary the Consoler Church—the very tip of the spire and a part of the graceful tower. Aurelita Bonopartovna slept in the other room with her young daughter Ewa Gerbertovna, while at night in the kitchen their mother and grandmother Helena Brzostowska would drink red wine thinned with boiled water, listen to Penderecki and Vivaldi records, and sit up until dawn carving ritual masks out of blocks of linden, masks that were full of evil fantasies—of Mardi Gras, Japanese, and Užupis inhabitants. But no, maybe I made it up. Only one thing is for sure: awaking in the night, I'd immediately see the little triple-nave church's tower—apparently I knew it was a triple-nave. It was vivid even in the darkest sky. I knew a lot more—it had been a long time since the old lady Daszewska lived next to the Virgin Mary the Consoler, with her slutty daughters and crazy son Tadek who went nuts the day he was bested at the open ring final in Philharmonic Hall—it wasn't just his fiancée Angonita Brandys who abandoned him, but all of his friends and drinking buddies. That happened in 1956, right after the 20th Communist Party Congress—when talking about this event to me and my colleague Teodoras von Četras, *pani* Daszewska always mentioned the Congress. She was in the Hall herself at the time, so it's not surprising that every time she remembered her beaten-to-a-pulp son (when the fight was over, someone thrashed him in the locker room too), the old lady's voice trembled. Zofia, a suburban letter-carrier and a great one for nookie, understood her brother's insanity completely differently: listen, Tadek went crazy from eau de cologne and acetone glue in jail; you can see for yourself how puny he is, what a puke pack he is! But young Maria, who used to get me and Teodoras cheap socks from her Sparta factory, the beautiful Mariana, with whom we would dance at the Arklių Club, the dreary dance hall belonging to the Interior Ministry, avoided talking about her little brother entirely. The biography of *pani* Daszewska, widow of a legionnaire *chorąży* or ensign, in "our" time already a wrinkled and slovenly but still energetic and crazy old lady, would perhaps be worth further study, even though I don't doubt that most people would much rather read the spicy memoirs of the late letter carrier Zofia—no, no, not about the tiresome delivery of letters and newspapers, not about the mean mutts of Filaretų and Olandų Streets—what else then, but her neverending, dangerous, and breath-taking adventures in bed! Actually, Zosia in her youth was as pretty as a church painting—the pictures prove it!—but to us, *Almae Matris Vilnensis* liberal arts graduates taking shelter in one corner of the Daszewska den in the fall of 1967, she no longer, unfortunately, looked as charming and seductive as she had, for example, to the Soviet cadets of 1949, or to the boxing trainer who, they say, talked Tadek into fighting with the trained soldiers in the garrison's club. Zosia liked to stop by our little room, separated from the stinking kitchen by a width of flowered cotton, sit on the creaking stool and, puffing on a cigarette, start reminiscing. Četras and I tried to fix her up with Francas, a well-fed French student who was always desperate for a woman, but when he saw Zosia, Francas vanished backwards from the door, and he practically never stopped by our furnished hole anymore, even though Zosia always asked: *nu, gde vash tot usach*—well, where's your bewhiskered one? I had already lost Tūla (did I ever have her?) when I discovered, quite unexpectedly, that in this very same tiny little room where I with my colleague Četras once wasted pleasant days of half-starvation with the alley cats, the rats scurrying under the floor, and Tadek wailing one minute and cackling the next, yes, in the very same den, in 1907 I believe, Mikalojus Čiurlionis once lived, the one and only officially recognized (even by the Russians!) genius of our nation. When I found this out, I got the urge to find von Četras, buy a bottle or two of some more decent wine, and go to that courtyard—all of the Daszewski family, excepting maybe Mariana and her kids, had died out already—to glance once more at the black window frames and the copper door handle that had survived through some miracle, and at least try to imagine the genius's silhouette in the gateway or pressing that handle... wine helps, doesn't it? But as it turned out, Teodoras was away in Vienna—I guzzled down the wine under the Daszewski windows with some scabby guy. When we finished, he started demanding more, and I barely managed to escape. Once more I turn in circles, just so I won't have to immediately reveal everything about Tūla, about THULLA with two l's. Tūla, whose name I wrote in six-foot letters of green paint on the narrow wall of the Bernadine shrine, not far from the Great Altar...

I had managed, back then, to write only one German word, of my own invention, *"VOLKSHÜTTE,"* on *pani* Daszewska's wooden, never-locked door with the copper handle. It was supposed to mean something along the lines of "The people's shack." I thought it sweet and pretty. *Pani*, I remember, got upset immediately—hey, this word seemed to prove our pretensions, or even intentions, of taking over her dwelling! The old lady calmed down only when Uncle Hans, a theoretical physicist and Teodoras's uncle, stopped by on his usual visit. I don't know if I've ever met a nicer person. A politician, a gentleman with a terribly sharp tongue who knew all of Vilnius's elite and demimondes. Uncle Hans took *pani* by the hand, led her into our tiny little room, poured her a brimming cut-glass tumbler of wine as bluish as potassium permanganate, with his wet lips smacked her dirty little hand, and immediately convinced her that the *khlopchiki*, that is, we rascals, were just joking, no one had any intentions on her mansion! The old lady backed down at once—*dobrze, dobrze*—fine, fine! After another glass, she started giggling unattractively and hanging onto Uncle Hans as if she were sixteen instead of seventy. Uncle rather discreetly remarked that there really were people who wouldn't like that sign at all, but he himself laughed aloud, treated everyone to wine and Tresor cigarettes, and asked us to bring some real babes over—he was going to show them—in the dark!—some completely new conjuring trick he had just learned. The theoretic physicist wasn't indifferent to the arts; if he had as much as suspected that Čiurlionis had penned his fugues or painted his cosmos under this smoky vault the cockroaches fell from, he would have immediately written to the newspapers, or even brought some musician friend of his from the Neringa Restaurant over—look, Vaclovas, now what's this? But, like us, he didn't suspect it. Besides, if the genius really did live there, then it must have been in the big living room, where, in our time, *pani* Daszewska, her daughters, and strange men with tattooed chests slept on mattresses laid on the floor, along with the cats and the filthy children, and where sometimes Tadek, the unfortunate boxer from 1956, returning briefly from jail or the madhouse, would rave a while.

I had the chance to bring Tūla to this yard: I showed her the low window nearly even with the floor, through which cats streaked onto our study table—they would befoul the place and escape outside again. And the girls? Tūla narrowed her eyes, but I snorted: What for? The doors were open night and day anyway; I'd frequently find completely strange men and women there, even in my little bed: *pani* would say, it's just for a little while! And if you want to know, I told Tūla, the only ones who came to visit us were three singing English majors—Athos, Porthos, and Aramis—quiet, decent girls. We'd drink natural apple wine, sometimes beer; they would sing "My Bonnie Lies Over the Ocean," "Delilah," and maybe "Brave Abdullah the Dreadful Robber." Or else we'd just listen to Vanda Stankus's little songs—and then off they'd go!

At night, smoking under Aurelita Bonopartovna's pink window, I'd wander back many years; living in a city for nearly a quarter of a century, your glance, your footsteps, your dust and your residue remain in almost every little corner...

But the churches! The churches are paramount; at least they force you to turn your head upwards, and upwards there's always the heavens—low, ashy, grim, but the heavens all the same. When I see this bellowing neighborhood, flowing with blood, full of rats and people—a neighborhood of drifters, the poor, the sick, the disabled, the soul-starved (we're just feeble creatures, Uncle Hans liked to emphasize, there's no need to be ashamed of our weakness, physiology, or the flaws we've inherited from unknown ancestors!)—my neck flushes, my head starts spinning—no, no, not so much as a ray of sunshine! That's why there's churches. If they didn't force me to kneel and fold my hands in prayer, then at least, like I said, they lifted my eyes upward; in those days that was a great deal, to me at least.

I was a toy in the hands of Aurelita Bonopartovna, the maker of masks; I was her voluntary slave, whose slightest revolt had to end with expulsion from a relative paradise into the dirty street with the rats, cats, and the hulking figures standing all day long next to the mutt market and *Tėvo kapas*—Father's Tomb, nicknamed after the masoleum in Red Square—the beer stalls there gushed adulterated beer. I was the emotional Aurelita's whim—like all emancipated women's whims, it was short-lived and immediately forgotten. Neither Aurelita nor I gave the slightest thought to sparing ourselves: we partied like madmen, lived a closed night-time life, an almost closed daytime life, and only in the evenings were we open to sincere but trivial conversations, random guests, good wine. We'd wander through cemeteries, abandoned parks and basements, imagine we were being persecuted, easily talk ourselves into feelings, visions, and a great deal of similar things—you can read about it to your heart's content in second-rate translated novels. It's painful to write and say this, because I don't regret those days at all; like I said, my enslavement was voluntary! On those clear, moonlit Užupis nights, looking out Aurelita Bonopartovna's window—the yellow brick house stood on a hill—I kept thinking: the caprices will come to an end soon; I should make it easier on them—Aurelita and her household—I should drink even more, carouse, run riot—then they can throw me out into the street with a clear conscience; the weather is pleasant now, it would even be quieter! Helena Brzostowska will carry my books out to the woodpile herself; maybe she'd even make me a present of some mask... or maybe that *swinski* blond will immortalize us all? He's everywhere! After all, he's a photographer too, not just a lithographer. Is his surname Mishustin or Jevgrafov?

Although the little church of Saint Bartholomew juts out above Užupis's blackened roofs much closer than the Consoler, I couldn't see it through Aurelita's window—the trees and walls blocked the view. At night I would just feel how close it was, beyond the maples, the street's incline, the bristling tiles... During the day I would forget it, even though it was there, in Bartholomew's Church, that I spent the night drinking Tokay with Aurelita. Afterwards she left me there alone; I lounged about the nave crammed full of unfinished statues: wood carvers worked there. Beyond Aurelita's window, in the neighboring yard, a painful light would fall through the thickness of the maples during the day—sometimes even entire bursts of reddish-gold rays—while the neighbor's little girl with her name, Maria, knitted onto her chest would loudly call for her mother: "Mammmammmamm—Mammmammma!!" The stout, pretty, healthy five-year-old Maria was the work of a healthy, talented man who rarely showed up there. Hail, Maria! Her mother, as tiny as an ant, would immediately rush off the porch—later she would remind me about Tūla, it seems she knew her?—she'd snatch that heavy child up in her arms, and I easily believed that ants really do lift loads so and so many times their own weight. Maria would frequently throw back her little blond head and look at the window, where I, leaning out, whistled a melody from Carmen: Maria would literally shriek in glee, even though I have no ear and I'm a lousy whistler. Ewa Gerbertovna, Aurelita's daughter, a sweet, dark-haired little girl, would rock all day long on the swing hung between the doors; she gave me nothing but dirty looks, and when I came home once with a black eye, her eyes lit up: just what you deserve! The silly little thing apparently thought her father—a bricklayer, the leader of a Robin-Hood type group and an amateur philosopher—had thrashed me. No, I'd feel safe in that house only at night, smoking next to the window, sometimes with one ear catching a phrase of Penderecki's from the kitchen, where the old lady was still carving masks more horrible than even this life. If I had even suspected that Tūla lived on the bank next to the shoal, I would have immediately shinned down the chestnut's trunk and run over to her, not to the artist Herbert Stein, meditating all night long, not to the silkscreen master Valentinas Grajauskas, but only to her, to Tūla. But Tūla didn't live there yet. I hadn't met her yet. The shoal murmured only in the head of her landlord-to-be, the widower Petryla. But every day, drunk or sober, I'd walk across the concrete bridge past her windows-to-be; from the uncovered cellar across from that Pilsudski transformer I stole lumps of coal for the little stove in Aurelita's workshop and spoke to the eagle-woman—hadn't she lived here during the war, and if she did, then didn't she know my mother—you know, she lived in a carpenter's family, yes, he was a policeman too, yes, he moved here from Smalininkai, yes, my mother was a teacher at the Lab School, not far from the university, now there's a square there, a beer stall and toilets; you know it, don't you?

Yes, on that same bridge where the Americans to-be, my cousins Florijonas and Zigmas, hurried to their gymnasium, my mother, also to-be, walked across to classes at the Lab School. Today I think that perhaps their life in Malūnų Street wasn't perhaps so very grim; first of all, they weren't buried under a mass of information, and rumors frequently remained just that. Well, as long as airplanes didn't fly overhead, of course—for those who weren't pious, it was hard then. For my mother, for example. In general, Aunt Lydija was outrageously thrifty; this characteristic stood her in good stead in Irkutsk, and no one died of hunger there. I had the opportunity to experience Auntie's thriftiness myself—as gifts from Irkutsk she brought home not only cedar nuts, but several sport sweaters as well; one of them fit me perfectly, and the other my brother. Beautifully looked after, no moth holes; I'd never had one like that before. But they were from before the war, perhaps even worn by Florukas or Zigmutis!

The monasteries and all the churches survived, and here they bombed the Lab School—at the time my mother was praying in the chapel at the Gates of Dawn, truly a rare occurrence! Tūla's building was untouched, too. But there were no bridges to the Bernadine side yet. No, wait, wait! There was, of course there was! Didn't this unattractive old guy with round eyeglasses, cheap sandals, and a long, dark blue cloth coat take us, the freshmen, through old Vilnius? When he led our troop next to this cloister, he waved his arm—as thin as a willow switch!—at the foundations, green from age, right next to the shore, and proudly explained: Do you see? Once upon a time a covered wooden bridge stood here. When it burned down, the monks would go wading and wallowing across to prayers—yes, even to the very earliest ones! That's what that old man said, who, I later found out, was the author of an old textbook on Vilnius, a Latin scholar. When the field trip was over, in the churchyard of Peter and Paul we collected twenty kopeks apiece for him: the class leader, redheaded Onelė, presented it to him. Five rubles. For some new sandals. I couldn't get those monks out of my head for a long time, so much so, that during one military studies class (if I remember right, *ognevaya podgotovka*—firearm training), I wrote in a notebook with an orange cover:

At night it froze and snowed
The rumpled cot grew cold.
His habit lifted high,
The monk waded through the river.
He waded to the tall church,
Where the brothers prayed to God…
By accident his foot slipped,
The old monk fell down.
Like one of its own, he was carried off
by the furious stream, by time…
Only his bones glistened for a long while
Like a stripped-down willow…

By accident his foot slipped… What do I know!?

But even in those grim but not boring days I had looked over Tūla's future house, its second floor. Tūla, by the way, lived on the first floor, on the end where the apse is. When one day *pani* Daszewska made Teodoras and me give up Čiurlionis's low-arched room, when the rain had time to wash away the "expanded" writing *VOLKSHÜTTE. HIER WOHNEN ZWEI GERMANISTEN—* Folk cabin. Here live two German students—I stopped there first to ask about shelter. There, where twenty years later, completely unexpectedly, Tūla settled in, a young designer without a clue as to what she needed in this neighborhood, in Vilnius, or in the world…

One of Daszewska's daughters gave birth again (Lord, I nearly said calved!) to two more children—we had to do the twenty-three skidoo. I had already tied a couple of books and clothes into a bundle and looked over a different shelter under the autumn sky, when a lecturer of mine, Cecilia Perelstein, the passionate researcher of Western literature, urgently needed this rare book; I was quite possibly the only one in our university town with a copy. Iris Lorscheider Pohl, a young German woman I barely knew from Riesa, not far

from Dresden, had just sent me this prose collection of an expres-
sionist writer who had died young. The honorable lecturer had such
an itch to hold that book, smelling of Germany's post-war auster-
ity, in her slender bejeweled hands that it even occurred to her to
accompany me to the famous Daszewska-Čiurlionis yard next to the
Blessed Virgin the Consoler. It was just that little holiness was left in
this world now—church or not, hadn't it been used as a warehouse
since just after the war? Trucks and scooters dragging little silver
carts clattered over its threshold, so when the literature researcher
and I stepped into the *Volkshütte* yard, smelling of wash water, kerosene, and vinegar, I coughed quietly and asked, "Maybe you should
wait, professor, I'll just be a minute..." She just smiled understand-
ingly and whispered: "Yes, yes, of course!" Cecilia Perelstein was a
pretty, slender woman, wonderfully gracious, and didn't look Jewish
at all. Well, Jewish, but she could just as well have looked Spanish
or French. At the time she hadn't yet reached thirty, and I was still
under twenty. Who knows, it sometimes occurs to me, if she now,
in her sunny Haifa, hasn't at least once remembered this dilapidated,
washed-out, but immensely lively little corner of Vilnius? Perhaps.
But our visit continued like this: I quickly dived into the stinking
corridor: in the corner of the kitchen I saw the *pani* squatting over the
deep sink—it was already too difficult for Daszewska to get herself to
the nearby sewer, the yard's outhouse. I quickly found my rare book,
but when I ran out into the yard, the *pani,* fixing her sagging skirts
around her waist, was already sternly shaming my elegant guest in
passable Polish. Roughly like this: *lakhudra*—slut! What are you, you
tramtararam, doing visiting boys, huh? Go on, *tram tram,* go to the
Officers' Club, you'll find what you want there, *tram!* Even though
she was dreadfully pale, Cecilia Perelstein only smiled. The frames
of her glasses were very thin, but the glass was darkened—I couldn't
see the lecturer's eyes. I rushed to apologize, but she just thanked
me for the book and didn't say anything more. She was research-
ing modern literature—surely she had met similar old ladies there,
maybe even worse ones. She walked out as straight as the spire of the

Blessed Virgin the Consoler and didn't turn back once. It's unlikely she would have been comforted by the fact that the *pani* called her own daughters *gavno kusok*—piece of shit—and *zhopa negramotnaya*— illiterate ass—it's one thing to meet literary characters in books, and a completely different thing in a filthy courtyard.

Why did I remember Cecilia Perelstein when I was talking about Tūla? Well, it's because to me there's some resemblance between the two, not just the shyness, or the passive smile of someone who's bumped into life head-on. Perhaps the quiet nonchalance too—oh well, the world will never be perfect!—which isn't particularly characteristic of either Jews or Lithuanians. Or maybe some grandfather of Tūla's was a Tatar, or half Jewish at least? Unlikely, except perhaps for the one from my home town which, interjecting itself into the valley of the Nemunas, snoozed, scarcely visible, between Helsinki and Brest. By the way, I could have put it much more plainly— between Simnas and Daugai. Only much later did it become clear that I had confused Tūla's grandparents, her step-uncles, and even more distant relatives, whom I knew much better than I knew her—they were the ones who, regardless of their membership in the Communist Party, carried out their Christian duty and helped bury her—plumbers, dentists, judo trainers, and even security agents of that other government. I won't say anything more about them, even though I know that brown-haired plumber quite well. It's not necessary, since after all, if I hadn't come from that particular little town, if I hadn't known all that clan by sight at least—grandparents, gap-toothed handy uncles, the likable lady dentist, and the strict lecturer on the strength of materials—quite likely everything would have turned out a bit differently, perhaps even so differently that Tūla would still be alive today.

There's nothing to be done except make silly speculations, and here I'm standing on the covered bridge again, watching the workers slowly raising Tūla's former dwelling from the dead—tossing pieces of brick, smelly papers, tile debris, old shoes, and mattresses

with escaped springs out the windows: the only thing I don't see is
the unmatched chair I had left there. My head raised to the nettle-
covered slope, through the gray branches I think I can see the drawn
pink curtains in Aurelita Bonopartovna's window—she apparently
doesn't live there anymore, either. How close by everything here is!
But Aurelita, I heard, moved somewhere; maybe she even ran away,
but from what? I suppose there's nothing growing there but a truly
beautiful pale-faced girl who looks a little like a civilized Indian
and her great-grandmother Helena Brzostowska—the craftsman of
masks, a descendant of the Kiszka or Sobieski families. There they go
down the street—past the bakery, the produce store, the pharmacy
(do they have valerian drops in stock?), past the arch of the studio
belonging to the eternally young Herbert Stein (is there a wooden
grave marker still lying around under the window?), past the book
store, the gas office, Felix Dzerzhinsky's memorial plaque (so that's
where the future cannibal hid from the Tsar's Okhranka!), and turn
into that same courtyard of Tūla, aunt Lydija, the eagle, and other
personalities, into the Bernardine cloister's enfilade of little yards,
where dirty chickens are kept, where motorcycles are disassembled
and put back together again, where moonshine made from sugar is
distilled and sold, where each day the cultural (or some other) layer
thickens by at least a millimeter. Now the two of them are setting
foot on the "freight" bridge. In this gateway once, with a cold cres-
cent moon shining, the old lady helped me drag home a thrown-
away white dresser with an oval mirror, a little secret shelf and an
indentation for a wash basin—the work of a master craftsman! Now
the two of them are walking, a brisk, willful old age and a ripening
youth, both smiling, their faces reddened from the breeze, and the
chasm of time shrinks to the size of a perfectly ripened rowan berry,
or at least it looks that way at this dignified moment. They're greeted
by every other inhabitant of Užupis; they're greeted by that gray-
eared gentleman too, whom I used to snort at when I met him earlier,
but now I just smile. A professor of chemistry, a Communist Party
member—well, what of it? Dear departed Uncle Hans was right

when he said there's no need to be ashamed of either your weaknesses or your physiology! So why did I snort? Well, wasn't he the one, this honorable gentleman who didn't have the slightest intention of leaving his party, that Aurelita Bonopartovna and I stumbled upon one dark evening at the very foot of Bekęšo and Panoniečio Hill? Oh, I remember perfectly well why the two of us had snuck off there—she was the one who craved a bed of nature's green, and I, of course, didn't object. Then we crawled out from under the bushes wet from the rain, still breathing hard, pale, exhausted, holding each other's hand—if we fall, then together!—but Aurelita suddenly hissed, and her peg nose got sharper still: "Shh! Look!" I, her caprice, stood up behind her and put my hands around her bare, wet, belly. Then I saw, too: next to a low, brightly-lit window—the cottages there were literally crawling atop one another, cutting and carving into the slope—some man wearing a hat stood with a briefcase set between his legs. He stood there completely motionless, as if waiting for something. We could see his slightest movement—the slightest uncertain little twitch—but total darkness hid his face, that's how low the cottage window was! Beyond the uncovered window you could see a narrow kitchen, utensils, pots and pans—nothing out of the ordinary. But I saw the man's pants collapsed below his knees; with one hand, I suppose, he was holding his stiff rod. But I still didn't get it; after all, the two of us hadn't recovered yet from our green passions. Suddenly the man knocked on the window with his free hand—impatiently, or so at least it seemed to me—and stepped one step closer, literally pressing himself up against the bright glass. An inside door banged, a still-youngish woman quickly approached the window, gave a shriek, and the light immediately went out. We heard the relief in the man's breathing, he was panting even harder than we were; he deftly buttoned up his pants, straightened his hat, and grabbed his briefcase, nearly brushing us with his coat as he took off into crooked Baltasis Lane, where, under the Colonel's apartment, the windows of Aurelita Bonopartovna's garden apartment studio loomed in the dark—sometimes I believed that every other

person in Užupis had tied his fate to art and science, and to life—
every last one!

Later, from a distance, Aurelita pointed out that elegant-look-
ing man next to the underground toilet across from the mutt market, and still later I myself read somewhere that exhibitionism is, of
course, an unhealthy phenomenon traumatizing teenage girls, but,
compared to violence and other perversions, it's completely harmless
to both the exhibitionist and his victim. It's true—Aurelita pointed
out the woman too, an Užupis aboriginal: she was walking along
carrying two sacks of potatoes, cheerfully laughing at something—
no spiritual trauma!

The gray-eared professor (gray tufts of hair stuck out from his
ears) looked lively too, still upright and athletic, even if he was an ex-
communist. The briefcase was pure calfskin; the raincoat, let's say
it was white, with epaulettes and a fashionable pleat on the back. By
now he's a bit bent over, actually. Maybe he's shaken off that inappropriate habit? Hardly!

III

Why on earth did I wander off to Užupis again, which I could, in a certain sense, inherit? So I could find endless pretexts to justify my meanderings through the yards, cemeteries, slopes, half-basements and nooks? Maybe some part of my spiritual heritage really is hiding here somewhere? After all, I could look for that eagle-woman again, who said she remembered both the carpenter-policeman and his domineering wife Lydija, the polite and pious—but you wouldn't say unwholesomely religious—high school boys Florijonas and Zigmas, and even my arrogant cousin Domicėlė, who hated her "hick" name more than anything—surely she hates it to this day! All her life Domicėlė was convinced, and probably still is, that she never married only on account of her worthless name, although it seems to me it's really something else. I'm convinced it's my cousin's limitless pride that's to blame; her immoderate scorn, with no exceptions, for anything in pants and her hatred for married women. Domicėlė couldn't have inherited a hatred like that from her God-fearing parents—she developed it herself, or if she did inherit it, then probably from the ones I know nothing about; Aunt Lydija spoke of them only obliquely, that branch of our family, who, as far back as the middle of the nineteenth century, under persecution for confessing the Calvinist religion—Aunt's words!—ran from Salzburg to southwestern Lithuania, to Suvalkija, quickly assimilated there, and rapidly melted into the sea of Balts, Slavs, and Jews—the salty spray of this sea has most likely splashed my puny body, too. In her youth, I remember,

Domicėlė was a real troublemaker: sharp-tongued and quick to make fun of everyone; talented at languages, natural sciences, the arts, physics, and religion. She knew how to dress, to take care of her things; she rode a Viatka, a graceful motorbike, and, it seems to me, was always fighting for some kind of justice—and did she ever fight! She didn't like my father's handwriting; she scorned my modest attempts at literature; she gently mocked our distant cousin— the mumbling physicist and boxer who spent all summer preparing her for her entrance exams. Ah, Domicėlė! All our clan avoided her, even Father. But she didn't marry after all: today she flies to Chicago with a distant relative—an unassertive, practically speechless little biddy—or else she takes along some friend, another inveterate old maid. If I've inherited all my worthless characteristics from those unknown Salzburgers who are long since rotting in their graves in Suvalkija, then maybe they're balanced a bit by the genes from my other grandfather, a blacksmith in Aukštaitija? It seems to me I'm more tolerant of the world and its vanity or its depths than Domicėlė.

But what does Tūla, whom I keep seeming to forget even though it was because of her that I took up these unpleasant notes, have to do with this? She doesn't resemble Domicėlė in the least: if they had known each other, Tūla would surely have become Domicėlė's slave. At least now Tūla will never have a motorbike, won't go to Germany, will never turn sixty... no, not now! But if Tūla's grandfather, whom I used to see with a hat and a cane back in the city park on Sundays in my childhood, was a true destitute Dzūkian, then her grandmother... Oh, Tūla's grandmother! Even at the end of April, when the entire city was already soaking in the Nemunas (well, not everyone!), she would toddle down Birutės or Vytauto Avenue with both hands stuck into a fur muff, paying no attention to either the passersby or natural phenomena. She was, I think, a true cosmopolitan, but was she really Tūla's grandmother, or just a step-grandmother? To me she resembled an old peahen, still giving off flashes of bygone beauty, who hated mirrors, puddles or other flat water surfaces and the young girls hurrying by on the way to gymnastics training.

Ah, Tūla's grandmother! Surely she had blue blood too, at least my
mother said so once. How badly I wanted back then for that old lady
to cut her finger somewhere! Not a chance, her hands were always
stuck into a soft, warm muff. Tūla and I never discussed our genes;
we probably felt we were real Europeans anyway. Or perhaps we
simply didn't have the time—after all, our strange, regardless, shy,
but nevertheless intensely close connection lasted for all of a week,
but I feel it yet today. Apparently connections like that can't break
off entirely. They didn't just knit together, but changed so much that
it's impossible to shake them off, in either the past or in the present. Domicėlė, of course, would just laugh—so she was the one who
kicked you aside like a worm-eaten mushroom! No, maybe she's
not to blame for her unfortunate character, maybe she knows that
herself? How many postcards and books she sent me from distant
Irkutsk when I was still a child! And when she first returned from
there she behaved like a human—she was still young, still hoped to
marry. There's one thing I can't forgive her for, although a wise person would have forgotten it too. At the time I was still studying; I
was crashing in the university's photo laboratory, even though I was
already one step away from being a student. The military department, together with the hero of the Soviet Union, Wolf Wilensky,
in the fore or in the behind, had already thrown me out of the Alma
Mater, even though I had no intention of becoming either a regular or a reserve officer. I shuffled around the streets waiting for the
final order: Dismissed! That's the shape I was in when sharp-eyed
Domicėlė ran into me, and I didn't even notice her at first—I was
going past the stone walls of the Dominican Monastery, my eyes
glued on the crumbling sidewalk. Actually, I did see her later, but she
and her companions were already turning in at that door where for a
long time a barrel hung overhead. I would have forgotten—and I did
forget!—that meeting, but when I went home, my mother reminded
me of it immediately: Doma saw you in Vilnius! Domcė? Well, what
of it? I was surprised. So what, if she saw me? My mother spoke hotly
and reproachfully: You were walking along, she said, ragged, torn,

your shoes full of holes and worn down at the heels! She was afraid, she said, that you'd see her and greet her—she was going out to eat with the Germans! So, there's the rub! I surely would have nodded at least, or even lifted my non-existent hat! Domicėlė would have sunk straight into the ground from shame? But it wasn't that touchiness of hers that made me furious, no. After all, it was Mother she was trying to hurt, not me! Now that's dirty; now that's something else entirely. I know, Domicėlė has no use for either my forgiveness nor my fury—what for? She lives on quite well in her old, girlish world, baking apple and cottage cheese cakes by the recipes, living wholesomely, although she no longer drives a motorbike or spins a hula-hoop next to the river as she once did, just after she made her way back from Irkutsk. I wouldn't fume now because of those words she said once upon a time. It's just that when we're young we're very easily offended, and terribly proud; later that passes almost of its own accord. When this refined aesthete I know recently admitted to me, smiling: "I was so ashamed to walk next to you when we first met! I kept looking around to make sure some acquaintance didn't pop up!" I just shrugged my shoulders, and immediately remembered Tūla. When she saw me the first time, I really did look quite pathetic; for sure worse than I did on that autumn-steeped avenue in Palanga when I met that inquisitive aesthete—Hiacinta is her name; "Gothic Hiacinta," was what the small, artistically-inclined clique called her. Come on now, in my opinion, I looked like a "real person" in Palanga! There's no comparison! And by the next day Tūla had already given me her soft plaid Chinese shirt—it fit me just fine, but on Tūla it was a bit oversized.

IV

I'm so often annoyed by the talk and all the writing about one's love for Vilnius, by vows to return from the ends of the earth to this immortal city: I don't believe either thoughtful and coherent reasonings or heartfelt sighs, and of course I'm wrong. Who am I to judge people's feelings for stone walls, landscapes, topography, that dip over there or this little street's bend? But why someone else, and not me? I can have an opinion too, if only a threepenny's worth—for three pennies in old Vilnius you could drink a quart of vodka! Now I'll be more precise: I don't believe it when my peers make this claim—it always induces an indecent suspicion that they want to sell their love for Vilnius at the highest price, to get something tangible and pleasant, I can't say what, in exchange for it. That's why I want to believe the sighs and even vows of the old folks who don't need anything, even though they're mostly insincere too: few people really don't need anything anymore, when even a spot in the cemetery is chosen on the basis of a name's fame among people, or the sonority of a voice. No, all of them, those claimants, are fond of the city in their own way, they're horrified at hideous crimes, splutter on account of the disorder, fume over the discomforts, but really wouldn't want to live and die anywhere else but here. But do they love it? I'm not condemning anyone, or chastening—however short a man's time is, he doesn't succeed in realizing his true insignificance anyway, and stops being ashamed of physiology only when he's become childish again.

My trump cards are pretty weak, too; I don't know if I can love a
city where I experienced so much contempt, poverty, and failure. In
any event, I got to know it as well as I was destined to.
Take, say, that monastery on Malūnų Street, between the three
bridges. Between the Orthodox church and the flock of Catholic
churches. That one—it's on the other side of the Vilnelė River, inside
Užupis, as if inside some other, practically independent republic; the
river isn't just a natural wall, but the boundary of a sphere of influence. Take the gallery, and the door behind which my mother lived
when my future father visited her. My American cousins ran about
and Domicėlė crammed German grammar there. Perhaps I wouldn't
want to live there anymore. Tūla's building with the apse is much
roomier. But I was attracted to that place before I ever knew a thing
about the war years or the Lab School. More precisely: I had heard
this or that, but I didn't know the actual addresses. Now at least I
know why I keep unconsciously ending up here, taking a side trip
from some route of mine through the city, pretending I'm simply out
to saunter along the river, or when I've found an excuse to visit the
graphic artist with the lush facial hair. It's Tūla, that's what. She was
here; this is where I heard her husky voice, her delicate laugh; where
her tiny dragon-fly head twinkled above Bekešo Hill and above my
head, under the room's arch...
But if all of that hadn't been, I surely would still find an excuse to
come here. And not just because my mother lived here... my aunt...
my uncle the carpenter... their children... No, I'm not visiting graves;
this neighborhood quite nicely recalls people who are still alive and
about—if they sinned, they'd all be accused. It recalls Herbert and
Valentinas, Aurelita with little Ewa, even Helena Brzostowska and the
Colonel from Baltasis Lane—the retired warrior who was as dumb as
a Swedish turnip and his pleasant *supruga,* his spouse, Mrs. Colonel.
Staring at the empty mutt market, in whose gateway stands a filthy
bloodshot-eyed man with an even filthier mutt (he'd give it away in
a heartbeat for a couple bottles of strong ale), looking at the three-
corned square with the shallow underground toilet, I remember not

just these people, not just Tūla's husky laugh or—from a still earlier
time—the chubby nurse Ofelija, devotedly attending hopeless can-
cer patients in the Oncology Dispensary, no; I remember a still warm
fall afternoon, when, outside the now-shuttered summer theater, I
ran into the late Vandalinas Janavičius—a teacher from the juvenile
correctional school who wore a vinyl raincoat and had a nose like a
potato—he dragged me along all of those little bridges to the bank
that was once the Paplauja possession and suburb, insistently tried
to fix me up with some rumpled seamstress from Vileyka in Belarus
who was tiptoeing behind us, sympathized with me, told me about
the difficulties of education—you have to beat, beat, beat, and beat
them!—repeated banal Latin phrases: *Panem et circenses*—Bread and
circuses! *Quod licet Jovi, non licet bovi*—What Jupiter may do, the ox
may not! or: *Medice, cura te ipsum*—Physician, heal thyself! He could
have applied that one to himself. He talked non-stop and kept pouring me brown Azerbaijani Agdam. But I didn't get drunk as much
as I got tired from his grandiloquence—the content was the same
as it was two decades before in a dormitory full of bedbugs, where
Vandalinas, lying in bed, would translate excerpts from Caesar's *de
Bellum Gallicum* for the freshmen for a couple of beers—so, when
some lady on the Užupis side waved—looking up the steep slope,
overgrown with underbrush and shabby sheds, her breasts covered
half the sky—I, with my shoes and all, without even rolling up my
pant legs, holding the last bottle of wine above my head, waded to
the other shore, to drunken Užupis, and shaking myself like a puppy,
started climbing up, slipping and sliding, to the top—the big-breasted
woman was still waving invitingly. It was embarrassing: even now
it's unpleasant to remember. All I recall is that Vandalinas Janavičius's
gargling laugh suddenly stopped: on the slope three guys suddenly
appeared out of nowhere to meet me. No, no big deal at first, *priviet,
priviet,* hi, hello. We drank the wine, and they said that in exchange
for my watch they would—instantly!—bring me several bottles of
vodka. Watches were still as cheap as mushrooms. They really did
bring it; we drank; the big-breasted woman, too. For a laugh (really?)

I touched her swaying bust with both hands, and they kicked me so hard all over, battered me so bad—Vandalinas would never have dared to beat his delinquents that way. I spent three days tossing and turning in Herbert Stein's garden apartment while he just giggled, but maybe he was right: They beat you just out of boredom, out of petty annoyance, because there wasn't anything more they could take from you. After all, you gave them your watch? You, yourself!

Herbert Stein's tiny, round, dark, old-fashioned glasses couldn't hide my black eyes, much less my crushed nose, when, the moment I stepped out into the street, I ran into Tūla. At first she just covered her mouth and looked like she was going to scream, but then she stepped backward and, quickening her step, disappeared among the crowd. We had already said goodbye: I would only see her from afar, catching a glimpse of her flashing by somewhere across from the Astorija or at the curve on Antokolskio Street. I'd run into her brother more often; sometimes we even sat down to smoke a cigarette, but both he and I avoided so much as a mention of Tūla. It seems to me that he and I would have gotten along okay, too—what am I saying, we did get along. And at least I used to see Tūla from a distance. And now, too! I relished my pain—I never tried to catch up with her, never tried to either talk to her or stop her. It never even occurred to me to ask her to some café for coffee or to accompany her to the next turn, no. It was enough just to see her, to nod when I met her, and plod onwards with my head down. Look! I'd say to her in my thoughts when, still from afar, she would spot me with a mug in my hand in front of Father's Tomb; there was this "spot," there was, with something even of a bohemian flavor; on occasion it would be flooded by journalists, restorers, and people like me, with shiny elbows and perpetually runny noses. Look, Tūla! I would shout in my heart. You're the one who's to blame that I'm standing here! I saw myself how bitterly she smiled when she met me on the street with a staggering Kaira Primea, an alcoholic Estonian; didn't her business trip to Vilnius take three years? You're to blame, I'd sternly condemn her, for me dragging this drunken bed-sheet to her damp cot somewhere in Markučiai, instead of sitting with you under the vaulted ceiling, instead of seeing your flat body hanging above me in the greenish moonlight... you're to blame! But that was just the disgustingly sweet cry of a half-drunk soul, along with the darkest exasperation—why did she have to meet me with this scarecrow! After all, I never saw her, Tūla, the little animal, the dragonfly, the sleepy dormouse, with some athlete or wasted genius. Always alone. In the same brown fur jacket. Always cowering, always seeming afraid of something.

Well, no, I did actually see a thing or two myself. At the time I couldn't restrain myself, and as if I were driving something away, I stuffed my fingers into my mouth and whistled sharply. In the grass below Tūla's windows a little group of long-hairs were sitting and lying, including that *swinski* blond—this time a real blond pig, while she, in a long flowered skirt, walked between them pouring some kind of drink from a plastic jug. I whistled from the cement bridge; they looked, Tūla turned around, too, but I was already scooting off, as if I were driving myself away. Running to the center of the house, I clattered up the stairs to the gallery, leaned on the rusted railing, and had a cigarette. She saw me. Smiled. Lowered her eyes. And laughed so musically that I immediately lost all desire to stand there and smoke. On top of that, some female resident as big as a navy cruiser poked me in the back and in a bass voice thundered, "So that's where my *belizna*—whiteness—goes!" See, she meant the bedding she apparently hangs out to dry there. And yet all my relations, who began in Salzburg, Krosno, and Grodno, had lived beyond the door she came out of. By then I knew that was where it was. In my childhood there was a stiff postcard floating around the house with the Hill of Three Crosses and a mustachioed Hitler on a reddish postage stamp, on which, above the line *Deutsche Reichspost* in Gothic letters, *OSTLAND* was printed in gothic letters too. Wartime mail. Malūnų 3, to *pani* Domicėlė. And just a few words in black ink: "Domut, go to that store and see if that pullover with black shoulders and (unreadable) buttons is still there? Kisses—Hana." Or something like that. I don't guarantee it word for word.

There was a gray stationery supply notebook with graph paper from the Ashelm company in the house too, yet another witness that my dear relatives really did once live next to Tūla. True, she hadn't arrived in this world yet, as neither had I, but they probably stopped by the house with an apse to borrow kerosene, matches, salt, chicory, or just to chat. Say that my gray cousins stopped by to see the girls who lived in that same apartment where, after nearly forty years, Tūla came to reside with Petryla. Perhaps they played records, solved their algebra problems, and listened to the distant cannonade from the east. I don't know what the teenaged Petryla was doing then, and Herbert Stein, Valentinas Grajauskas, Aurelita, and the others weren't in the demographic scheme yet, either. But I have reason to suspect my future parents were already mentioning the possibility of my appearance in this world. How desperately I searched for the flimsiest hints of my ties to Vilnius, as if not just my past, but my future life, or even my death, depended upon it. These efforts frequently seemed a bit comical to me, but not always. Aha, that dark gray Ashelm notebook, father's wartime journal! Even then father was an incorrigible pedant: returning from Germany, he meticulously, in detail, in a beautiful clear hand (where's that Doma's eyes!), flooded line after line of that notebook with his impressions—exactly that, impressions; no outpouring of feelings, even though there was a poem written on the very first page, by Brazdžionis the bard. "THE RETURN TO THE HOMELAND" was written first, in printed letters, and a bit below:

The amber sun shines in gold
Below the little clouds it'll be bright,
When we return once more from the ends of the earth,
From all the crossroads of this world.

I'd semi-secretly paged through the Ashelm earlier, too; as far as I know, there wasn't anything particularly intimate there, but it was only later, much later, that I realized that "B.B." under the poem didn't stand for Brigitte Bardot, but Bernardas Brazdžionis. I was fascinated with Brigitte Bardot when I was still in the tenth grade; we all fell out of our chairs laughing back then, watching the comedy *Babette Goes to War*. Today, besides the pedantry and the "longing for the homeland" in my father's notebook, I'm surprised to encounter a bit of bravado, humor of a sort, and a sincere letting off of steam. Even conceit. The first entry is dated September 11, 1945, so even Japan had surrendered, and father was still knocking about Austria and Germany. Like a diligent tourist, he immediately wrote down all that month's "notable events." Here's those events:

1945, September 11, Tuesday, 7:30. Start off from the yard of a dairy in Neuruppin;

September 19: a "tour" through the ruins of Berlin;

September 20–21: a "turtle" race at Anhalter Bahn, refereed by American soldiers, our time: twenty-four hours. Distance: from the street to the platform;

September 21–22: lodging with Lukenwalde's whores—our innocence is under attack!

September 22: in the evening, two prodigal sons with a broken *handwagen* knocked at the closed gates on which was written *"Mat Rodina zhdet vas*—the Motherland waits for you!"

September 22–October 11: bivouac at Camp 251;

October 11: we pack up and move out;

October 13: my friend Cottbus was thrashed and disgraced by the Russians, and carried a cross on his shoulders.

October 15: In Sorau, the first Polish soldiers;

October 16–18: Sorau: piles of manure, echelons…

Glogau, October 19 (…) The city is completely destroyed, deserted, the ruins already overgrown. There's something rather romantic hovering over them, not like in Berlin, where the bricks, dust, and ashes are gloomy. But because of its size, Berlin still had some life, while I'd never seen a city as completely destroyed as

Glogau before. Grim impressions traveling through the destruction of Germany. The worst is that the Germans, with such a high standard of living, started a war that didn't just destroy them, but forced other nations to suffer hardships, too.

Father's echelon stood around in the fields of Poland for a long time; together with the others he boiled gruel out of flour along the railroad tracks, was no longer surprised at ruined Minsk, bartered and wondered what he would find on his return to Lithuania. And then:

1945, November 4, Vilnius. Last night with a pounding heart I went to Malūnų 3. When I climbed the stairs to the gallery, I saw it wasn't Lydija living there: there were other things at the door, there wasn't that cleanliness that Lydija and her family so valued. I knocked, but no one opened the door beyond which, when opened, I used to see Her quite often. Not getting any reply, I stopped by *pani* Hanulka, and found out a thing or two there...

With a pounding heart, swiftly flapping animal-bird wings, I flew in—can it be that even now I'm still not flying in?—through the broken window, through the glass encrusted in dust and sawdust, into a room as bare as an emptied bottle of wine, where it smells so harshly of paint and lime, something acid and disgusting; only the smell of humans no longer remains. It no longer smells of Tūla's body, her hair; even the dusty picture albums no longer smell. No matter how much you sniff, you won't even smell the musky scent of Petryla or his pimply son, the stench of shoe polish, flat beer—nothing! It's as if you'd landed in an old burial crypt: the whitewashed plaster walls with barely visible little spiders look horribly eternal, worse than any image of death, worse than the wards in the madhouse or the Butterflies Cemetery next to the Ritual Services Bureau, where, at one time, when a strange fad or merely a collective insanity had taken hold, young drug addicts and young damsels would march over to commit suicide, and curious eccentrics, too. I've wandered around it—it's more comfortable over there, and warmer.

Some years back, when I dropped into your (or our?) already

emptied dwelling, I came across a strange couple in the kitchen: a
man covered in rotten debris and a fat deaf-mute woman with a dirty
puppy. They ate, and slept, and emptied their bowels there—in the
kitchen. They would build a little fire on a sheet of tin and boil something to eat. Stories had already started appearing about people like
that—there were almost as many people of that sort showing up in
the city's garbage dumps as crows—but here, in the middle of town?
They invited me to sit down and drink some beer, but I just glanced
into the room where your cot once stood, had a cigarette, and slipped
off to the Vilnelė, where a bony lady was feeding white bread to some
fat ducklings. Other people, Tūla, were already preparing to adapt
your dwelling to the needs of the insatiable public—they've decided
to put in artists' studios here, for the children of good parents. But
at least it's for painting! Before, barely living ghosts hung around
there; later the Satanists, the homeless, couples in love, and teenagers
obsessed with finding God showed up, the kind that in the long term
could grow up into real bible thumpers; the Führer shoved those
types into concentration camps, and Sruoga suffered with the likes
of them in Stutthof. In the end the construction workers came—for
the long term. They moved in with all of their ammunition, nailed
together a shed for their materials, repaired Petryla's old stove in the
kitchen, and it seems they'll be tending it for a long time, until…
until sometime someone really will set up easels there.

   I flew in—it's fall, the weather's raw, but it's still light. It's just
there's nothing to grab onto with my tiny clingy bat's feet anymore,
it's so empty, smooth, round, bare, and lifeless in here. Here, Tūla,
in your former dwelling next to Petryla's kitchen—his former scul-
lery, roguery, sanctuary for Bacchus and Lucifer; next to the hard
hats left by the construction workers, shards of bottles, and a mountain of food waste. I thrashed around in that nearly airless space until
I bashed my way out the window's eye sockets again. Exhausted,
I perched on a thick eglantine bush; below yawned an abyss, or at
least it looked that way to me—a wide, steep-sided deep chasm—
who dug it out here and why? While the rather dim October sun still

shone, I saw at its bottom a barely sloping ditch, a gutter lined with round stones, and a bit further on some larger boulders and thick oak logs that were hollowed out inside. Aha, the old city water supply, I thought, blocked up long ago, choked on a stream no longer pure. Tūla will never learn of this; in her day, this was just a burdock plantation and a little meadow, where she once poured drinks for her guests from a pitcher. What else was there? Squadrons of rats and mice, hordes of mosquitoes, gnats, green flesh flies, bluebottle flies, temporary—eternally temporary!—sheds, garages patched together with corrugated tin sheets rusting right in front of your eyes, and that greenish-blue moonlight on our momentarily resting bodies— did everything really look that way back then? Maybe...

We said goodbye, Tūla, but that's exactly why I learned to turn myself into a flying mouse whenever I wanted—a being with a bird's heart and a beast's teeth. It was I who perched on your breasts while you would sleep a dreamless sleep and wake up in the morning with nothing to write into your thick notebook of dreams ornamented in a square, girlish handwriting with strange loops on the "y"—for some reason, to me those loops resembled the dropped pants of the dwarf on the door of Petryla's stinking toilet. I spent many hours darting about in the air above the remains of the excavated clogged old water supply and above the city's little red pumping station No. 1 on the other side of the stream—it still fed the old city with ground water. When he saw me, the blue-coated, green-hatted water supply security guard—there was a star with two crossed rifles on his cockade and a piercing whistle always held ready in his metal teeth— couldn't stand it, and whistled like a kid, or at least clapped his veined hands. There aren't many people who like us bats.

I would perch then on the Bernardine spire, on whose heights the pillars of Gediminas are architecturally encoded, and from there I would survey your former windows, Tūla. Just as I did when you still lived there, but by then without me and, I dare presume, without some small part of yourself. How eagerly I'd wait for you to come home! Most of the time you would show up just as it started to get

dark and immediately go to bed; then I'd fly over to visit you, hang
with my head downwards from the vault in the ceiling—how sooty
it was back then, covered in dark, greasy nuggets, stuck with grime,
cobwebs, dead flies… I'd smell the barely noticeable scent of wax,
oil, urine, and stale food—the kitchen was, after all, right next door.

By then I was just watching you, Tūla, we no longer spoke; not
since that time I crawled over here for the last time from dark little
Filaretų Street, which, not having the Philomaths at its side, coiled
and forked through the dark woods of Belmontas almost up to the
red-brick KGB officers' houses across from the *Negyvėlių namas*,
the House of the Dead. I never did have the time to tell you about
the House of the Dead, the one next to Marytės Margytės Street,
known locally as Mary Margot—the famous Soviet partisan—not at
all far from Baltasis Lane and the Polocko route. Listen, Tūla, when
you ended up in the kingdom of the dead, didn't you, at least in the
beginning, feel the living's morbid curiosity about death, a nasty
curiosity, somehow similar to what a person does when he smells a
disgusting smell but doesn't run off, doesn't turn his nose away, but
just the opposite—sticks that nose just as close as courage will allow,
snuffles, looks around, bends over, greedily drinks in that smell, follows behind it like a dog, until in the end he does himself in? Isn't
that how it is, my dear? This is the first time I've call you "dear" and
you're already dead; when you were alive, I only called you Tūla, but
I wrote "THULLA" in green letters on the Bernardine's walls before
they were probed. How long ago that was! But listen now. The House
of the Dead is a horrible little building made of silicate blocks, always
sealed closed, with windows covered to the middle in white paint.
A morgue. Clearly too small for all the city's dead to fit and breaking at least fifty of the necessary sanitary and moral standards, not to
mention God's commandments. It was always looming right behind
the gardens that belonged to the Colonel and Rikard the butcher.
And it didn't bother either one of them in the least. Although both
men—the waxy, flabby Colonel and the dark-complected, sanguine
butcher—knew full well what was going on day and night behind

those white walls, what kind of trucks and buses rolled in and out through the rusty gates. It was completely immaterial to them; the Colonel worried about moral matters in madcap Aurelita's workshop on the floor below him, and Rikard had other things on his mind— all he thought about was how to carry more and better cuts of meat out the shop door. Although it's true they had both—without agreeing on it in advance!—planted deadly nightshade they never picked at the ends of the gardens bordering the morgue's fence, while nettles glowered by the fence of their own accord.

One of Aurelita Bonopartovna's windows looked out on the House of the Dead too—the bathroom window. Once, while the two of us were bathing, Aurelita unexpectedly climbed out of the narrow tub and I could stretch out my legs and float around on my own. Leaving wet footprints, she went over to the window, with her little hand quickly swiped the fogged-up surface, and covered her mouth as if she had choked on something. Then, without turning around, she waved to me—come on, come on! Looking out the bathroom, those white-painted windows no longer blocked the view of what was going on inside at all: on a table covered with galvanized steel I saw a corpse—naked like me and Aurelita—with a dissected stomach. I stood behind Aurelita's back, hugging her, but she trembled anyway. She trembled, but she didn't retreat from the window: wild horses couldn't have dragged her away! Probably a still-young man, I thought, even though his face couldn't be seen. But it seemed to me I saw a blue tattoo on his forearm. We could both clearly see his blackened feet, the arms lying calmly next to the body; when one of the two examiners moved aside, his genitalia showed too—the light there was painfully bright. Come on, let's go, it's enough, I whispered, but Aurelita's nails, sunk into the window sill, didn't let go; she stood there frozen, silent, and her eyes devoured the clearly lit space on the other side of the narrow street. The two thick-set men in white coats sometimes returned briefly to their dissected client, seemed to do something to him, then turned again to the window daubed with paint, quickly poured something into a beaker, downed it, frowned, and grabbed a crust of bread. I don't even know how long it lasted, our observation and that cycle of theirs: scalpel, beaker, crust... in any case, I didn't get terrified, Tūla, although it's true I felt even more insignificant, but after that sleepless night awash in wine it seems nothing's horrible or scary to me anymore. It was just that Aurelita wouldn't let me sleep—the wine glass knocked against her teeth—I took her to the bathroom again, stood her in front of the window and pointed out into the dark: Look, there's nothing there anymore. They've taken him away. They'll bring another one soon, she whispered, just wait. No, I said, they have to rest, too, let's go to bed. But sleep wasn't in the cards; every rattle, every car going by drove her out of her mind, she kept asking over and over: It'll be like that for us too? Me, too? And after all, she had climbed out of the bathtub and gone straight over to that window herself, as if someone were pushing her. Who was pushing her, Tūla, what do you think? And how are you there, underground, above ground, in the heights where your soul hovers? Will you be able to tell me sometime what you felt just after you died?

I flew by the House of the Dead, too, the same night I scattered your resting body with lilac blossoms—I knew the air vent was open, that you needed more and more fresh air at night—and then I flew over to you at night all spring long. From the ceiling I'd look at your flat, quivering body, darker groin, your legs as white as paraffin candles; I listened to you breathing, turning over on your other side, and, after moaning in an unnatural voice, weeping soundlessly in your sleep—not for yourself; not for me; not for anything else, but just in your dreams... because you no longer know how to weep when you're not sleeping, when you're sober, when in a cracking voice you told me about your strange friend who, after putting on an amber necklace, lies down on unread books, sharp knitting needles, and honed knives, and sleeps so soundly that she doesn't so much as stir until morning—and all the wisdom of those books transfers to her during the night. Why do you talk such nonsense, Tūla? And do you really have even one friend?

Often I'd fly over to you from the madhouse, too, from the woods at Olandų, Vasaros, and Rudens streets—no one would have let me out, but I'd slip into the attic and from there, through a broken skylight, I'd rise above the forested hills, above the triangulation tower across from the Butterflies Cemetery and, making a loop, dive at an insane speed into your poor dwelling. If I saw strange shoes at your door, I'd squeal in a bird-beast voice, unable to slip in through the darkened windows and the closed air vent. One time I perched to rest on the octagonal Bekešo tower: the rustling of my wings scared a woman lying below, under a soldier. The soldier, swearing, got up and threw a rock or a clod at me. "They get tangled in your hair!" the woman shrieked and covered her head, although I was already perched in a tree farther off. The soldier tried to calm her, to lay her back on the grass again, but she wouldn't give in: Let's go, let's go!

When they disappeared, I looked with open eyes at the soot-covered city, wrapped in a network of wires, with radars, prohibitory signs, cordons, and all sorts of impediments erected everywhere, worn out by a sad existence, but an insatiable, hungry, covetous, and brutal city all the same, and I already knew: I'm condemned to remain here, even as a bat who is either hated, feared, or completely and utterly unknown! Condemned to live a shadowy life, to always be on my guard, not just from people, but from the bats themselves as well, the real ones. To hide from the sun and the stars, to not show myself even at dusk, to either you, Tūla, or to those clear-eyed women at the Red Cross hospital where a blue van took me one night, beaten and bloody; they pulled me out and laid me outside next to the reception door. Those *milítsiya*—the people's police—of the same blue and the clear-eyed women dragged me into a corridor smelling of carbolic acid and left me there: a drunk!

Those were blessed nights, Tūla, when I could fly over and observe you, flutter my wings, even if it was next to a closed window, watch you knit furiously, unravel that knitting, and start all over again, knitting something awful and never-ending, and then suddenly laugh, pour yourself some cooled tea, stand up and lean on the window sill, and in the scruffy notebook of dreams write a few disconnected sentences... were they really disconnected, really sentences? Did you sometimes dream, my dear, of my protruding, wide ears, my little mouse snout, and the clinging nails on my little feet? Oh, hanging upside down is an art too, quite an art, believe me! Thrown onto the chair—I brought you that chair!—I would see your olive skirt with a little carmine spot there where, when you buttoned it up, your right thigh would hide itself. I would see you undress for the night (after checking the door bolt that separated your chamber from Petryla's kitchen), throw off your flannel shirt (the same one you had given me to wear), pull down the gray tights, pull off the narrow black underpants too, and dive completely naked into the cold bedclothes on the mattress... roll into a little ball and try, try to put yourself to sleep... What did you think about those lonely nights, Tūla? Did you stir in your sleep when you felt my closeness? But at last, after coughing dryly, you would fall asleep; on the ceiling or beyond the window, I would snooze a bit myself—the little creature's sensitive ears would catch the wheeze of your lungs, the murmuring bronchi, the drone of blood in your temples, hear the kefir drunk for a cheap dinner cruising through your bluish intestines—getting ever sourer and darker... I was in your home that evening, too, when you couldn't stand it anymore and completely cleaned out Petryla's foul, fetid kitchen—you shined everything it was at all possible to shine, hauled out mountains of trash and old newspapers, at last even gathered up all the empty bottles out of all the corners, took them to the recycling center, and bought Petryla three bottles of Tauras beer, detergent, and some dental paste; it would still show up in the stores every now and then. And I saw when that solid, already thickening man stepped in the door, fell silent at the sight of the shining kitchen, shook off his misshapen shoes—he reeked all over of enzymes or some other product of his mysterious enterprise—opened the beer bottle fragrant with hops, drank it down in one draw, burped in satisfaction, and then in surprise looked at you, Tūla; I saw everything! Listen, kid, he, your landlord, said in a wheezing voice, my son's already grown, they're taking him into the army soon, we could shack up, huh? And quieted, clammed up—the way you looked at him. Well, sorry, he muttered, I guess I was barking up the wrong tree… forget it, I didn't say anything. It was only later that you laughed; you even shrieked in laughter while telling your friend about this proposal, maybe it was the same one who piles knitting needles and unread books onto her bed at night.

I would frequently hang in your room until daybreak, but I never stayed long enough to see you get up—at dawn I'd hurry through the hills and valleys back to Olandų Street, slip under the thin blanket, and once more turn into a patient of the Second Section (I'll tell you more about that Section, Tūla!)—one of those harmless inhabitants of a madhouse who diligently swallow the ordered medications, willingly tell the doctors about their weaknesses, and with each and every day become more resigned to their illness, even coming to love it in a peculiar way. No, no, I wasn't like that yet—I still found it funny to listen to the nonsense in the smoking rooms or bathrooms, or while sipping strong black tea as hot as fire—the heated enamel mug went from hand to hand, it was so hot that no one could possibly take more than three little sips. That's when the breathtaking stories of the insane would start—any wise man would listen to them with pleasure! If, Tūla, you've read Hauff's fairytale about the caliph stork; if you still remember the magic word "Mutabor!" you, too, Tūla, would have been able to sit next to me and the former *militsiya* sergeant Nazarova, next to the trembling ex-surgeon L., whose articles, he said, even the *Lancet* used to publish, and a green student who had managed not just to drink up his inheritance, but his memory too. Or next to a homeless old man with his hardened crown of arteries and a hoary master of alchemy. What fantastic and wonderful storytellers they all were!

It was only when I flew out at night to visit you that I would for a while forget all that routine, the colored and white tablets and the preparation called MGB, or something; you know, they inject the medicine in a vein and instantly your anus gets so hot it seems it'll start smoking any minute, but a few seconds later it all passes, your body strengthens—that's how they heal the majority of the milder madmen—they're hungry all the time anyway, constantly want to smoke, and complain endlessly that no one visits them and no one wants to sign them out of there. I won't tell you everything about the Second Section yet, Tūla, I'll just say that during the day I devoured books there—*Folktales of the Soviet Peoples, Tales of Uzbekistan* and a wonderful find, forgotten since childhood—Kipling's *The Butterfly That Stamped*—do you remember that little book, Tūla? Together with this reading I slowly returned to my childhood; I felt just fine there, I liked the endings of the Eastern tales, and Kipling too. Now I even remember his first name—Rudyard. I even read it several times in a row—no one passed new books out here for nothing, you had to earn the right to exchange books at the hospital library—only the most disciplined and diligent patients got them, and I already had two strikes: I'd smoked in a forbidden spot—on the stairway—and I was a few minutes late to the general meeting of patients and staff... Yes, yes! My other friends in misfortune, who had long since stopped worrying about reading, either secretly played cards or walked around the grounds giggling with some young, pretty madwoman. Practically all of the madwomen were still young—seamstresses or students (but maybe it just seemed that way to me?), all of them rouged their cheeks, put on lipstick, and darkened their eyebrows; they all wanted to be loved, even though it was love's charms that got them there in the first place! Almost all of them. I'd frequently see a cheerful couple like that turn into the hilly pine forest after dinner and disappear between the low aspens and spruce. The doctors punished patients of both sexes rather strictly for this; they would shame them publicly, but no punishment was enough to restrain them from their pleasures—I've already said they didn't read books, and they were so accustomed to the injections—even Aminazine!—that the doctors just waved a hand helplessly—screw yourselves, shove it, go to the dogs! One evening—the others had already gone to bed—your brother and his tall friend, the one who liked to shave his skull and grow a thick beard, came to visit me. The one who painted the Tashkent market and announced he was not just Vaitiekūnas's student, but Chagall's, too. He would have fit in perfectly with our company; when I said so, he just nodded his bare head and laughed. He was unbelievably arrogant and expected a great deal of the future—the very near future. We sat in the hospital garage, which was being remodeled, and then we went out to a gazebo at the edge of the park. Your brother was quiet; he poured Black Aronija—a wine as dark as a September night—in a glass he had brought along. He didn't mention you that time either, and neither did I. I was waiting for them to leave as soon as possible—we drank in silence, quickly—and as soon as they stuffed both empty bottles into a leather artist's portfolio and walked off across Olandų Street, I was overcome by an infinite sadness: the sadness of loneliness, the sadness of the forthcoming night, the sadness of a bat hanging upside down above your cot, Tūla—a bat who will now never descend to your body again, or if he did descend, then just so that awaking suddenly from sleep you would scream in an ungodly voice, and from the shriek the dirty carafe with its "dead water" would shatter into pieces: you used it at someone's advice—was it your fatalistic friend's?—to heal yourself from exhaustion, heart problems, bronchial asthma, and several more real or imaginary illnesses.

That evening I flew out just as it got dark—I fluttered around the roof ridge of the Church of St. Bartholomew, twice swooped over Herbert Stein's yard, nearly bumped into his bandages and shirts hung out to dry (Herbert had recently been injured in the street by bruisers from the pan-Slavic organization Severozapad), and it was only then, past the underbrush, the garbage dumps, the couples hurriedly making love, and the drunks sleeping in the bushes, that I dived into Malūnų Street. You didn't come home alone; you were bringing that lithographer and photographer with the white eyelashes, a world-famous man in green velour pants—his photographs had traveled to Asia, the Caribbean Islands, and even Nepal, the land of prayer mills, lamas, and monasteries. The land of bats and slowly

clotting blood. The two of you stopped by the exterior double door:
the little predatory beast bared its fangs and its bird's heart resolved
to fly—it tore at the chest, ticked like a tiny motor, capable of turning
a paper windmill or lighting a night light. I pushed myself off and,
breaking the air vent with my body, managed to cling to the vault
before you stepped in; I still didn't know what I was going to do. The
wine drove my wings; the wine hammered in the leathery ribs of the
wings' membrane—the membrane flushed, perhaps even turned a
purple color: it was the wine your brother had brought—my blood
was that way, too; it wasn't dripping yet, not yet. I hung upside down
and swung, getting dizzier and dizzier. Oh, I was of no concern to
you two! You spoke in short sentences, you mentioned several pictures, white lashes spoke of the wonderful mess in your little room,
went over to my chair with the khaki skirt thrown over the back, and
with his thin white little fingers felt the carmine spot and smiled—
how I hated him! But I just swung—you started dressing; he effi-
ciently checked the tripod and hung the lights he had brought, and
you were already lying on the mattress in a pseudo-Spanish dress
brought from his workshop. One lamp accidentally flashed right
into my weak eyes—I hated that light and I hated him, the foreign
body in this house, this neighborhood, and maybe this entire city.
You smiled wanly. I retreated to the side, but shortly the dazzling
light reached me there too. Now you were sitting in the unmatched
chair I had left: I didn't see anything, I just heard the folds in your
clothes rustle, heard him ordering you about in a friendly way, and
approaching you, turn you together with the chair and cry out,
"Good! Don't move!" while the dress's heavy rustling even rung in
my ears. I pushed off the wall and, crashing painfully, tumbled into
a dark corner. The two of you looked, and he said something, wasn't
it: "You're a rich woman if spirits visit you!" And while he photographed you, while you sat, lay down, kneeled, stretched out, and
looked over your shoulder, I sprawled on my back on the cold floor
and didn't see anything, didn't want to see anything. After all, I knew
how it would all end, this artistic séance! Routinely and sublimely;

boringly and quietly. Out of duty, and out of misery, out of seeming decency, and a desire to not lie alone in the dark. While you two
drank Hungarian vermouth, I got up thrashing and knocked over
the little vase with cranesbill, which had been brought over recently
by that episodic and exotic supposed friend of yours—the cranesbill
were wilting and drying, but continued to stand forgotten on the
wide windowsill. And only when the light went out, when I began to
see again, when the blood instantly rushed into my tiny beast's skull,
I fell like a rock between you two; I sunk my nails into to the albino's chest, but oddly, he didn't even get scared. You quietly gasped
in horror, while he firmly grabbed me by the scruff, took my glider
with his flabby hands, and threw me out the air vent in disgust. I felt
his blood streaming down my body—what nails! I heard you sob, I
heard him angrily trying to calm you down. Good-bye! I flew off to
the old willow on the other side of the little bridge—I perched there
and waited. And it paid off—the albino left immediately: his hand
bandaged, his footsteps firm and angry. I saw you standing in the
dark doorway next to the blue mail box, into which my letters were
yet to fall and fall, and quietly see him off: "Don't ever, ever come
here again! Never, never!" You never stopped me when I was leaving
either, nor waited in the doorway for me. Never.

Inside the little room, you crossed your arms on the table and
put your head down, but after all, you didn't cry: I saw. You fell asleep
without turning off the light or pulling the frayed cotton curtains
shut. I flapped off to the eave across from the gutter and remembered
the evening when, returning from Užupis via the covered bridge,
we found a corpse on it, a still quite young man. He really was dead
already; the blood on his forehead had actually dried and his arms
were thrown out to the side just like they are in pictures and movies—it was only later that I thought about that. Why did we turn onto
the covered bridge? Oh, I think we'd decided to stop at the Bernardine Church—a light still shone in the restorers' window—I wanted
to show you the wooden statues. Or maybe we wanted to stop at
some coffee house? I don't know anymore. After all, we were going

straight to your hard cot—the mattress thrown down on red, pitted bricks, propped up with books and scraps of wood, and we turned onto the covered bridge without discussing it. That lonely restorers' window was the only one shining; it was probably what attracted me. I leaned over; the dead man's eyes were open. For some reason we sat him up and propped him against the railings. His head rolled down on to his chest. There was nothing we could do to help him—the morgue stood up on the hill, but... We left, our footsteps quickening, without looking back, holding hands. In the morning he was no longer there; just as it was getting light I went out into the yard and saw from a distance—no, he wasn't there. I returned, trembling, to the cot—all night we lay embracing each other tightly, not sleeping, irritable, guilt gnawing at us; all the same, I don't want to call that gnawing conscience. It wasn't conscience gnawing at us—it was cold, slimy fear. The other time, watching the man being dissected, I didn't feel anything like it. But you, Tūla, shook so, your teeth chattered so badly I forced myself to wake up Petryla and ask for a glass of wine—I knew he almost always set a bottle next to his bed at night, so if he woke up he'd be able to immediately guzzle down a glass and collapse back into a drunken sleep again. But the wine wasn't of much help—I caught your shaking, too: I didn't believe you loved me; you didn't believe that I loved you; even though we had already said those dangerous words and now we were both waiting impatiently for which one of us would repeat them first without asking. In the morning I walked you to work past the cloister, past the shoe and fish stores, just so you wouldn't have to cross either bridge. At a round table at the Užupis bakery we drank a cup of bad, bitter coffee—you weren't in any hurry to get to work. I'll be truthful—you didn't like your work; you didn't know how to do it and didn't want to know, either. Nothing there was dear to you. We waited for the bus for a long time, and when it arrived, you didn't get on—I could see you didn't want to go anywhere; you held on tight to my sleeve, looked at the slender Missionary spires in the cold fog, and were silent. I love you, you murmured, and buried your little nose into the scarf sticking out of my jacket. I loved you, I was afraid you'd go off, get lost in the city, fall down a sewer or gas line opening they'd forgotten to cover, or simply melt into the fog. We wandered arm in arm through the meager autumn light until nightfall, and in the evening Petryla put the afternoon paper on the table. See, he poked it with a yellowish finger, on that bridge! Yesterday's murder was written up, someone had confessed. But the item had an unusual title: "Suspect arrested." You sighed heavily and Petryla laughed foolishly: What, is it better now?

I loved you. I warmed you, your hands, I flexed your fingers, laid you on top of myself so you'd warm up faster. I enjoyed every moment spent with you, yes, every moment—I already knew then that it was every one—how else could I have remembered everything so well later? I'd never met anyone like you, Tūla—shy, seemingly careless, but endlessly sensitive and vulnerable. True, I'd probably met people who spoke with a husky, hollow voice before, it's just that I never liked the silent and phlegmatic type; to me they looked as if they were always full of tranquilizers and walked around half-dreaming; they didn't get involved in anything, or if they did, then only in something completely inappropriate. I was amazed at how generous, genuine, and quietly curious you were, at your refined sense of humor, your somewhat wicked irony, and how sincerely you knew how to marvel—I'd forgotten myself what marvel is. I was charmed even when you let your tongue run away with you, at your naive belief that we hadn't met by accident. When we were wandering through the park, I saw you squat next to a black cat, and as you petted it, speak to it as if it were me.

Yes, I can say for sure that I remember every minute; I could remind you of a thousand similar ones, details of the most trivial sort. There, riding towards Belmontas, with your finger you draw on the fogged-up bus window, and throwing back your head laugh at my story about the "Volkshütte" and Uncle Hans. You chew on a pear and a seed sticks to your chin like a mole, I take it off with a kiss, and you lock your fingers around my neck... No, it couldn't last long; later I would have started to forget, or simply not pay attention. But we were together for such a short time, we were so close, that nothing had a chance to repeat itself. The world neither brightened nor darkened, but there was light constantly, like in that horrifyingly whitewashed building that smelled of the eternal... constant hell.

I would remember it all while hanging upside down above your poor cot. And it was just then, that evening when I no longer found you there, that the day and the hour I met you for the first time stood quite clearly in front of my eyes. You saw me maybe an instant earlier, because the art expert sitting next to me immediately noticed your eyes and poked me in the side: "Hey, are you blind? Don't tell me you don't see the way she's looking at you?"

Then I raised my eyes and looked across: beyond the flowers sitting in water, beyond the greenish glasses and the coffee mugs with cracked or chewed edges, I saw you, Tūla.

V

Even now I remember life before Tūla only with great reluctance, as I do "life after Tūla." Actually, I haven't divided it into stages, nor periods, nor anything of the sort for a long time now. If I do remember my "pre-Tūlian" life, then I try not to go into it too deeply, or at least not to torment myself over it too much—it was neither smooth, nor pleasant, nor easy. Such a dank, sad life—after all, I never knew where I would sleep the next night, had no idea of where my feet would take me or whether the day that dawned wouldn't be the one the blue-jacketed officials would finally snatch me up, coming across me somewhere in a helpless state, and cart me off to their stuffy cells: an interrogation rooms and monthly ripening in the hole would be my lot for a couple of years because "I'm worthless, I don't contribute to *building*" and, in general, I'm trash amongst the gleaming courtyards and mansions! That's the way it had been for about a year before I met Tūla. They were quick to punish, particularly when "Vagrant Roundup Week" came along. After all, back then every fall started with "Traffic Safety Week," followed by "Letter Week," and after the letters were written, it would be the turn of "Clean Nails Week." For all it's worth, I would have approved of such an action myself earlier, why not? But not then. When it started, out of all the cracks, holes, heating tunnels, and basements of dilapidated buildings, the rank and file and their bosses, assisted by the more zealous citizens—most often retired women and reserve soldiers looking for something to do—would dredge up all manner of poor people as if they were cockroaches or crickets—the poor, the unfortunate, the exhausted, the lame, the degenerate, the drunk—true, they were all drunks!—and stuff them into overflowing "temporary arrest" cells, until after a good month, or even two, they'd decide what to do with them: to plant them in the pokey, or, threatening that pokey, to release them again into the fresh air until the next law and order campaign. It was easy to fall into that contingent. It would have sufficed just to doze off on a bench in some little square, to take a turn without your documents at or near the railroad station, or stop once too many times by the ruins on Latako Street, where the dour and surly homeless, and not just them, gathered to guzzle wine and push time along: there they evened scores, remembered who was six feet under, who was behind bars, sometimes pulled japes on one another. There would be still-young women there, too, with thin violet-colored legs and ragged little coats—despite everything they'd make up their faces! I got to know quite a few of them a bit, I'd call them by name or, more often, nickname, but we never got "tight"—they avoided me a little, didn't entirely trust me; when asked about a place to stay, they'd mumble something vague and I'd go on my way, which would end in temporary shelter with some decent unattached person from among the acquaintances of better times, or, more frequently, in the attic of the graduate students' dormitory—I could nod off there at practically no risk. I was still attracted to people living a stable life, but in most cases they couldn't help me with anything: they were living cramped and frugal lives themselves, consumed and controlled by people and driven by bosses, while those who had it all, you know yourselves how they squint, how sincere the aversion with which they look at the ratty hems of your pants and your lopsided shoes. Almost like Domicėlė twenty years ago. Much later, when my little affairs had gotten considerably better, when I was able to speak ironically of myself, remembering those charmingly grim times, I often just smiled and muttered: *vivere pericolosamente*—live dangerously! I even knew that once upon a time that was Benito Mussolini's favorite saying. Actually, living on the street was dangerous—constantly dangerous. In fact, it would occur to me then too: I need to get out of the city! Drive out, find myself a bed and work at some forest post or a woodland farm and manage somehow—exactly how, I didn't, alas, know. These refined dreams of mine, despite their unfeigned fervor, were quickly dispelled by this tall skinny guy—a metal-toothed man of the pen with a reddish scar above his eyebrow. A professional journalist, his feature stories were works of art! A master of news briefs and summaries, a man who had not just been through thick and thin—he'd even been injured defending a woman from assault. Later he wrote up this incident in detail in an "artistic" feature story published in the local newspaper—he changed the woman's name, but not his own. At Father's Tomb, he bought me two bottles of watered-down beer, then, getting into it, he bought me two more and said straight to my face:

"You're not going anywhere. That's first. Second, why would they need a hatrack like you in the woods?"

"I'd trim branches!" I retorted boldly. "Why?"

He snorted beer:

"I'll tell you, just wait! You'd maybe spend a day trimming out of stupidity or stubbornness. Maybe two. That's it! The third day you couldn't pick up an axe, my brother boozer! It's a forest there! Better men than you can't stay on their feet. If you want, come by sometime for a rest. I have this overgrown place in the country. Some time."

He waved it off, took some more beer, and started in telling about his own, journalistic, kitchen—also overflowing with dangers, like my drifter life. About how he got lost by himself in the desert—he came across an aul only four days later, and nearly got married there! How he spent two days in ambush with a camera waiting for poachers and later—black storks. How the car inspectors tried to get even with him because of a critical article: the bullets, you know, whizzed by above his head like ducks! Was the beer really going to his head so badly, or was he desperately trying to impress me? He moved from his forest to the Caucasus in the blink of an eye; see, he had made himself a hangglider, couldn't get permission here, so he trekked off to Georgia, no less.

"I was flying above the valley," here he leaned his head forward and spread both arms with mugs to the sides, so that even the dazed fellow drinkers took note, "but suddenly—hey, stop making faces!—I was attacked by eagles! Listen, you! I'm circling above a ravine; I set down on a bare rock; the abyss below! They harassed me anyway, maybe they took me for something else. It was my good luck I'd taken along a sandwich with smoked sausage. You know, I fed them, nourished them—they backed off!"

It's true that Benito Mussolini was a fascist, but those same words of his would have suited this bold journalist perfectly—*vivere pericolosamente!* This man had already done his branch-trimming, and his fingers were itching in longing for a pen! He was now—at this point for some reason he wrinkled his brow—writing a study—"Beehives and Oaks"—it only seems they have nothing in common at first glance. But listen, who was going to publish it? Maybe after he was dead! He was clearly regretful to be talking this way, that's why he scowled, raised his eyebrows, looked me straight in the eye, and I was already thinking: It's getting dark, it's drizzling, where am I going to settle down tonight? It's nice, of course, to be here swilling free beer with you, listening to pretty fairy tales, but where were my feet going to take me? It keeps getting colder in that graduate students' attic, even though winter never really came this year. It's the beginning of March—the worst of it is the constantly wet feet and runny nose. We parted warmly: he went off over the little hill to his train, and fate took pity on me again—an old jazz fan, a friend from my time at the Alma Mater, showed up out of the blue. The one who, even back then, constantly listened to nothing but jazz and had a stack of the magazine *Jazz Podium*. Maybe he really did know something about that music, it was just that he hardly ever spoke. He would mutter something vague. He was nearly as poor as I was, but at least he had a tiny little room not far from the Clinics—enough to fit a bed, a table and a stack of books, records, his rather old tape recorder, and a couple of his aunt's paintings: his aunt was famous. A literate man, a man of the arts, in any event. A quiet alcoholic, and a bit of a rascal. Even back then he was immersed in wine, as all true jazz fans are. In his school days he lived in a bigger room in the same house—a chest of drawers stuffed with old copies of the cultural magazines *Židinys* and *Naujoji Romuva* fit in it—but now his brother, an economist, had settled in that chamber with his family. Once this kid brought home paint and brushes from his aunt, and in his free time painted a fresco in the half-niche: "The Russian Grand Duke Lays his Flags Before Grand Duke Kęstutis's Feet." A long, lovely name! And actually, it was pretty good—Kęstutis's shining helmet, the kneeling bearded Russians—when the sun shone in that half-niche, you could recognize everything. I'd stop by there quite often. But not just me. The quiet jazzman wondered for a long time who could have "turned in" his creation to the "art committee"—one Sunday morning the class advisor came over, this curly-haired, fat-lipped athlete; my friend made coffee, even set out a bottle of Aligote. But the advisor just nodded his head. "Paint over that shit, my man, what do you need it for? The historians wouldn't go along with it, either—Kęstutis practically didn't battle with the Russians; he was worried about the West. But don't draw Algirdas, either, no need!" "So what should I draw then?" The fresco painter, emboldened by the wine, got a bit angry. The advisor chewed on the end of a Kazbekas with his fat lips: Put Grunwald up there! The Battle of Grunwald, get it? And after a pause, quickly: Or Stalingrad! But it seems that fresco survived; just that the brother who moved in shoved a three-doored armoire in there—one day the grandchildren will be surprised! So, a drunk with a home and something of a social position. When I said this out loud, he giggled. Just like old times: frescoes and jazz. An editor of labels at a toy factory, a journalist as well, apparently. He'd seen "better times" too. So what was he doing at Father's Tomb? Why was he so happy to see me? Living that way you always get suspicious; you never expect anything good. No reason, he smiled, I just saw you through the trolleybus window and got out. What, I was surprised, trolleybuses go by Father's Tomb? Sometimes, he grinned, look, there's a number eight going by! Really, how could I not even notice? He punched me in the side—are we going? He had money from a debt he'd long since given up on and it was burning a hole in his pocket. At Sonia's he bought white rum, red wine, even cigars and red peppers—he always had a fancy for the exotic. But no *vivere pericolosamente!* No conflicts with family or former wives: sophisticated women, artists, of course! It wasn't just his brother and his family living next to his tiny little room, his "autonomous zone," but an entire flock of relatives: no dramas!

When we blew in by taxi to Klinikų Street, it was clear no one there was happy to see us, no one shouted in joy, but they didn't get in the way of drinking rum and smoking in the warmth of his cubbyhole, either. No one, not even the nephews. We both belonged to the same caste of failures, but his situation was much better: waking up in the night he could shuffle off to the toilet and, lighting a cigarette, examine the table of the USSR soccer championship pinned to the bathroom wall; the nephews carefully filled in the newest results—our "aces" were on its first half. Perhaps he was superior in other ways, but he didn't brag about it. Well, that wasn't his style. He only bragged that he "made ends meet" transcribing music, entire scores. It's doubtful he understood half of what he was writing, but he transcribed them anyway! When he smiled, a thousand little wrinkles would show up on his face, but it seems to me that in even his youth—early youth, not twenty yet—he was wrinkled; not the same way old people are, but wrinkled nevertheless, at least when he smiled, and he smiled almost all the time. Even when he was terribly wretched. The majority of our generation had already overcome their allotment of obstacles: they had fallen from their steeds, splashed and rolled in the mud, sold and again bought cars, beliefs, and outlooks, and either long since stopped writing poems, playing music, or painting, or else earned good money at these arts. Now, still aglow from the ride, the heat of the race, the jolting, the deceptive banked turns and the blows, they deservedly relaxed in the shade of thinly-leafed laurel trees and admired their own tenacity, vitality, and life skills, which they themselves, without even a crumb of modesty, call a lightning mutation. There's nothing more to add. But in my opinion, they could have repeated it too—*vivere pericolosamente!* But of course not at all like me, sitting in this friend's shoe box with a bottle of white rum—Fidel's gift to Soviet alcoholics.

I got drunk instantly; I started blathering nonsense, but he made me some particularly strong tea and we smoked cigars in silence. Following his example, I soaked them in the rum too, but we were a long way off from a real Daiquiri like the one suggested in the recipe written in Russian on the long-necked bottle, since we were missing most of the ingredients.

How could I have known that I would meet you the next day, Tūla? There were no signs, at least as far as I could tell, in either heaven or on earth. I was still a long way off from the webbed, sharp-eared bat with a mouse's soft little belly, a long way off from the bloody flight into the breaking glass.

In the morning I got up and had no idea where I was going next. There's nothing I can do, said the landlord of the cubbyhole, that shaggy-haired child of fortune, you can see for yourself... He spoke the truth, the truth of the one who has a place to stay, even though he was just as much of a lumpen as I. It was all the more painful for that. He was quiet, his hands stuffed into his pockets, then he suddenly decided to make a one-time, non-returnable loan of ten rubles and unexpectedly said: Wait! He immediately returned from his brother's with a swiped bottle of cheap wine, which we drank down in a flash, straight from the bottle. Now, go, go, he pushed me towards the door, go!

The pink ten-ruble bill with Lenin's profile was fairly serious money and for me it was a real fortune on this Sunday morning. Yeah, I already knew where to go—into the warmth and light! A little café on Olandų Street above the Rytas—Morning—grocery, where on the weekends spirits were sold practically without a mark-up, was already open. I knew that on Sundays before lunch, sodden hung-over artists, intellectuals who hadn't managed to make up with their wives yet, and unshaven, greasy-haired plowmen of the street

gathered there—a somewhat grim, but not a rude, even a rather dis-
creet company. This unkempt guy with blue glasses would always be
sitting next to the window by the door—an unrecognized grandee of
the graphic arts. Of course, there were well-fed Luftwaffe aces, too,
who would make girls with reddened cheeks and matrons with big
rings on fat fingers—from sixteen to seventy—giggle. You would see
the "soul" of Old Town here, too: poor Milutė, smeared with vivid
makeup, who plied the oldest trade until she was on her last legs
and nowadays extinguished the sparks of life everywhere, ergo at the
Rytas too, a little café with even a certain amount of pretentious-
ness; two or three painted works hung on the walls and the arm-
chairs were upholstered in dark brown hide, which, although fake,
still struck the visitor as substantial. I headed through the warming
thaw to the trolleybus stop and already saw myself climbing out at
the fire station not far from Peter and Paul Church, carefully cross-
ing the busy street, and heading straight for the Rytas: a little island
of warmth and relative peace in an uncomfortable, hungry, soaking
wet city. And even the more respectable clients of the neighborhood
madhouse found warmth there, the ones who came changed into
normal clothes. The warning hanging above the coffee machine, dis-
concerting at first glance, was no accident: "We don't serve those in
pajamas!"

I had already almost reached the bus stop when it suddenly
struck me; why not stop by my former wifey, I'll get a look at the
child, from a distance at least! Just a few steps! Here's the clinic where
the boy was born three years ago, and there's the milk-formula
kitchen where I used to get him little bottles with porridge and cottage cheese. Really! At the same time as this insanely bold and risky
"*vivere pericolo*" deed, I'll take the little sheepskin coat with a removable lining I'd left there—I could use it! No, that morning wine was
to blame, otherwise I'd never have gone through that communal
apartment block's plywood door next to the toilet. Well, why? To
marvel at how well she manages to live without me, and get enraged?
To gnaw at my nails, because I've lost that which practically everyone

has? No, that bottle of classic rotgut from my friend's brother's untouchable reserve—saved for a delivery man or a plumber—was to blame. No, I thought as I went, the fact that you tied your fate to the commie party wasn't the reason the two of us had such an ugly breakup; I would have borne the connection somehow! And probably not because several times when returning from my duties I ran smack into a famous person in the doorway—the bearded genius who hadn't managed to paint a landscape or a nude for a long time, Romanas Būkas! Well, enough! Būkas, Būkas! I'll grab my coat, take a look at the child, and disappear into thin air. There's nothing I can do to help them anymore, absolutely nothing. And they don't need my help—not in the least!

From a distance I saw a slightly open window: they're home. They hadn't yet left for party training in Petersburg. Of course, the Party never leaves its children like I did. The Party, you see, is incomparably richer; not just richer than the drifters, not just richer than that brother hiding wine from his loved ones, but richer even than those Georgians or Armenians selling garlic, melons, condoms, and fake gold. Yes, even the ones who haunt the front of the Kronika Cinema day and night, even during blizzards, who burn candles in the dark and offer shiny gems from the South. It was wonderfully apt that one of the drunks nicknamed the sculpture group of bronze Soviet partisans in the depths of the square "The Frozen Georgians." What am I going on about, I need to get hold of myself, prepare myself morally, if I'm about to step over the threshold of this house!

There's the perfectly familiar bare little lobby, and there's Katerina Filipovna, the doorkeeper, with her truly powerful bust thrown over the railing. It's really rather unpleasant to remember: Yeah, it was the drunk theater mechanic Leonė who crashed in on me that time, when he'd just bought his breast-feeding wife a breast pump—the first time I'd ever seen such a strange apparatus! He was the one who, guffawing, pressed up to Filipovna's mountains with that milk pump, squeezing its red bulb—the reservoir—while she giggled and blushed, pretending to protest, tickled by curly-haired

Leonė's attention. That didn't stop her from badmouthing me later and complaining to the entire apartment complex's administration—the retired general Gregori Shikin and his right hand man, the Turk Zija Akhotovich. They guffawed, and in their turn abused me with *matushka*—various extremely profane Russian swear words. When she saw me, Katerina smiled wryly, but didn't say anything—this powerful matron knew everything, too! Or almost everything.

My ex-wife was one of those determined women who fought tooth and nail for her place under both the sun and the moon. The Communist Party, into which she had been accepted with such difficulty, shined like the sun for her, and the face of the brunet painter Būkas, stung by life, tobacco, and paint, sparkled like the moon above her. The Party itself calls people like that spirited and principled—always responsible for someone, constantly hurrying, anxious and furious, my better half was perfectly suited both to be a functionary and to be at Romanas Būkas's side. It was only deep in her heart that she mocked her party; perhaps even hated it, the same way she hated a plugged toilet, sewage in the shower, or the rats dashing by outside the window. And my drunken talk that the Party would soon die out of its own accord.

Out in the corridor I could already hear hoarse voices coming from that room and brown cockroaches still crawled under the ragged little carpet by the door just as they had a few years before—I used to smash them without any anger, smoking, right after the child had been brought home from the medical clinic. Even more often I would just watch them nimbly creeping about here and there, disappearing into the cracks and then again sticking out their long, practically elegant antennae—they didn't make me feel any pathological disgust, no lump in the throat or anything of that sort.

Aha, not one voice, but several, well then? And women. Laughter, giggling. I've already raised my fist to knock when I distinguish one voice, I know it: Būkas! Romanas Būkas, the stocky, swarthy genius. Nudes and landscapes. Not Toulouse-Lautrec, but a genius. Shows in Scandinavia, Moscow, Kraków. True, this was in the past—maybe a decade ago. Yes, that's his voice; it's unmistakable. The others there have apparently quieted: he appreciates an attentive audience. I introduced them myself—the wifey and Būkas, who else. With shaking fingers I lit a good-sized damp cigarette butt.

"...and the ice is green, clear, not a flake of snow yet," I clearly heard every one of Būkas's words, even more hollow than usual. "Just—crack! As soon as I plopped into the water I remembered... a dam, a dam ten yards away! Off I go, under the ice, under the ice, to the side! Why I had enough air, why I didn't explode, I don't know to this day! I smashed through the ice with my head! Then on my side, back, on my side again..."

No, it's a far cry from that metal-toothed journalist to Būkas's mastery! The pauses, the intonations, the nuances, and I'm not seeing the eyes or hands, either. I've heard this fantastic story ten times, and now here I am, behind the door, the cigarette butt forgotten, my mouth open, once more listening to how he once miraculously saved himself ice fishing (for all I know it was the holy truth!), how he crawled, wet, dripping, solidifying into a rock, to the nearest farmhouse... drank... lay there, ran a fever, hallucinated... got better...

The second story reached back to even darker times—at that time the narrator served in a unit of border guards. In the Carpathians, in Chop, I believe. I'd heard this detective story from Būkas before too, but more colorfully—during the time he'd come by our house as a friend of the family: always a bit drunk, always sarcastic, but at the same time terribly sad and unhappy. He wasn't, after all, a fool: he knew his fount had already gone dry.

"... and Gribko, our sergeant major, knew—if they undress the countess and find nothing, his stripes would fly, and not just them, oh no! He'd followed her all the way from Moscow—she was riding in a compartment, this trembling old lady with her granddaughter, I think. And then right near the border Gribko noticed that neither the loaf of bread nor the jar of jam on their little table had been touched since the beginning of the journey! Then Gribko..."

I knew already: Sergeant Major Gribko grabbed the bread, the jar, called Būkas and two other sergeants, and as they watched, he broke open the bread, stirred the jam with a spoon; it was full of gold, gems, rings. The old lady fainted, the young one went into hysterics, and they, Gribko and his group, drank like mad for a week—*bez prosveta*—nonstop!

"Then Gribko..." Būkas began, and I stepped inside—Mother Goose shut up and glared at me irately, but pretended to not be in the least surprised. Oh yeah, he was surprised all right! But he managed to control himself so well, carried off the pretense with so much talent, that neither a muscle on his dark face under the bushy eyebrows nor the ends of his mustache so much as trembled. It was the eyebrows and mustache that Lavinija—I mean the wifey—valued him most for; apparently it reminded her of something. A great master! Although by now he hadn't painted either nudes or landscapes for quite some time. Didn't even visit the Literati's Salon anymore. Every last bit of him had moved into everyday reality, into communal apartments like this one, where ears still caught every word of his tales—actual, polished short stories. Oh, Būkas, men and women used to say to him, you should write your stories down some time!

No, he wasn't preparing to start life anew, or even partway. "Why?" Būkas asked, blowing out his cheeks. "I know a lot of people like that! They get the urge for a new life, and change not just their passports, but their first names, last names, and even nicknames, put up with the toughest operations, surgical ones too, and then they suddenly see—it's all shit, not worth bothering with! Everything comes out like a pile of manure in the snow (a vivid, beautiful saying of Būkas's!) and nothing's left but a noose! What for?" He, an extraordinary talent, could even now be sitting in a pale-faced ladies' parlor, where he'd be honored and his slightest wish tended to, rather than in this musty cockroach haven. But no, he's here anyway, next to a stinking squat-hole, surrounded by ordinary little cogs in the works. Really? After all, the still-unfaded Iveta was sitting there, and her intimate friend, the poet Netsaryov, and a couple more sympathetic listeners. Every one of them listening and lending an ear just to him, Būkas; he gave the command to drink, to take a bite; he let sarcastic, witty observations fly, apparently masking his injured soul that way. I was convinced that it wasn't my wifey's soft spots that brought him here. It was loneliness.

I'd barely stepped inside when Lavinija leapt up from the sofa and from under Būkas's arm and started shouting: she won't stand for this! It's her birthday, she's the boss here! There she was mistaken—there was only one boss there: Būkas. But she kept shouting. Shoved me back to the cockroaches in the hallway, but Būkas— well, you see now!—waved a hand, and she let me go. And Romanas Būkas up and invited me to the table, asked me to sit down, poured some wine into a green goblet (I'd brought that goblet home from Lvov once as a gift, and he, apparently, knew it!), pushed a plate of salad towards me:

"Have a heart, woman! Can't you see what a wreck he is!?"

He greatly exaggerated saying that, but what of it. I gave him an angry glance. Būkas laughed:

"He's not dead yet! See, how pissed off he is! You know, I had a dog once…"

And he started telling about a dog, an old Pomeranian, that he was ready to take down to the river and finish off, but… I should have let him have that salad in the beard, but… I really wanted to eat.

Ivan Netsaryov looked at me and Būkas with bloodshot, slightly protruding eyes. He knew everything, too—everything! You won't believe it: I've never met a nicer person. Unbelievably sweet, helpful, perpetually torturing himself over his nation's conceit and pride. I was already planning to ask Netsaryov for at least a fiver, I knew he'd give it without so much as a blink of the eye. Būkas filled my glass again.

"Drink!"

"And get lost!" Lavinija, the beloved wifey, hissed. She saw what bad shape I was in; she saw how angry I was, and she was very pleased.

"Let the man sit for a while!" Būkas graciously allowed. "I'm just warning you—no excesses!" He intentionally used an international word. "No extremism!"

God's rooster, this Būkas was, a wind of fire, you never knew from what direction he'd wallop you with his broad tongue! But even drunk, I would never have overcome him by force, either. And why? He'd just get up—loved and fed—and go off to some other communal apartment, where he'd be planted at the table again, laid in a soft bed, and once more tell stories about green ice and sergeant Gribko's sense of smell.

Netsaryov offered me a cigarette and handed me a lighter. I felt something else in my palm. Well, a fiver—that's a man of gold, he gave it without being asked!

Now I was getting ready to get up and go myself. I forgot that sheepskin coat with the removable lining. But on my way out, I got the urge to tell Būkas who and what he is. He was sitting there spread out on the sofa I had assembled, his feet stuck into my worn slippers; for some reason the slippers particularly infuriated me, and the second glass encouraged bold speech.

"You're shit, Būkas!" I began. "You go through beds like an evil spirit, pretending to be some wise man, a sexosaurus, God knows what! But in the end..."

I shut up—everyone started laughing so hard—even quiet Netsaryov!—that even I got it: who was I to moralize!? Even to someone like Būkas. He himself smiled quite pleasantly, not getting in the least angry, not at all.

"Drink!"

I drank, and Būkas made his only mistake—standing up, he tried to hug my shoulders. I smacked him with my elbow without even looking, and hit him below the chin. Būkas fell down on the sofa and surely would have killed me in another minute, but all he managed was to tear my last shirt—the thin flannel tore almost soundlessly, right to the stomach. I was only saved by Netsaryov and Iveta, ordinary Russians, who were perhaps merely visiting this house by chance.

"Get lost!" Lavinija hissed. "Before I call the police! Bum!"

I got lost, lost, lost... to slide down the green ice the children have trampled down, whee! And no lagoons, no dams! Nor gold fish under the ice. It's snowed, it's winter again, so what if it's the beginning of March—it's warm. If it wasn't for that torn shirt... why did I pull my sweater off? You could suffocate in there; how does the child take it? The child was sleeping; he didn't wake up from the voices or the laugher; the child slept, he didn't wake up, that's good.

I kicked a dead crow. No, a drifter has to live differently than they do: like a drifter. There's no time to torture yourself, blame yourself, or sit with your head in your hands. Without pause, each and every minute, you have to protect your pathetic life, think only of this day and hour, worry about what you'll eat, what you'll drink, where you'll spend the night. If you just start thinking about the time of year, or go digging in your memory, or consider what will be a year or two down the road—amen! You have to worry over every worthless detail, to not let the slightest opportunity to eat or drink go by, to not be ashamed to ask for worn-out shoes or dry socks. And furthermore—you must pay absolutely no further attention to either your physiology or your weakness, your worthlessness. At your horrible envy of the satisfied, or at your fury. Otherwise, it's amen, too. Traits of vagrancy don't manifest themselves in a person right away; for a long time still you're ashamed of your poverty, hunger, and thirst; it's unpleasant when looks follow you down the street. Particularly when you've seen "better times," even though that was exactly what you were running away from, to the street, the fog, the homelessness. In the long run, all of that gets dull and wears away; living under the skies gets much easier. You no longer fear the night, the dark little streets, the nooks and crannies, the strange women—they sense what sort you are from a distance and know they won't get anything out of you. You start getting to know a lot of people you wouldn't have paid the slightest attention to earlier; they talk to you, call you by name or nickname, and now you know, you must know: Never ask what you don't need to ask, never stick your nose into strangers' business.

And don't put on that you're any better, even if you are. If you can, if it's possible, retreat to a distant corner, if you should have such a thing. Like an animal, you have to adapt to new conditions, to merge with the street, the fog, a stall by the market, or a tile in the sidewalk, with the steam, the smoke, the tar, the curses, and the whirlwind of dry dust above the suburban wasteland. Then you'll survive for a while longer—even a drifter's life has its rare highlights—if you don't die, don't stumble under some wheels, if no one pushes you off a cliff, or you don't jump off a bridge yourself, if... When they get to the age of thirty, people aren't suited to be drifters anymore, they're just homeless. Normal thirty-year-olds who could have been drifters have either died by then, or else they have a dwelling, a nest, a home of some sort or another—they've shackled themselves so tightly with unwritten agreements, habits, even feelings, that they no longer have the strength to either leave their homes or live in them. Maybe that's why I don't have my own "to-the-death" gang that would support me and trust me, just as I would have to support them and trust them. I'm too old for them, too boring, too hesitant; they don't trust me with their hiding places and empty apartments, they're too distrustful to let just anyone that comes along into their ranks, and I don't cling to them, no. Even when they end up in cells, in prisons, they don't worry about it too much; they immediately make connections, help each other out, but far more frequently they drown each other... Yes, yes: drown, swamp, save their shabby little hides, lie to your face, behind your back, betray you, settle old scores. No, better to drown alone; it's sweeter that way, and the descent to the bottom is slower.

The theory of vagrancy differs painfully from practice, at least in our geographic latitude. How many excellent books I've read about about unfortunates, the Gavroches, the vagabonds, *der Schlendrian!* One of Hesse's wanderers in the Middle Ages went from monastery to monastery, spent the winter next to a flaming hearth, and tickled the servant girls in the baron's castle until spring! Or sang his severe, endlessly righteous songs somewhere near Baikal, you remember: *Brodyaga k Baykalu podkhodit*—the tramp heads for Baikal! And how many Russian intellectuals with loose shirt-tails, bearded and bold, wandered along the Volga, the steppes, through forests of all kinds, floated with rafts, and tramped from one *stanitsa*—Cossack settlement—to the next. That's something else entirely. In those books and in that life, people were much more tolerant of drifters. They'd take them in for the night, give them some soup. And me? I turn circle after circle in this same soaked, dripping, soot-covered city... circle after circle... Did I live some kind of spiritual life before? Strange question! Of course I did. And now I'd find spirituality even in a flock of sparrows next to the Halės market. A crow's flight from one roof to another frequently seemed difficult and spiritual to me, and only the blue *milítsiya* jeeps, or the painfully yellow ones with blue like a single belt around its belly, eventually triggered a sharp pain in my guts—a hideous cold emptiness would show up there. Just one night in their quarters was enough for me, that time they picked me up with Kardokas, a quiet, gentle young man, a future architect, a friend of Tūla's brother, as it turned out later. No, they didn't beat me there, or the master flutist either (Kardokas played the flute). I suffered all night anyway, not just with a hideous thirst, but with the thought: It's over, they won't let you out again, you're done for! But they released us. When we woke up, Sunday morning was dawning, and on Sundays even the 'pigs' were too lazy to mess with the *brodyagi*—tramps. Besides, I was still registered—they checked. The flutist stayed—inside Kardokas's waterproof bag (how could I know?) the pigs found about thirty yards of denim from Latvia. They didn't want to believe the musician intended to cover his pad's walls with it.

It was stupid of me, of course, to fall into their hands. After all, I didn't even flee from the café in the Exhibition Building when the barmaid Zoselė—and every one of us heard her!—summoned a patrol. "Never been like this here before!" the straw-haired woman shouted, "Never!" Kardokas and I had brought some cheaper wine to this little café, sipped it quietly, like everyone else smoked half-surreptitiously, and weren't paying any attention, not even to Romanas Būkas wildly waving his arms about—he was there encircled by artistic ladies—every one identical!—wearing leather pants, heavy sweaters, and delicate pendants on bloodless necks. Būkas, I remember, was telling this story:

"Then I climbed up on the van's roof, opened the window to the restaurant, opened the curtains .. and plop, my foot went right into all those aspics with caviar! On all their beauty and tastiness! Good grief!"

Perhaps his story inspired the amateur flutist? We were sitting with our backs to Būkas and his ladies, we heard everything. He hadn't managed to tell me this story yet, so I was listening, too.

"...The furies are shrieking, their calves bleating, and I'm tromping around in the middle of the table, like... well, like a bull in a china shop! I stomped on roses and lilies, and then whoosh! onto the floor and I'm out the door... Well, no! All three waiters jumped me, arms behind my back, dragged me off to their little room, and smack! Smack, smack! Hey!"

Maybe it just seems to me now that the phlegmatic flutist pricked up his ears and started drumming his fingers and tapping his feet?

"...they beat me up, turned my pockets inside out, found three rubles, so they took those too, of course! Well, I retreat, all bloody, to the door and say: 'Dear Iveta, there really is no room in this nightclub!' "

For some reason, it was just as he heard these words that Kardokas, the flutist and clarinetist too, the architect, the Kaunas native, the phlegmatic, jumped up, with one bound leapt over to the bar and turned it over, knocked all the glasses stacked up in the case to the ground, a lot of glasses—maybe a hundred, maybe even more. Four or five shelves—trays, glasses, trays, more glasses... Some survived intact, of course, but the floor was full of shards. Even Būkas and his lady admirers were shocked—now you've done it! That's when Zoselė called. The patrol arrived. Told me to get up, too, shoved me in the back, and led me into the street where the yellow jeep was already waiting. And after all, I could have left quite calmly a hundred times over; no one would have lifted a finger!

Why did I remember all that while walking from the fire station towards the Rytas? I don't know. Maybe because a siren went off with flashing lights and two of those same jeeps, yellow with a blue belt, flew by. Sometimes they're a disgusting green too, maybe I've already mentioned that? The green of a pregnant cat's shit, some contemporary literary protagonist would say. A drifter—never. *Voronokas* was what we called them, from the Russian for a paddy wagon.

Maybe I did make a blunder? After all, if I had behaved properly... No! I would have either insulted someone or broken something anyway. A plate, a flower pot... No, no. But what's this? Here's the door to the Rytas already, faster, clump, clomp, there's such a sleet plopping down that everything's instantly plashing. Some kind of yellowish precipitation, painted as it were, sort of the color of Hungarian vermouth. And what do I see? Today Indėnė's at the bar: slender, dark, firm, strong. And fast—the glasses, bottles, mugs, plates simply fly in her hands; it's a pleasure to watch her work!

Standing at the end of the line, I looked over the small "salon." The same people. Hats placed on the knees or the window sill, red-faced girlfriends set beside them; mustachioed, bearded, bald; they all look a little like losers, somewhat unhappy and tired. There's no fire flaming out of their nostrils anymore, and the gleam in their eyes is slowly fading. Just reflections, shimmers, and the stench of hangovers from half-toothless mouths. But now, when a wet snow is falling outside, life doesn't look either gloomy or hopeless to them; more likely the opposite, at least as long as they can still buy a glass and whisper something into a gold-toothed woman's ear.

With a glass of white Havana Club, I sat down next to three men—there was only one I didn't know. Dignified. Big-nosed. A gray mustache and goatee. A green jacket and a tobacco-colored shirt. Practically the only one sitting here with his coat off. Nails clean, darkened glasses. His nose really did resemble De Gaulle's, only the height wasn't even close. The two other lumpen, compared to him, were boring, half-drunk television men. Actually, they were pompous, unbelievably important and meaningful to themselves, but I saw right through them; pennies jingle, even I'm richer today!

The gentleman in the tobacco-colored shirt impressed me; he spoke freely, teased his colleagues, and didn't advertise himself. It was just that he, too, had come to the end of his resources. When those two staggered out, I bought some rum for him too—unheard-of generosity! De Gaulle immediately appreciated my gesture; he got it into his head to drive over together to his aristocratic friends, borrow a lot of money, and party just with me, in some nice surroundings, without any hassle. I sacrificed my last two rubles for the taxi and we drove to Klaipėda Street where he—it'll just be a minute!—disappeared in the darkness of a baroque door. The minute took a half-hour, but apparently the negotiations weren't in vain; as soon as he appeared in the doorway I understood: he got it! That's yet another drifter's trait: from the slightest gesture, even a faked one, you instantly understand—success, failure! De Gaulle stopped a sedan, even though we only needed to walk just a few steps. Settling with the taxi driver, he ordered me to take the change—for my "autonomy." We sat in the same little café where once the clarinetist and denim material trader had knocked the entire display case of glasses and tumblers to the floor. We squeezed into the very corner. I sat next to the big window covered with blinds and lazily blew smoke. Apparently another gathering of art people. But here there was a great deal more vanity, freethinking, a bit more dress, and less in the way of *mat*—cussing in Russian. Just an occasional bleepity bleep, for the sake of weightiness. I see that corner table next to the door as if it were yesterday—not next to the bar, where the entrance was earlier, but in the depths of the café. A wide, long table, enough maybe for eight exhibition visitors. This time Būkas was nowhere to be seen. Kanutas "de Gaulle" and I in the very corner, next to us a tiny linguist with a face etched in fine veins and his dignified friend, some clerk from the Culture Ministry. Or maybe Education. Beyond the blinds evening had already fallen. Think less about what you'll do with yourself today, I said to myself, there's still a whole hour before this corner of heaven closes. De Gaulle spoke loftily about those dark times when he was a young man and didn't have a cent: wonderful, hungry, bohemian times! Turning around, he agreed with the linguist that our surnames are either Slavic or just simply uninventive: almost all of them should be changed! The surprised linguist smiled and waved a childish little hand: "What are you going on about, Kanas, that's enough!" Turning to me again, he went on—boringly, drearily, even though entirely correctly: "Everything comes when you don't have either the health or the energy anymore!" He kept tugging at my sleeve: "Hey, do you hear me?" I heard everything! Now he had money up to his ears, but what of it? I drank his expensive brandy, boldly smoked his cigarettes, slurped lukewarm coffee, and under my breath, neither to myself nor him, recited Aistis:

> It's a day as colorless as spirits,
> Like glass, like the purest spring!
> It's all one to me that gravediggers
> scatter the amber sand

A couple of girls looked at me—they were sitting opposite, swilling dry wine and blowing lots of smoke alternately at the ceiling or at de Gaulle's goatee. I saw one smirk mockingly.

"A Capricorn!" Her neighbor pointed at me, but she didn't concern me either, not in the least. I was already sobering up, a question mark writhed together with the smoke: So, where will you retreat to, wanderer? De Gaulle poked me in the side:

"Hey, maestro! Maybe you're blind? The way she's looking at you! Lord, the way she's looking!"

It was rhetoric. His speech was not just smooth; it had a constant passionate intensity as well. At first this impressed me, but by now I was tired of it. I let the blast from the other table go by as if I hadn't heard it either: "A Capricorn!" Yeah, a Capricorn, what of it? All I wanted was to stretch out my legs, have a smoke, and after stubbing it out—for sure stubbing it out!—go to sleep.

"Listen, you catch up with her," de Gaulle urged me, "Believe me, it's been a long time since I've seen a look like that! The way she was looking!"

I shook myself like a dog, put on my plaid coat lying next to me, and took off—okay, I'll catch up. The place is closing, anyway. What came over me—I have no idea. The vestibule was empty; the girls have gone out already, I thought, but they can't have gotten far. Aha, there they are! The brown fur jacket is next to Kapsukas's greatcoat now—she's going past it, one turned off... Faster! Someone stuck a fist out a car window—what are you up to?—but I was already panting next to Micky-Mickevičius's pedestal. Next to the object of my pursuit (a delicate little girl to look at), her friend—the tall one—strode along in striped soccer leggings. I'll find out later that she carpets her bed with knitting needles and unread books. Breathing heavily after I'd stopped running, I walked along next to them, and neither said nor asked anything. I walked, that was all. No reaction, even though they see I'm intentionally walking next to them, and they saw me chase after them. To my pleasant surprise, the soccer player waved in parting and ducked into an archway across from the bookstore. She turned back once from the sculptor Petras Repšys's decorative metal window netting and then vanished. She, Tūla, was walking next to me. I didn't know her odd name yet. I didn't sense anything yet. It made no difference to me what she would do—continue along a bit together and then disappear without a word, like her long-legged friend did, or immediately retreat to the side, casting off some word—goodbye, Capricorn! She'll dart off like a weasel—she's so tiny, even with that jacket! But we were still going down Maksimo Gorkio Street towards the Cathedral.

> So-o-o-ldiers marching through the sand,
> You've left your homes be-e-e-hind!

The high guys started singing unexpectedly right next to us. She giggled, I smiled, but we continued without a word. I was breathing more evenly now. I stuffed my hands into my roomy pockets and, feeling the change from the taxi driver there, figured it would cover some beer. When the two of us, still not saying a word, neared the miraculously still-open deli at Jono Biliūno Lane, I acted rather sensibly, or at least it seemed so to me then.

"You could wait here," I said, "I'll go in and buy some beer!"

If she wants, she'll wait, if she wants—she won't. Is waiting a commitment? Beer, too. If she waits, well then… I stood in a line of several people and glanced uneasily through the steamed window into the street, even though I didn't see anything there except for the ghostly silhouettes of people going by. Tūla waited. Waited with her green fabric bag ready. Well then… I piled five bottles of Tauras beer in there.

"Carry it yourself!" My mute traveling companion spoke at last. No, I didn't even know what to call her. It was the first time I'd heard her voice from so close. I was astounded—a throaty, hollow voice; isn't that how trampled moss, stirred depths, a spirit speaks? I don't even know what I could have compared that quality to.

Now, I thought, we'll go down to the Vilnelė—there now, it's not sleeting anymore, it's not even freezing anymore!—we'll find a spot there, even if it's on that little covered bridge!—I'll open a couple of bottles… offer her one… will she drink it or not? Maybe she won't, but she'll at least sit or stand next to me. She took my arm. I grasped the bag with the beer more comfortably and bent my other arm more comfortably, too. I glanced into her face under the street lamp in Biliūno Lane. A bright, calm face. She raised her eyes and smiled.

The concrete bridge; the cloister; the Water Safety's quarters not far from Malūnų Street—everything in this neighborhood is perpetually etched into my memory, just as it is in Kamarauskas's watercolors, the topographical and military maps of the city, and the memoirs of notables. I gave an expansive wave towards the covered bridge:

"Maybe we should go over there, my dear? Under the roof?"

"No, my dear." she answered in a voice I never from that moment forgot. "Let's go to my place. I live here. Over there, the lit window, Petryla's at home."

She laughed. "Petryla's my landlord!"

That same house with the apse I've already talked so much about. The one next to the cloister, next to the dug-up remains of the old water conduit.

Back then, all there was in the apse was a tiny door and stairs to the second floor; I looked it over later, when a major renovation had begun. Still later, I had the chance to see Kamarauskas's watercolor too—there's a patient man! He drew every window, every crumbling masonry patch, every cornice and chimney; he didn't forget anything. That house was in that 1896 aquarelle wash, too, but brighter and merrier. The same footpaths next to the same creek, the same trees, and even the same flimsy little fences and sheds, what else. Only the high fences are long gone, and townsfolk's lush gardens grew in the spot where the mugwort and the dug-up water conduit are now.

"Let's go," Tūla tugged at my sleeve. "It's my place, too."

We stopped at the door.

"Now you wait."

And coming out a few minutes later:

"You're an old friend of mine. We haven't seen each other in two years!"

I agreed to it all—why not stop in? I stepped over the threshold, followed her down a dark corridor up to a whitish door. Someone coughed in the kitchen—a man with the heavy cough of a smoker. Aha, Mr. Petryla!

The moment I stepped inside I glanced at the room's graceful, nicely proportioned vault. How could I have known that with my tiny, thin bat's feet I would spend long nights hanging there, that this, Tūla, would be where bluish lilac would shower over your body... I saw none of it coming.

VI

With nearly fifteen years gone by since that damp week in March, every time I remember Tūla I think she was a terribly lonely person. This sort of beautiful, sad foreign body in a city mad with worries and greed—with slightly puffy lips and a carmine spot on a khaki skirt. Easily hurt and lonely, as if she were living in the parallel universe everyone so likes to talk about now. After all, it was only because of that loneliness that she invited me then into her vaulted hall, where I tripped on a box, fell on her low cot, and announced: I'm not going anywhere! For an entire week we didn't part, neither day nor night; we didn't let one another either out of sight or out of touch. We couldn't get enough of either the sight or the joy of one another, but I cherished no illusions it would last for long—I avoided commitments and responsibilities, I feared hurting her. But when at the end of that week she meekly offered that we up and visit her parental home—she hid nothing, absolutely nothing, from her mother!—I, the fool, immediately agreed, and lost everything at once: Tūla, the desire to live "like a human" or even just a bit more decently and more spiritually. Actually, I had nothing to lose yet; those riches still shone only vaguely, like the dim streetlights on Užupis's hills, like will-o'-the-wisps, or glowworms.

Even now I still find myself wondering—well, maybe I didn't even love her? Maybe the two of us just blazed up like naked wires blindly touching in the dark; we sparked, and that was it, total darkness again? Maybe. But no… no. After all, I remember her more and more often with pain and frustration, even more so today, now that I cannot find out whether with the years her husky voice didn't turn into a bass, if the down on her upper lip didn't grow into a black forest, if she still laughs with that crackling laugh that so drove me out of my mind? If it's just my frustration at the inconclusiveness, then it's much too vigorous and strong; after all, there's so much I've forgotten, buried, covered with the dirt of oblivion, and the dirt's long since subsided, nobody underground is complaining to me anymore! I don't even remember the people who helped me so much; I don't remember the faces of those women in whose tiresome embrace I would wake up in some dingy suburb—and I don't want to remember anymore! But Tūla keeps emerging from the crowd on the streets, from the ripples in the creek; she drifts down like a maple leaf brushing against my bare neck. I get the shivers when I see a young artist resembling her, with a portfolio under her arm; no, it's probably not frustration, not just that. After all, she was the one who forced me to kick my feet against the muddy bottom, to give myself a shake and at least look about; I felt that I wanted to live yet, to stroke Tūla's breasts bright as onionskin, to dive into her depths, to emerge and look into her frightened eyes, and together with her swim off above the burdock and the apse, even up to the rooftops, and together furiously swinging our cracked heels, to flap up even higher, and when we'd descended to the earth, to again blow smoke through that air vent barely holding on its hinges, into the wasteland where today the water conduit from Sigismund's time—is it really Sigismund?—is dug up, where, at the end of the nineteenth century, beets and dill flourished and salmon swam the Vilnelė to spawn.

After all, the two of us were neither naive nor green; we weren't even terribly derelict, Tūla wasn't, that's for sure. Most likely we were both pierced at the same time by a desire to save ourselves, a lucky instinct knocked us over into your puny cot and didn't disappoint; we felt a spiritual connection almost instantly, there was no need to go groping about scrutinizing—are you really the one? Are you her? You know, I said to her the next morning, we're Mongols.

Why Mongols? Well, in the course of a single night, out of a primitive society we've achieved mature socialism, actually, a great deal more, speaking seriously, or maybe not? She was already prepared to laugh, everything still made us laugh like little kids. But she started laughing almost hysterically, truly unto tears; she shook with laughter, all of her little body trembled, I could barely hold Tūla in my arms. She was no longer laughing; out of breath, she just nodded her head somewhere under my armpit: "Really, really, really!" I was lying barely a foot above the ground, with a woman collapsed in laughter whom I didn't even know yesterday, and felt happier than I had ever been. There's just no words; actually, I'd never yet experienced happiness like that. I was cheered by the dim March morning, for some reason I was cheered by her lodging's poverty and smells, the boxes stuffed with papers, clothes and memories, the empty bottles of paint, lotion, iodine, and crusted kefir set on the windowsill, and the shadows of early crows flashing past the window—they were out catching the worms. "We'd just gotten lost somewhere… Now we've found each other," she said to her brother who stopped by. She smiled saying that, and burst out laughing; so sincerely, that in that laugh I heard everything I was missing: warmth and tenderness, a woman's pride in her man or even mate, a little bit of doubt, and finally, an open confession—I don't know what will come of it, but what's happened is wonderful!

I could have investigated every little thing in her room, but time was short then, and now, even though I've forgotten nothing, I have neither the desire nor the strength to rummage about in that vaulted dwelling where the two of us, lying on our stomachs, turned the pages of a worn album of reproductions and laughed at Petrov-Vodkin or maybe some other Peredvizhniki realist's picture, not because they were funny—we were, quite simply, happy! And those pictures! Look for yourselves: on a bench in a square sits this red-shirted, hatted young man with an accordion on his knees and a red-cheeked girl with a bundle rests her head on his shoulder. "A Visit to the City," or something. That square, by the way, was remarkably similar to the little three-cornered square next to the mutt market, the toilets, and the taxi stand, so how could you not laugh?

That morning she saw my torn shirt too. But of course she didn't ask anything, just pulled hers out of a plywood box and threw it to me—soft, flannel, Chinese—and said it was way too big for her. We didn't leave the house the entire first day; her brother brought beer, and spring, real spring, was still a long way off.

It's only now that that week with Tūla seems endless to me. I've said it, haven't I: I remember every minute, every spot we were, where I met her, where she accompanied me. I remember that when I showed up the second evening, Petryla just cleared his throat; on the third evening, unwillingly laying out my grim life for her, I found out, completely unexpectedly, that her grandfather and step-grandmother, her step-uncle and even more distant relatives—in a word, an entire broad branch of her family—budded, blossomed, and set fruit under the sunny skies of my tiny town! She wasn't surprised; she listened to all my opinions about the town and that vigorous branch, didn't interrupt me once, and didn't ask anything. What for? After all, we would still have lots of time, time to tell one another everything, both about little towns and distant relatives. She had even been to my town; they all went to visit her grandfather, a long time ago. She remembered only the boulevards—such a thing in the provinces seemed particularly beautiful and strange to her—and the coal cars on some side tracks. I'd seen that house covered with yellow tiles, yeah, I knew where it was. Now it's long since been sold, and the tiles have been replaced with slate as gray as the fog after a thaw. That was the first time I felt something like unease; that home town of mine is small, everyone knows everything about everyone else, so that family has its opinion of me! Up until then, of course, they weren't at all interested in me. And now? But I just pressed my palm more firmly on her frog-like little belly—like anyone there cares about me!

As soon as the two of us extricated ourselves and went out—and I do mean extricate, since the week crept by mostly under Tūla's vaults—she would immediately cling to my arm. I hated that kind of clinging as much earlier as I do now! I always felt restricted; this kind of intimacy, in my opinion, blocked traffic too—it's a worthless bourgeois custom. If you had only seen how happy and even proud I was, feeling her arm! If I regret anything, then it was just that it wasn't summer yet, so I couldn't feel Tūla's bare arm while hurrying across Pilies Street or climbing up Bekešo Hill; as soon as the snow melts, that's where we'll clamber up, first thing!

Tūla's quiet and husky voice reaches my ear yet today, but now I'll never again feel her sneaking up from behind and giving me a warm little snuggle, her breathing on the back of my neck or the top of my head, her damp cheek in the little yard next to the Bernadine façade—not from tears, but from the rain and snow...

Tūla had the time to make discoveries, too. "I can with you," she said when, snickering and giggling, she slurped on a lukewarm bottle of beer not far from the Orthodox Church of the Holy Mother of God; there was a fad at that time to sell supposedly warm beer on the streets.

On our fourth day together, success visited me: Herbert Stein, meeting us by Gannibal's tiny Orthodox church, delivered a remittance receipt. Since I had no address, I gave those wanting it Herbert's box number at the Central Post Office; see, it came in handy! And how handy! Tūla and I didn't have a cent left. The money—seventy some rubles—came from a journal for disabled people: I had, some time before, translated an intelligent article for them: "Suicide: Not a Solution!" or something like that. What timing! It was like it fell from the heavens; at the same time, it was clear evidence that I wasn't completely ruined yet, see, sometimes valuable remittance papers fall into that guy's box!

I immediately took Tūla to the Daina, a little café smelling of mold and the kitchen on what's now Vokiečių Street. (It's not there anymore, either.) Back then it even seemed cosy to me, partitioned, like Tūla's room, with decorative wooden panels. An inexpensive, sort of clean café with a tiny bar and a coat clerk who was always a little drunk. I wanted to always be with Tūla, to slurp plain cafeteria borscht together, drink wine, smoke in the courtyards or stairways, to wander around the chilly soot-covered city, collect sorrel alongside the railroad tracks in the spring... And even more: to slowly turn gray, old, and babble more and more nonsense. That's probably the way two people who aren't afraid of losing anything anymore should live, people who no longer expect much from either the world or themselves, who are happy with what's given to them—sleeping when they're tired, and awakened, climbing the hills beyond the city again, waving to the birds and airplanes, amusing serious people a bit and irritating the eggheads a bit; they'd like to behave that way themselves, but they can't, so they squirm, mumble, and get furious with themselves. You see, they look for a causal relationship everywhere. I was already somewhat past thirty. Tūla was six years younger. What more?

We sat in that half-empty café under a shepherd blowing a *lumz-delis*—a pipe—on a decorative shelf, slurped noodle soup with dumplings, and chewed on a piece of low-grade meat labelled an entrecôte. Later we drank coffee and red wine: an entire bottle of Gamza. Like in a picture, I thought, elated, watching her raising a tall glass in the murky dusk of the café, watching her set it on the table without taking her fingers off the wide stem; what luck, that not many find her as beautiful and fetching as I do—her slow movements are beautiful, the stir of her voluptuous lips before uttering some meaningless word is beautiful, even the little unbuttoned button on her boots is beautiful. How nice she's not one of those the young bucks turn to look at in the street. She wasn't ashamed of her so-called plainness, just as she wasn't ashamed of the carmine paint spots on her skirt; she gently mocked the peacocks and fashion hounds sitting at the next table, and asked me: listen, is a man supposed to wear a jabot in a place like this? And without waiting for an answer she choked back laughter. It's allowed! Unhappy about something, she would just shake her short dark hair, and during the entire week she only once asked me: do you really love me? I nodded so vigorously that one of the vertebrae in my neck cracked—she heard it and laughed: I believe you! Aha, it was in this café she asked that, before the gloomy customer sat down next to us. We were just drinking our wine, about to finish. We chattered endlessly and boundlessly. Giggled. It was Saturday afternoon, no, Friday; on Saturday we left town. Half the café was filled with decent Vilnius intellectuals, winos, self-styled and real artists, students with the faces of idiots and geniuses, and workers from the neighboring offices; they didn't bother us a bit, we simply didn't notice them. But when the gloomy man sat down next to us, we instantly quieted, for just a bit, of course. But even he didn't concern us: some kind of awkward, clumsy, true stranger in this half-way decent salon. He obviously didn't care for us—he didn't even try to hide it—he grumbled in his chair, waiting for his order of vodka and herring with onions. It was only when Tūla couldn't resist and pecked me somewhere on the ear that the man couldn't take it anymore:

"Listen, this is a café, after all, not..."

He spoke, and then got flustered; his pockmarked face turned red and darkened, and not just from the vodka. He poured out what was left in the carafe, downed it in one fell swoop, wiped his fleshy lips with his sleeve, and fixing his eyes on the table announced to us:

"I just came from the morgue. My son hung himself yesterday!"

Then he muttered, "Excuse me, what am I doing!?" waved his hand, and standing up, turned for the door. Now I could, of course, convince myself that it was a sign, a warning; we needed to stand up and take off, each in our own direction: she—to Malūnų Street, and I—not to Malūnų Street.

But we both went, very slowly, to Malūnų Street: we went to bed very early. The round government cable radio speaker quietly played, spoke, and sang in Petryla's empty kitchen; there was no other radio technology in that house, thank God. We lay down practically without undressing, just throwing on an old plaid blanket; we didn't even open the bottle of wine we'd brought home, just held each other by the hand and listened to the music. Classical music poured out the door open to the kitchen; the radio was broadcasting extracts from world-famous operas, so famous even I could guess them: Aida, Turandot, Carmen, Rigoletto. Someone knocked quietly on the window glass; even though I was lying there without saying a word, Tūla lifted a finger and put it on my lips: we aren't at home for anyone. The world outside the window flew, fermented, buzzed, rotted, sharpened its teeth, and sparked, while I felt Tūla's breast under her sweater on my palm: the bird's heart throbbed under the thin threads. The world was full of poverty, fear, uncertainty, violence, and cosmic mysteries; full of the shuffling of wet feet and the ringing of glass, but out of the kitchen, as Radamès's warriors tromped in, the march of triumph echoed. I held her in my embrace; I could have tied her to myself with belts, cording, ropes—Tūla was already asleep—but I was swept by deep despair: I knew I could lose her any minute now, even feeling the warmth of her body under my palms, even hearing her quiet breathing in her shallow early evening sleep. A despair like that sometimes so sharpens the eyesight and keens the hearing that some people instantly see through things, while others instantly go blind. I was just waking Tūla from sleep; she hadn't really lived yet. I wasn't in a hurry to solve the riddle—why didn't she want to live? After all, she was already waking; she'd wind her arms and legs around me even in her sleep, but in her awakened eyes I saw emptiness and mistrust—who's that lying next to me, who are you, you who have penetrated my body and aim to penetrate my soul? Go away, her back seemed to say, leaning over the basket of potatoes, I don't know yet… And the next moment, she'd turn around, her slender arms would wrap around my neck, and I had no idea anymore: would she get better, or not? I was certain I would sense myself what she needed most: Quiet? Activity? I would know everything from her snuggling, her glances, her silence; not just from her walk, but from how she stood and how she lay. Of course.

Isolde suffered waiting for Tristan in Petryla's kitchen, while I, finally opening the wine, poured it for her, kissed her hair and ears, intruded on her business, crawled into her flat, narrow, and already

so familiar body, but I didn't ask about a thing—my soul fluttered
under the vault and watched us as if from the side. Probably by now
our bodies' bacteria had already gotten used to each other, mixed
together, and no longer fought among themselves; our spittle and
lymphatic fluids had mingled—her tears turned into rheum in the
corner of my eye, or maybe the other way around? Carmen raged
before dying in the kitchen; Tūla quietly moaned several times and
dug her nails into my back. Then she whispered right in my ear, shivers even went down my spine: "I thought, I thought I didn't need
this anymore. I thought!" Boredom did not threaten our exhausted
bodies, our vitamin-craving cells, our eyes, our ears, or the tips of
our fingers. But I should have tempered her slowly, I should have
arranged romantic meetings next to the Vilnelė's shoals or one of
the little bridges, I should have brought flowers and quoted Ovid,
Catullus, and Radauskas! I should have been charmed by her, been
concerned about her, amaze her with my abilities: Tūla was worth all
of that. I didn't do anything; I didn't have anywhere to live myself.
Yeah, I did tell her everything right away—but was it really everything? She didn't go to work that week; she would just call someone
and not go. They didn't miss her much there, I guess. Tūla didn't like
her job, her employer, or talking about her job. She worked at a toy
design office; that was all I ever knew about her job. She didn't say
anything, but I understood anyway; if she left her job, the men and
women there would just breathe easier.

Tūla had been gone for some time—gone to me—but I kept
stopping by the house with the apse; when Tūla left to go live in
Kaunas, the Second City, her brother moved in there. Later he vanished too, along with all of his boxes, but I stopped in anyway, by then
to see Petryla, the unhealthy enzyme factory worker. In the filthy,
smelly kitchen, the radio broadcast variety shows and folk songs and
trumpeted arias from operas and operettas, while we would guzzle
wine until the landlord fell asleep collapsed on the table. Waking up,
he would stagger off to his cell, and I'd curl up on an empty mattress

in *that same* room. Sometimes I'd doze off, but if that insomnia well-known to drunkards would come over me, when even though you're worn down to the nubs you can't manage to fall asleep, I'd page through all the old journals and magazines, older even than the old inhabitants who'd left them here—from *Mokslas ir gyvenimas* (Science and life) to *Pozharnoye delo* (Firefighting science). Yes, there are such things! Back then Petryla wasn't yet, comparatively speaking, an old man, but he was already marked too; his panting, coughing and spitting kept getting louder. And how old he seemed to me at the time! Now I've almost caught up to Petryla as he was then! He just seemed so decrepit, cranky, and mean; he'd buried two wives and his freckled, skinny son went into the army. Petryla was from somewhere near the Curonian Lagoon; neither his old house nor the stream babbling nearby produced any sentiment in him. We'd sit in the kitchen with a bottle, but we never talked about Tūla. In a certain sense, we'd both been rejected by her. Only once—and how much water had already gone under the bridge since that week!—Petryla slammed a large enameled pot down on the dirty oilcloth: There! I only just now found it in the snow! That's her doing, hers! Mixed her paint in it, was too lazy to wash it up, and threw it out! Petryla actually got heated in his anger; he hurled that pot down on the floor. On its once-white side was drawn—in the factory, of course—two horses with their heads lowered: a mare and a colt. "Who does things like that!?" Petryla fumed, as if Tūla were still living there. I picked up that pot with the dark paint dried in it and asked him to give it to me; Petryla just waved his hand: "Whatever! Take it." So why was he so angry, huh?

So Tūla still connected us: Petryla the enzyme cooker and me the drifter. But Petryla didn't grieve over Tūla in the least; he drank purely out of boredom, or maybe because he already had a presentiment. He'd occasionally bring some little lady from his milieu home to grope in the dark; he had a place to take them to. While I wandered over there solely so it would once more hurt and ache: I'd come to once more toss and turn on that same mattress, especially since

I was still wandering the city at the time. Well, regardless, Petryla wasn't a bad guy. Once he gave me the keys: Here! You can live there until some renter shows up. Then leave, and see to it that I don't have to remind you of it!

Renters showed up after some two weeks; they came with baskets, portfolios, and suitcases along the bank of the Vilnelė, put five hundred rubles on the kitchen table, and Petryla just spread his short arms: You see yourself! What can I do? He immediately sent me out for vodka and wine, and by the time I brought them back, the table was already set for a feast. The girls—future painters—landed like tornados: They drank, sang, smoked, winked at me, nearly convinced Petryla to pose naked for them, drew an indecent silhouette of a man on the kitchen wall in charcoal, tossed raw eggs at it... Petryla was falling out of his chair laughing, pounding on his knees, but I knew—tomorrow he would be furious, hiss, ask, where did *that* come from!? We all three went to lie down; brown Joana and white Dovilė on the edges, and me in the middle. Lying on my back, I caressed both their substantial breasts and tried to see the vault's edge, as sharp as a razor; did I really hang up there? Then my hands almost in unison slid down to their dark groins; did they in the least suspect what my other hand was doing? Dovilė snored like a sea lion, but Joana knew what was going on; she so encouraged me, so provoked me, that I couldn't hold out; I banged her right there, next to her snoring friend, who didn't even wake up.

I didn't go there for a long time, maybe a year, and when I stopped by, a completely unfamiliar girl opened the door. Neither Joana, nor Dovilė. It was thundering outside, I was already sopping wet, dirty, drunk, rude. I never did figure out why that sturdy, somewhat clumsy girl didn't boot me out the door, but instead pulled me inside. No, no, she didn't know any Dovilė, no Joana, but she knew me! Petryla's in the hospital, she whispered (I wouldn't recognize her today in the street). Come on in, she said, wiped my face dry, and then she was rubbing my entire body—with spirits and with herself—you're so frozen! I know you, really I do... I've seen you in Skarga's courtyard,

you were talking to my professor... so I know you, come closer..."
She lay down next to me, gave me tea to drink, poured some diluted
alcohol, rubbed and massaged me again, until she started snorting
and panting, and all of her powerful and blindingly white body—at
least so it seemed to me—began to tremble threateningly. I was lying
on my back; as if it were today, I see two giant breasts swinging above
me, looking like the wrecking balls tied to a cable they use to smash
and wreck old buildings. She fell on me as if on an innocent child,
I sank... and was out of action. But I do remember the next morning: how that gloomy room shone! Clean, tidy, expensive things;
mirrors, little carpets, runners, pungent scents, and horrifying oleo-
graphs where Tūla's paintings once hung. I was rested and managed
without any problem to do what I apparently couldn't or didn't want
to the night before. Stop by, she said, after all, I saw you in Skarga's
courtyard, yes, Skarga's! She hammered on that courtyard! Ofelija
was the name of that big-breasted student of Lithuanian, Ofelija
Ordaitė. She read me her delicate poems, but I barely managed to
get a drop for my hangover from her. "From this day forth you won't
drink a a drop!" was what she declared. Lord, I sighed, how patient
you are! For some reason she had decided to make something out of
me even if it was in a hurry. She sat down to peel potatoes and gave
me a good-sized bill: "Get some butter, cream and rolls!" I managed
a smile and left. I don't know, maybe she's still waiting for me today
with some hot potatoes? A Lithuanian major, Ofelija Ordaitė. O.O.;
I don't remember anything more. It was my last visit to that house
with the apse while there were still people living in it. While it still
lived that gloomy, poor, but human life of its own, and not just in
Kamarauskas's watercolor.

A few years later, after I returned from the Drunkard's Prison—
if it will be allowed, I'll talk a bit more about that later—I went back
there again, and before I had gotten up to the Water Safety Zone's
red-brick house, a long ways away on the other side of the Vilnelė,
I saw the the black eye sockets of Tūla's former windows. She was
still alive herself somewhere; she still was, then. No one looked out

those windows, only darkness; no one lived there anymore: my heart ached. I don't know how else to describe it. I smoked on the covered bridge until a woman came out of the Institute building—maybe a security guard?—who up and asked: what are you standing here for? Apparently I looked suspicious; my hair hadn't even had time to grow back yet.

Famished ginger cats and fat gray tabby cats slunk below the window sills of Tūla's house; wild hemp and mugwort burgeoned right up to the windows; a bit lower there was an entire plot choked by burdock—a real wasteland! But the blue mail box was still hanging on the door that barely held, and inside a perhaps forgotten lamp shone dimly. On the second floor, through a window covered in rags, a rumpled, gray old lady poked her sharp nose out. She giggled and disappeared. Like a shade, I thought; just like a shade.

The house was no longer alive. But Tūla still lived; it's just that I didn't know a thing about that life. Maybe I didn't even want to know?

VII

Sometimes it seems to me that I invented you myself, Tūla; that you actually never even existed. I created you out of air, water, algae, sparks, and the quiet rumbling beyond the hills of Vilnius. Or: that I'm grateful to you that we lived together for only one week; that that week took the place of—for me, of course, just me!—many years. After all, even then, when it was only just over, I realized with horror that I would miss you, Tūla, for a long time, maybe even for the rest of my life; even on the other side of life, where more and more today our, the transients', eyes turn with such curiosity and longing. That's just what happened—even now it's hard for me to believe it! But you aren't, in any event, invented or imagined; I have my own hard evidence. There are a few short letters, a broken tile from your old abode, and finally there's the photograph your brother took: almost all of your face is in shadow; in the dusk, one leg in flowery pants is carelessly thrown over the other. Only someone who knew you well could confirm: Yes, that's her, that's Tūla...

Frequently I up and imagine you're still alive, just turned into a winged chimera on the roof, a young Old Town cat, or an agile lizard on the bank of the Vilnelė—that's in the summer. And sometimes it seems to me that you're following me, walking behind me, but as soon as I turn around, you disappear. It seems you'll catch up with me any minute, I even hear your breathing, footsteps, laughter; you'll catch up and we'll sneak into some courtyard or gateway for a smoke... but no, turning around I suddenly see only a stranger's surprised face—what's the matter with you, Mister?

There you are, Tūla! With a sphinx's head and a long, curled tail—you're standing on top of the pediment, it is you, isn't it? Staring for a long time with my head upturned, the sphinx up and moves—first the tail... then the jaws open... There's no need to swig so much, I say to myself, swig so much that even the black phlegmatic crow with gray underwings, perched on the railing of the little covered bridge, would seem to be Tūla. Oh, I know, you'd just laugh—briefly, sadly, maybe angrily. You're still laughing in my murky memory. After all, both fervor and omniscience were always foreign to you. Writing down dreams only forces one to doubt the slightest reality. It seems to me that you constantly doubted almost everything, most of all, of course, yourself. Omniscience was foreign to you, too. Once, I remember, you asked me: Do you know what's at the end of Polocko Street? I cringed; I was even a bit creeped out, but you stubbornly looked me in the eye: Tell me, what? Oh, I answered, well, forest, of course, forest, what else? And... No, you shook your head vigorously—it's that shaking of the head I probably miss most now—there's just fog and sky, you know? Nothing more, I've already been there, don't you believe me? But you weren't much of a mystic, either. Like most solitary, slightly yawning people. No more, no less. All the same, magic attracted you too—your haphazard reading had an influence. Like that one evening when you needed to find out, immediately, what the symbols for gold and its color were! Apparently you had known, but suddenly forgot. You drew all kinds of little signs, symbols, little circles and arrows on a scrap of Whatman paper and muttered: No, no, that's not right! It struck me—Valentinas, the nitpicker and pedant, would surely know! Through all of ghostly-lit Užupis, through gateways reeking of urine and beer and the figures standing in them, we headed for secluded Žvirgždyno Lane, next to the Bernardine graveyard—it was there, in a damp garden apartment, leaning over his graphics, that Valentinas inhaled smoke and the steam from tea. Whenever I stopped by, it almost always occurred to me that a few meters away, at the same depth, inside decayed coffins, lay famous university professors, French and Polish generals, nineteenth-century spiritual leaders, lawyers, and even Ironman Felix's mother—and the cross on her grave. And it was never terrifying; it was never even strange that here Valentinas, coughing as he poured beet wine and tea, walked around, stirred inside his cramped workshop, while the spirits whispered to each other next door, even though I did imagine it all very vividly. I knocked at both the door and on the closed shutter—Valentinas sometimes worked "under cover." Nope, not home. We went over to the cemetery; at the gateway, a grayish, famished German shepherd halfheartedly whimpered—a job for a retiree. The two of us slipped between the black marble and cement crosses overgrown with green moss—their impressive volume lay in wide, nearly regular shadows; it looked like there were way more crosses here than there really were, at least three times as many. In the moonlight on the other bank of the Vilnelė loomed the motionless suburb with the Visitation cupola and the maximum security prison's pale structures, the industrial ones, or whatever they call them. I gazed in that direction too long, and when I came to, Tūla was no longer there; I didn't see her anywhere. I turned this way and that—no, nowhere to be seen. I got a bit peeved; tell me it wasn't on purpose! So I ferreted among the graves, not daring to either shout or clap my hands: Where are you, peanut? At last I turned to the brick gate: Tūla was standing in the street next to the Polocko intersection. Next to a telephone booth with broken windows and a cutoff receiver. Angry, I ran over, turned her towards me, and, taking her by her little shoulders, shook her. Oh, it's you, she glanced at me sullenly, where did you come from? How did I get here? Where's my home? You were afraid of something, or at least it seemed that way to me. But not the spirits or the gloomy, soulless street. Then what? I never did find out whether you really did have spells of amnesia, and at the time I didn't even think of memory loss. So it was awkward. You walked holding on to my arm and quietly asked about things out of nowhere. It was cold; why I hadn't I put on a winter hat? What hat? The one you were wearing when I went to Moscow with you last year. Oh, hadn't that friend with the leggings come by while she was gone?

When we got back—I didn't say "home," I just said "back," you, Tūla, didn't just fasten the bolt on the room's door; you also asked me to set a couple of boxes next to it, heavier ones, if possible. When you laid down, you immediately hugged me tightly and didn't let go, even in your sleep, when I tried to free myself. Awake, I sat up in your shallow cot; next to me you breathed deeply, trembled, opened your swollen lips as if you wanted to say something extremely important. You wrinkled your forehead, but at last smiled, while I lit a cigarette in the greenish moonlight pouring in the windows. The walls looked green now too, like the patina on copper. And the vault. And what about tomorrow? I thought, what about tomorrow? In your sleep you pulled back your warm thigh and unintentionally uncovered yourself; the green moonlight immediately perched on your breasts. Brown oak leaves curled on the window sill—and what about tomorrow?

I don't even know why I agreed to go with you, Tūla, to the Second City. I agreed with a light heart, nodded as soon as you said you couldn't do this much longer, even though visits of that sort seemed, of course, terribly old-fashioned. Yes, yes, I agreed solemnly, of course. Let's go, no problem. On the train, for some reason, you started telling me about an Estonian you barely knew who came to the Second City—you two met on the Avenue—and he lived for nearly a month in the attic of your parents' house. For entire days, you said wondering, that strange boy wandered through the city, what was he looking for there? And in the evenings when he'd come home, he'd gorge on dinner—buttering a fresh roll especially thick—and climb upstairs to sleep. Then he started bringing girls there, yes, Lithuanians, but you know yourself what kind. I listened to that "Estonian story" without a clue about why you started telling me this now, what it had to do with our serious trip; I had no plans to either live there, or to bring girls.

It was only several years later that your brother mentioned that

I shouldn't have gone there; he even muttered this somewhat guilt-
ily—I shouldn't have. I thought so myself. No one was prepared for
it; me least of all. Your parents, Tūla, although they had come to
terms with their daughter's solitariness and reserve, to your quiet
desire not to live and even a certain antagonism, nevertheless more
and more impatiently awaited the day you'd bring home and show
them a decent man who knew how to work, who looked at life very
"seriously" and was determined to take care of their daughter, that
is, you. The kind I clearly wasn't. I didn't even remotely resemble
someone like that. Not to mention the biography it was probably
also proper to relate on such an occasion. There was nothing I could
brag about. They were expecting a solid man, and you brought home
some dazed observer of life with a worn-out jacket and a hobo hat—
my cousin Domicėlė was right! In your mother's or father's place I
would have shown the door to a suitor like that myself: Go on, now,
please! *Skatertyu doroga*—good riddance, as our best friends the Russians say. Wind at your back! Don't tell me that even now I'm capable
of mocking innocent people that meanly?

But I felt practically no open hostility in that house. Polite questions about the trip. The father's unambiguous story about a charming evening party on the occasion of International Women's Day; just
think, not a drop of liquor, and an excellent mood! But on the whole,
no one there even noticed me. Nothing was asked about either my
past or my plans for the near future. You, Tūla, invited me to your
attic, where once the Estonian slept after a satisfying dinner. In the
attic, the four of us, or even maybe five—your brother and his friends
were there too—slowly sipped vodka with tomato juice. The walls
were covered with magazine clippings. A tall guest tried to torture
an old clavichord in the corner of the attic, inherited, as I later found
out, from the grandfather in my home town. You, Tūla, kept worrying: you kept standing up, going downstairs, and after some half-
hour returning more and more unhappy. I didn't pay attention to
those wanderings; I was foolishly convinced that whatever your parents said to you, you, without any doubt, would obey your heart—if

necessary, you'd stamp your foot and leave the house, taking me with you, and later, later everything would straighten itself out of its own accord and we would all just smile indulgently, remembering this unexpected visit. With these thoughts in mind I carefully examined the torso of a muscle-builder pasted on the wall—Good Lord! Only afterwards did my eyes fall upon the head: what's this? In place of the head there was a real photograph pasted on, a black-and-white one. Come on, really? It was someone I knew! Yes, it was that uncle of Tūla's, not a real uncle or at least not very, still a young man, who'd way back when worked as a lifeguard at the beach in our pleasant little town! He was the one who rowed his lightweight shallow boat to the bathing bay and sat there until sundown, waiting for the opportunity to save someone. But people drowned elsewhere—in the current next to the demolished bridge, or next to the slaughterhouse; as if deliberately, no one drowned where this athlete stood guard. When he finished work, the lifeguard used to plant some prettier girl in the boat and set off down the current for town. It was him, of course, him! Everything fit. "I wonder what he's doing now, who he's saving?" I asked your brother. He just mumbled something.

We slept apart for the first time since we'd met: I in that same attic with the nearly voiceless clavichord, and you somewhere below in the house. A typical Second City bourgeois house, more modest than its neighbors even. I lay for a while with my eyes open; maybe you'll come and lie down beside me? No, you didn't climb the stairs and lay down beside me. I fell asleep without the slightest suspicion that there, in the house, everything, oh everything, was already decided, signed, and sealed, that all there was left for me to do was to go out through the little house's white door for the first and only time, to sigh looking at the vines girdling the attic and say: Goodbye! And now it's your business, your choice, drifter, where your feet and eyes will lead you. *Vivere pericolosamente!*—how could I forget?

Even the next morning, when, after quietly breakfasting, we went out into this—to me—foreign city, I still didn't realize what was going on. You, Tūla, were strangely quiet, but after all, you had been strangely quiet before. You still held on to my sleeve. You smiled looking at my serious face and were quiet again. A cold emptiness appeared in my stomach; I began to sense something. And you were quiet. I didn't come here to make a marriage proposal, or show off my good side. You didn't warn me; you babbled about some Estonian—did you tell me everything? We went somewhere; somewhere we drank coffee with some disgusting liqueur, but I suddenly had a funny feeling: now you'll tell me. Some kind of pain was etched into your forehead, some wrinkles that hadn't been visible earlier appeared around your lips, or maybe it just seems that way to me now? But your eyes really were bigger, right next to mine. You shook your head and said: Take the train to Vilnius now, go on, and come by tonight. You shook your head again: For sure come by. But now, go on, go!

It seems at the time I hadn't completely lost my head over you yet, what a shame. Insulted, I growled: I'll decide for myself where I'm going now, understand!? Although my temples were already ringing, I shook in anger, and the pride that had just surfaced gripped my throat, which was already flooded with questions: What happened? Why? How's this now? I knew quite well what had happened, why this. And I immediately decided: there would be no Vilnius! I'll go wherever I want, I'm a drifter again, a free man, the master of my closed circuit! Saying something else to you, something pointless—Better go yourself, right now, take the express!—I was already making plans about who else I could visit here in the Second City. As much as I didn't care for it—a sign of good taste even among refined eggheads—I had a lot of acquaintances here, even friends. Now I know: I made a gross mistake. I should have listened to you, taken the train and come by in the evening. I shouldn't have let go of you for even a second; I should have held on to your hand. We already had our own love story—so what if it was banal and sentimental, burning only inside the rejected one, the disappointed one, there he is, unhappily stuffing his hands in his pockets and slowly disappearing down the foggy avenue. Well, well, now!

I walked with you to the funicular and we went up together. I pressed your fingers in the cold, antiquated car. You sat one level higher, as pale and motionless as a statue. I thought we'd have a cigarette together yet, but, climbing out, you walked a few little steps, suddenly turned around, and standing on tiptoe, wrapped both arms around my neck and kissed me hard on the lips. Only then did you run off. I'd lie if I said I felt that kiss for a long time, or that it was poisonous. No, it wasn't.

I turned towards the sprawling Second City looming down in the valley, descended with that same funicular, and right there, in the next café I came to, poured a glass of cheap booze into my cold stomach. Then I rode in an unpleasantly squeaking Ikarus bus to Šančiai, found my dear friend, the one who lived entirely on cards—bridge, bridge, and bridge once more!—and fishing,—both of these trades were, it's true, strictly forbidden, but does anyone pay attention? He was just then resting after a contest of many days; he had the time and the urge to chat—we sat there until morning. I didn't, of course, mention anything to him about any Tūlas. He kept saying: Oh, too bad you don't play! Oh, too bad you're afraid to risk it! Oh, oh, oh! He had no idea how much I play and risk—every day, every day, every day! So we talked. And the next day, Monday already, I didn't go anywhere; the bridge ace awarded me a "prize." Actually, a hundred with Lenin's portrait, even back then, wasn't much money in the Second City, but to me it was a real fortune! Bread with butter, ham, sausage, vodka, wine, beer, passenger tickets to the end of the world and even a bit further. Feeling stronger than ever, I walked around downtown, even stopping at a museum and exhibit; in surprise I watched a crowd of Georgians kneeling and weeping, listening to the Kaunas Carillon playing the Georgian folk tune Suliko—you can always see things in the Second City you won't see anywhere else! I felt unjustly wronged, but to my surprise realized the heartache burning me was, by some miraculous means, actually pleasant. But that's not normal, I thought, treading my way towards the Central Post Office. I had, you see, thought about sending you a telegram in Vilnius; I was just considering how to fit both my pain and freedom's fluttering into a few words—but then I ran right into this Erna, and in the evening, in her little one-room apartment with all the conveniences somewhere at the end of Vydūno Avenue, we were both already as drunk as skunks. Or as drunk as a lord, whatever. She muttered: I should make up a separate bed for you, but you'd sneak over anyway! She was right, I certainly would. I hadn't met a drinker like this Erna in a long time. As far as I know, she wasn't like that before. She was a friend from the university; once upon a time we'd been companions in a group traipsing through the Carpathians. Now she's an energetic, totally emancipated old maid; a chemist, she worked in a restoration workshop. Erna drank like a man, but never sank to the bottom. True, she waved her arms, swore, raised a ruckus, and bragged like all drunks do; what can you do. How many men rolled at her feet! The way they cried and begged! When she spoke that way, some kind of repulsive self-satisfaction appeared on her carnivorous face. But I was no longer concerned about whether she really could have married some academic or not. She wasn't a woman to me; she was a fellow drinker I ran into at the right time. We were already drunk, but kept drinking anyway. She started getting on my case, too: back then you pretended to be someone, now you've gone downhill, you're all grungy, listen, who needs you that way? She had a point. Fortunately, she didn't know what a fiasco I'd just been through; she would have kissed me all over! But she was making the bed already; she didn't even tell me to turn around. Not at all like those girls or women who start sobbing and raving as soon as they get a bit drunk, promising to kill themselves, and then spend the night retching in the toilet. She was even a bit older than me, that madwoman Erna; she was very happy to have solved the bed problem so subtly—lying down, she growled "good night" and turned to the wall. I turned her back towards me, took her in my arms, and she just sighed: whatever! I've already said it: I told her nothing about you, Tūla—why should I? Well, of course, maybe she wouldn't have made fun of me; maybe she would even have given me some "womanly" advice. In the morning she put Vysotsky's "Gimnastika" on full blast. "Get up, you wino!" And held a bottle of wine over my head: "You think I don't know?" She didn't drink a drop herself and was exceptionally proud of that as well: Listen, I'm no alcoholic, not some paisano guzzling valerian! Mornings—not a drop!

With my head splitting, I slugged down some red Agdam and seemed to remember something from the night before. Big deal! I decided. *Vivere pericolosamente*—I had no idea of what was waiting for me. The telephone and the doorbell both screeched at once; Erna opened the door. In walked a tall, good-looking guy in a leather coat, leather hat, and leather gloves. But not from any government "body," that was clear. He threw a leather bag down on the chair and lit up a cigarette pulled out of a leather case. "We're going?" Like most men with a "position" in life, he didn't pay the least attention to me. He invited Erna to go in his car to the Third City—Klaipėda, for those who don't know. Robertas was that good-looker's name. I'd seen guys like that here and there. He was an architect, a *fachwerk* specialist. The kind that know at least ten phrases in English and smoke good cigarettes. Cold and polite. Leather and sobriety! Erna was useful to him as a chemist, to test and treat framing wood. Maybe something more besides. Erna just shook her head aggressively, not at all like you, Tūla: you can all go take a shit, I'm not going anywhere! Robis, get him out of here! She pointed at me. Then the great *fachwerk* hotshot stooped to notice me. What of it, I can take him. At these words I felt like I was already on the road. I even wanted it to rain or snow. Erna introduced me to the guest without pulling any punches: This gentleman wants to marry me, too, understand, sweetheart? Sweetheart, that's me, apparently. "And here," she pointed me out to Robertas, "my ooooold, ooooold…" He wasn't blind: the bed still wasn't made and I'm sitting there barefoot, scratching between my toes and knocking back first thing in the morning.

Robertas didn't give a hoot. When I get back, I'll stop by, Erna.

A calm, pleasant voice. No, I hadn't come across anyone like that either for quite some time; being a drifter, I guess I really did distance myself from decent people. Everywhere I seemed to see nothing but yuppies, ditzes, and most of all the sincerely despised eggheads. Robertas had brought some beer; he saved a few bottles for the road, too. He waited for me to get washed up in Erna's shower. If he'd thought of it, he would have given me his clean shirt and socks. I pecked Erna on the jaw: Goodbye, my Mother Earth! Don't ever get married, maybe I'll stop by again some time, wait for me! And she: Don't be afraid, I didn't stick you with some disease, sweetheart! And she smiled wryly. Yes, without makeup an auntie of that age didn't look so great.

I had no idea what I was going to do in that Klaipėda; I couldn't remember when I'd last been there. But what difference did it make? Now it's time to get as far as possible from the Second City, just not to Vilnius. We put the pedal to the metal through Žaliakalnis towards the Žemaičių highway. Stopping at a stoplight, I saw you, Tūla—you stood there in that same brown fur jacket, your back turned and your head thrown back, chatting with an athlete even taller than Robertas. The little hat was the same, too—a coarse gray wool. But when we moved, I saw it wasn't you. A completely strange woman, much older. So now you're going to be showing up everywhere all the time? Everywhere, all the time!? In the suburbs, I asked to stop; the trip wasn't all that short. I bought some cigarettes and two bottles of Cabernet. Beer's just beer, but wine is wine! Robertas smiled, opened his leather bag, and gave me some soft cheese and a corkscrew—what a gem!

We buzzed down the expressway like bees. No rain, no snow, and thank God! We spent a long time passing a caravan of green armored cars, but armored cars don't intimidate me; they weren't *milítsiya* jeeps. I swigged wine and smoked. I knocked my ashes into the ashtray next to the radio, out of which Stasys Povilaitis tirelessly, and with increasing drama, asked: "Where are you go-o-o-ing? ... and the north winds howlin'!... But nothing will bring you back, and you could have been my happiness!!!" He finally tired, shut his trap, and the radio started crackling; in an icy voice, the announcer promised a freeze at night, a strong one. When the Kryžkalnis "madonna" showed up, leaning forward somewhat on the horizon, I already knew where I would head for when we got there. In the Third City, that fine port city, not too far from the stadium, a little tramp I knew might still be living with her friend. Well, of course, not a real tramp; after all, she did study at a branch of the Conservatory, burned with the desire to direct something, to act, to love. Once upon a time I'd put her up for the night in Herbert Stein's workshop; she was amazed at the stage sets and antique things there. I spent the night there myself, why not. It even occurred to me at the time that the young lady was sticking herself, because when I uncorked the wine, she just shook her head—there again, not like you, Tūla, or like Erna the chemist!—and sighed, "That's not what I need." And later, falling asleep, it occurred to me that the sweet thing was chewing something; monotonously, stopping from time to time—surely not a crust of bread? I had visited that attic, I even made a note of the address, and now, searching my memory, I suddenly lit up:

"Kulių seven-three! Kulių seven-three! Kulių seven-three!"

"Hallucinations?" the driver glanced at me. "So soon?"

"Kulių seven-three!!!"

Now, what was that little tramp's name? The surname seemed Latvian—Rozenkrancė or Rozenfeldė. And her name? Aha! I crowed again:

"Rodė! Rodė! Rodė!"

Worried, Robertas looked at me even more carefully, but I explained: everything's okay. It's the name of this lady. Rododendra. Rododendra Rozenbliumė. Only a northern Lithuanian farmer of unarguably Latvian blood could pick a name like that for his delicate infant. Her friends called her Rodė. Rodė claimed to be studying how to coordinate mass events. Life itself was a mass event to her: cafés, squares, parks, beaches, expressways, and gatherings in the gateways. Rodė lived in masses, too; embankments, markets, coffee houses, cafeterias; she resembled—at least to me—a disheveled northern lapwing, always friendly and approachable, and inclined to actively socialize with everyone. This was required by her profession—mass events. I ran into her unexpectedly and as a gift, like all things to a drifter. Back then she had accompanied a young Russian poet, a genius naturally, hitchhiking to Vilnius. Rodė and Denis— that was the poet's name—got good and soused while still on their way; when they arrived they hung around the dilapidated Alumnatas courtyard with a barely touched bottle of Rosu de Dessert. At that moment I happened to come out of the Bačka wine bar, and Denis— I'd met him earlier—grabbed me by the arm: take care of this girl, will you, I'll be right back… don't give her to anyone! Drunk, he apparently lost it; he suddenly got hot to visit his beautiful ex-wife and his son Salvador—you can guess, of course, in whose honor he was named. Rodė and I waited over at the foot of Gedimino Castle, on the rocks; we waited until sundown, and then with all the money we had thrown together bought—what? Wine, of course! When it got completely dark I took her to Herbert's workshop; the owner had gone to Kaluga for a show. Or maybe to Tula, I don't remember. Rodė didn't even taste the wine, I mentioned that already. She just collapsed on the couch and said: now, or a bit later? Now, I grumbled, and obviously later, but tell me, dearie, is this what your mass events are? She liked the question: Rodė laughed to the point of tears. That's what that Kulių Street inhabitant was like. A bold, vivacious, endlessly curious director of mass events. Rododendra! Maybe she won't throw me out?

I stretched the wine out to last as far as the port city; after all, Robertas wasn't going to stop whenever asked! And in any case. No, he was a real human being, to the letter—he drove me right to the gate of Kulių Street. When we stopped, I saw an old-fashioned "double" house number: Seven. A lucky number? Is it worth telling you how coldly, with what obvious watchfulness Rodė greeted her guest? Apparently she had fallen in love with the Executive Director and was engrossed in her studies; she was simmering some thick poppy dope and waiting on a more illustrious guest. But she made some coffee anyway, and smoked nervously, waiting for me to gulp it down.

I have to admit: she took pity on me, didn't drive me out, didn't ask about anything. When I finished a cigarette too, she took me to her friend on the other side of the street—a sad, chubby-faced blonde. I remember her name now too: Olyva. Olivija, Rodė introduced her, told me to call her Olyva, openly winked at both Olyva and me— you'll be okay—and immediately disappeared. It turned out Olyva was studying to be a director, too, but she just couldn't decide what kind of work to produce: a happy or a sad one? And which first: Chekhov or Kafka? She spoke slowly, as if she was asleep. She warmed up some Sangre de Toro for me, and asked if I knew Nekrošius. He was the only one, you see, who could understand her. Maybe. She told me about a wonderful vacation by the Azov Sea. About Albatross, her southern friend—did he wear her out! She glanced at me and clarified—with his chatter. She suddenly sobbed when she started talking about the seagulls—they knew how to die! As if she had seen it! She sucked down Prima cigarettes; stuffed them into a short cigarette holder and sucked on them nonstop. Chubby, gloomy, and sincere. Not even terribly wanton. I lived there for something like a week—she only invited me into her bed on the third day: "It seems to me we're starting to become friends now?" But she panted sincerely. She went to the train station with me—from a distance I saw Denis again, going to visit Salvador. "Olyyyvaaa!" He shrieked when he saw us, not in the least surprised. He tried to convince Olyva to come along: "Quick, let's get in, great, we'll go visit Begbis and Beetroot, huh, Olyva?" But Olyva didn't go. She asked me to write her at least one letter—she collected them all. She was a foot and a half taller than me and a hundred pounds heavier. Always in a philosophical mood, sometimes even when she was making love. Going out for a while, she'd always come back with wine and a dozen eggs. A specialist on Basque omelets. Kaf-ka, kaf-ka, Olyva's tame crow would croak above her destitute boudoir. I wonder where she is now? It was nice weather, calm, I thought, remembering Olyva, although we never did get to the seaside.

VIII

But then, Domine, I was already lying in the Second Section—
I've mentioned it rather vaguely. Vasaros, Rudens, and Olandų
streets, right up to the varying elevations of the Polocko line on
the southeast, were its natural boundaries, where I made myself at
home for almost two months. The hospital's territory was, obviously, much less extensive. On the east side rose a steep pine-covered
slope, which, when climbed, opened onto the valley of the Butterflies Cemetery. On sleepless nights, Domine, I would fly above it to
the corner of Filaretų, and there, making a turn to the west, I would
be fluttering into Malūnų Street...

There's no reason to hide it anymore; the Second Section was a
poorly disguised alcoholic sanatorium. Most of the time they'd write
into the hospital admission records that such and such a person suffered from a disturbance of the central nervous system. This was
certainly true, but about hallucinations or phobias, or about hangover syndromes or cirrhosis—not a word. An open secret, a finger on
the lips when someone from outside asked: Second Section? What is
that, really?

The dullest section. These slaves of the bottle—whose remains
of reason still whispered: go on, take a break, and then you can
booze it up "like a man!" again—accompanied by tearful wives or
girlfriends, or else alone like me, came to this shady park, lived in
barracks that had a coquettish summer-house style, and would loll
about there for a good month, guzzling vitamins and tranquilizers,

in their free time corrupting the unhinged young women who filled both the beautiful park and the woods around the nuthouse. Only an assemblage of alcoholic men rested in the beige barracks; in the other sections—brick buildings, some of their windows with bars no less, and a tall enclosure entwined in wire for walking—potential suicides, handsome young men beset by depression, curly-haired schizophrenics with Roman noses and fiery glances, unfortunate students who had decided it was better to spend some time in the nut house than go into the army, hysterical teenagers (whom you would hardly call teenagers anymore) in conflict with their parents, and lonely old men who no longer wanted to go anywhere except the kingdom of heaven, quietly went out of their minds. They were the ones who fluttered off to that vale, to the Butterflies Cemetery; there they would be quietly buried in a still quieter slope, usually at night for some reason—I saw it. The soft sand, the restless Butterfly graves, the pockets of the dead filled with wind-blown sand...

The alcoholics got better right in front of your eyes; they would lift a rusting two-pood weight by the door, hang around the kitchen, smack down playing cards, and almost everyone had a handle that would open almost every door.

As not just a drunk, but a homeless one, I felt particularly comfortable there. Clearly the Second Section was also, in a certain sense, a concentration camp, whose administration and personnel attempted to turn the "drinking animal" into a human again, even though the detox specialists and psychotherapists had long since given up believing in miracles and therefore in the meaning of their work. But they did what they could, or at least pretended to. A thin, nervous doctor with a sternly twitching cheek signed me up for the experimental group right away—I agreed to all the conditions. Every other afternoon he would take us, six or seven wretches, to the barracks' attic, lie us down on roughly chest-high cushioned platforms covered in brown oilcloth, and, slowly repeating pleasant words, urge us, or even force us to relax. Really... after a filling lunch, the body would grow lazy, the eyes would shut of their own accord. Gleb, a freight handler from the Krasnūcha district who lay on my right during the séances, would frequently, to all of our horror and his own dismay, start snoring. I'd want to laugh, but the psychotherapist, giving an angry shout, would poke Gleb in his bare stomach and begin the second half of the experiment. In a high voice, full of drama, he'd start passionately cursing vodka, wine, and beer, comparing the bottle's neck with a nipple; his eyes probably sparked. We couldn't see that—we'd been ordered to lie with our eyes tightly closed and not to stir, otherwise, we were told, everything would go to the dickens. But it's questionable whether he himself believed in the strength of his influence when, reaching the climax, he would suddenly spout:

"There it is, that damned vodka! There! That's the reason (he'd jab the nearest prone chest with a finger) you lost your job! It's only because of the vodka that your wife left you! (Here he could have jabbed just about anyone.) Vodka destroyed your brains! Vodka! Vodka did it!"

By now nearly hissing in fury, the doctor would order us to open our mouths as wide as we could and, pulling a full bottle of the just-now cursed vodka or spirits diluted in half out of somewhere, he'd start slopping it into our open mouths. And sloshing and splashing that way, it'd get onto your face and eyes—so that's why he'd tell us to close our eyes! Pouring out the entire bottle of spirits, he'd collapse limply into an armchair, cover his eyes with his palms, and brushing away the black hair that had fallen on his forehead, ask us, in a more normal voice, to get up slowly. There were red and blue plastic buckets set on the ground between the couches, but it was a rare patient, affected by suggestion or by the vodka splashed on his lips, who would throw up. But that was the purpose of this cruel treatment—to force vomiting, to cause as much disgust as possible. The pukers were encouraged by all means here, and held up as an example to the non-pukers.

"Well now," after a séance like this the doctor would ask each lab rat, "How do you feel? Do you still want to drink?" "Oh *doktor!*" my neighbor Gleb, the freight loader from Krasnūcha, would moan,

"*Nikogda bolshe, ey-bogu!*—Never again, God forbid! *Chto by ya etu gadost bolshe bukhal!*—That I ever drink this swill again! *Basta, zavja-zyvayu!*—That's it, I'm starting over!" The doctor's bad eye twitched and he marked something down in his observation notebook.

"Well, sir, and how are you doing?" he asked me one beautiful fall afternoon. Beyond the narrow white window, maple leaves bigger than your hand fell in pale green and red, and rays of warm sunlight glittered. How badly I wanted to answer this good person with something like Gleb did! Alas! The saddest part was probably that I, like the majority of the inhabitants of this colony of alcoholics, didn't imagine I was some kind of invalid, not by a long stretch. Well, maybe a tired wino who didn't have anywhere to spend the night, who didn't, in general, have a life. Nowhere. I was ashamed to look into this nervous, thin man's troubled eyes. After all, he addressed me politely. After all, it was actually his brother, an actor who hadn't yet had his pivotal role, who had helped set me up in this autumnal sanatorium. He even asked they not go overboard with me there and push the medications on me. It was this doctor I had to thank for a bed in the corner by the window, and for the fact that they had already, by the fifth day of my volunteer captivity, allowed me to go into town; I went down the street knowing I had somewhere to come home to and a blanket to crawl under. I don't know, I'd say to the doctor, the actor's brother, when I was asked, it's disgusting to me, of course... believe me, I try, but I don't get nauseated... I don't throw up! You know, a person gets used to all kinds of smells...
"No matter, no matter," he'd cry, fairly elated, "you just need to hold yourself together and not fall apart, and everything will be okay!" I'd nod and, together with my gray-faced colleagues, march out to rake armfuls of falling leaves and pile them into the little tractor's rusty trailer.

In the evenings, when the attendants would wipe the puddles of milk soup and brush the bacon rinds off the long tables (family would bring the smoked meat products; recovering alcoholics were swamped by a monstrous appetite!), I would often settle myself under this refectory's dim lamp. I could read there until the middle of the night, or, awakened by some neighbor's mighty snoring, when I just couldn't manage to fall asleep again or settle down, I would go there with a notebook and write down some impressions, try to compile a minimum of an explanatory slang dictionary, but mostly I'd write you letters, Tūla. I no longer sent them out, and not just because I didn't have an address for you. Frequently some other guy, also tortured by insomnia, would disturb me; most of the time they were overflowing with a passionate need to spill it all out, to tell everything, and I'd unwittingly fall into empty conversation, or listen to interminable monologues about riotous all-night parties, quarrels and fights with drinking buddies, about endless escapades in bed, and about constant battles with the authorities, with wives, with neighbors, with the entire world! Sitting around in the night-time cafeteria, I kept writing and writing letters to you. I no longer crossed anything out; I'd tell you about everything in turn, or just the opposite: I'd confuse everything so badly I'd no longer be able to myself distinguish what was true and what was an invention with a tinge of quiet insanity—no illusions!

> *Like a poison the spider's thread*
> *Stretches through the darkened streets*
> *Where buggies of blue will carry*
> *the sleepwalkers out of Tūla.*

Something like that. A poesy like that came into my head once; later I believe you liked it? Yes, you liked it; you even asked me to write it down—I scribbled it down on the gray wrapping paper the Rytas café used for napkins. I wrote you all kinds of things then. Nonsense. Excerpts from the life of a beetle or a wasp. Reflections on aminazine and amnesia. A short essay: "How do Ethics, Aesthetics, and Epithets differ?" The answer: Ethics and aesthetics are frequently only epithets, for which… Bah. Not so much as a glimmer between the clouds. In a hospital, you're supposed to sleep at night; that's the way the majority of our grim contingent behaved. Only Gleb, getting up after midnight, would start lifting the two-pood weight and pestering me with his silly questions—what do you think, if you poured kefir from one bottle to another for six months, would it really turn into pure alcohol?—and once, the same day he swore to the doctor to never drink again to the day he died, right in front of me he pulled a bottle of vodka out from inside his shirt, rummaging in the cabinet retrieved an onion and a dry crust of bread, and, turning up his head, emptied more than half the bottle. He would have drunk it all, but it didn't fit in one gulp and I coughed at the wrong moment. He gave me the little that remained: go on, drink it! I shook my head. Then Gleb clenched his freight-loader's fists—they looked like real boulders to me!—and grabbed me by the flimsy pajama's lapels: Well!? Gleb's eyes were already crazy—I drank it. I didn't have the slightest intention of turning him in to the jailers, what difference would it make to me!? I hadn't drunk in a long time; my head spun, my chest got hot, and opening the air vent wider, I flew out into the autumn night studded with stars. Gleb was left sitting there with his reddened eyes popping out—he didn't believe what he saw! Then he just snorted and fell head-down on the table. In the morning they found him dead.

That was the first time I flew to you, Tūla, without even knowing whether I'd find you at home, or whether you were still living next to the Vilnelė. Obeying entirely new instincts, I flapped my webbed wings, felt the never-before-experienced giddiness of flight, and rose ever higher. I flew above the Butterflies Cemetery; from above, the frosty grass looked like a white shroud. The woods of Belmontas, gripped in dampness, shone in the distance, but I turned to the west, to you, Tūla. There was nothing I wanted to say to you anymore, nor to remind you of, nor explain. I just wanted to see you for a while and, even if invisible, be near you, and what of it?

But I saw you only the next day, when, after it had gotten quite

dark, I got ready to go out to town again. A city getting ready to
entomb itself—I don't ever remember streets so dimly, so dismally
lit; the lanterns and arched lamps merely emphasized that grim-
ness. To me the passersby looked like victims of drowning, just now
pulled out of the water, who lifelessly staggered home, or somewhere
or another. It seemed the city had forgotten how to talk; only the car
engines coughed, sounding like they'd come down with a cold. A
coffin with glass windows, loaded with someone's dead planted side
by side, would soundlessly slide by like a real ghost: a yellow trolleybus. Maybe I didn't deserve a better life, I thought, skulking down
the cement embankment towards the dead downtown—the "heart"
of the city hardly throbbed, either—I'm of no use, not to anyone.
Many think otherwise: I'm harmful, to be exterminated, bound to
provoke the citizenry's intolerance; didn't the episode in the Second City confirm this? Well, then! Yesterday, flying back to the Second Section, my colleagues—several real bats, *chiroptera*, the common noctule—had attacked me; they didn't want to admit a stranger
into their domain, maybe they were from the pan-Slavic *Severozapad*
organization? Now my hand and shoulder hurt, but I got ready to
go to town anyway—the evenings had gotten longer with the howl-
ing and laughing of the real madmen, who'd been sent out for an
evening walk in the wire enclosure. Neither *"Ya uyedu v Komarovo*
(I'm leaving for Komarovo)!"* playing at full blast in our block, nor
the heart-rending cries of Gleb's wife—for the third day she hadn't
left the door of our barracks, unable to believe that her Glebchik was
no longer there—drowned out their voices. It seems they were ready
to admit her to the women's section; apparently she wasn't just wailing, but guzzling the wine she'd brought along. And they say no one
loves a drunk! They are loved— the same kind of drunks love them,
and how they mourn when they lose their loved ones! That summer-
house style barracks had been my feeding-trough and my bed for a
third week now.

　　　I headed down Gedimino Prospect—even drunk people (happened upon with practically every step!) rollicked, yelled, and shoved

as if unwillingly driven by a force greater than themselves. Misty shadows passed—women carrying huge bouquets of white chrysanthemums—All Souls' Day was coming. Nothing buzzed in my sober head; I had no object, and no one I wanted to see. I just walked along, and nothing more. And at the end of the Prospect, past the square, I ran smack into Tūla. She was walking by herself, just like everyone else—a drowning victim just pulled out of the water. We really did bump into one another: she mumbled, "msorry!" and was going on her way. I detained her by her shoddy sleeve; then she turned around and recognized me. Hello, hello, she stirred her swollen lips, hello... should we go somewhere? But she didn't take hold of my arm. The only difference? No.

Even that tiny, narrow, normally always jammed café, where petty passions constantly boiled over at the bar, where those waiting their turn to down a glass impatiently breathed on the necks of the drinkers, where almost everyone not only knew one another, but saw clear through them—even it was half-empty at the time. We sat down at the bar on the tall stools; Tūla next to the rough-textured square pillar, me next to her. Oh, she whispered, it's pretty dark, pretty dark in here. I asked for coffee and vermouth. I don't believe we talked about anything, or if we did, then it was just trivialities. I took her hand and together with my own put it on her cherry-colored wool dress—that was more important; understandably, more important to me. She drank greedily, if in small sips; I just watched her quietly. Then she ordered another round herself. Tasty, slightly bitter vermouth from the still brotherly land of Hungary. I felt her inspecting me with her eyes from her comfortable twilight; I was afraid to so much as stir. I just found out today where you are, she said, and here we meet each other, not bad, huh? We drank again; her eyes glistened, but I saw nothing in them, not the slightest desire to talk. Maybe I should have told her *everything*? Hardly.

When I remember that evening in that dim café now, when Tūla is no more, a shameful sorrow flows over me. Shameful?

Who knows. Hey, I don't display that sorrow, I don't wear it on my sleeve—and what of it, if I did? Then why am I ashamed? Maybe it's my lack of determination, my sheepish submissiveness, my thankfulness just because she's sitting next to me? Perhaps. That gloomy, half-empty café keeps coming to mind—as it never did before and never since. Now that evening seems to me like a clip from some sad Italian film, one of those black-and-white ones they used to call neorealist. At the time, of course, it didn't seem that way; it didn't even occur to me. A gloomy evening with a beloved person and vermouth that brings on sadness. Dusk; chrysanthemums outside the window; all that's breathing down your neck is the approaching All Souls' Day and a draft when someone opens the door. Maybe you would remember everything exactly the same way, Tūla. Still quiet. A distinctive but barely detectable kitchen smell from behind the scenes. Two stools away from me sits, as I remember, a gray conductor with a pointy goatee, feeding his cat tender boiled beef and slowly sipping brandy himself. He's already quite drunk—would he really take his cat to a café otherwise? The conductor doesn't pay any attention to me either, even though we're acquainted. Not far from the big window is a young film and theater actor, practically a genius. He's so modest that even in an empty café he shrinks from the glances of chance admirers. See, I show Tūla. I see, she says, what of it? Take my hand again, take my hand. I take her hand, but look at the actor. An artist: a black, thick mustache, a wide, low forehead, the neck of a champion wrestler. Stocky, sturdy, angry. I know he's an excellent gymnast, fencer, marksman, horseman. His only shortcoming—he can't pronounce short vowels; he stretches them out like blades of grass. But is that really important? If necessary, he's Romeo. If necessary, a Red Commissar or an SS Bannführer. Or else Hamlet, Gasparone, Oedipus. A fiery glance—the kind that makes the ladies' groins wet. Hey, Tūla tugs at me, where are you? I turn to her face again, she's in the shadow— she orders us both another glass of vermouth and a piece of cake—you'll get in trouble there, won't you? They let you rot there in solitary, don't they? Yes,

I said, we get in trouble for everything, they let us rot in solitary, stick us with needles... how do you know everything? Oh, Tūla says seriously, not everything... I just make an effort, just try to guess... Her cherry dress is nearly black, too. We drink vermouth and get glum, like that gray rough-textured pillar with nothing beyond it. Like beyond Polocko Street? She draws the symbol for gold on the napkin—you still got them sometimes in cafés. With lipstick. You started using makeup? No, I just carry lipstick, so that when I meet you I can draw the symbol for gold. Depressing talk. My stiffened fingers on the constantly darkening dress. The meowing of the conductor's satiated cat. When I look at that single photograph of you I have left now, I always remember that café—and it hasn't been there for some time now!—the same shadows, twilight, and somewhere beyond the edge of the photograph, a glass of vermouth giving off the scent of absinth. And not just absinth—maybe gall. Outside the window, white and pink chrysanthemum blossoms keep floating by. The superman actor's hair shines like crow's feathers above a battlefield—he's drinking vodka; his girlie, champagne, of course. I see the fleshy barmaid press the old-fashioned tape-recorder button; the tape screeches, the machine blares, at last a passionate woman's voice whacks you right in the ear—my ear, your ear, the bat's sizable ear—"She was a crazy woman!!!" The barmaid sways off stage somewhere; what else does she have to do here? Cold wafts from the door, and only Gerasim Mucha, a former Young Pioneer captain and now a doorman, can stand it next to the vestibule, and that only because from time to time he downs some visitor's proffered glass of firewater. It's dim inside; outside it's dark. I see the tape in the recorder tangle up; I see the theater and film actor get behind the bar, first discreetly and respectfully consulting with his lady—a remarkably thin big-mouthed girl with fishnet stockings—press one button; another; a third—the tape slowly straightens out, stretches, crackles, blares again, and... and this evening I want for nothing more—Adriano Celentano sings "Yuppi Du"! It was still the time of "Yuppi Du"! For some it was yupidoo, for some not, of course. I'm still yupidoo.

Yupidoo, yupidoo, yupidooo... yupidoodoodoooo... To others it was
a time of hopelessness, of "Sturm und Drang," of souls and gloomy
indifference. But there, in that narrow, cramped café, that dramatic
"Yuppi Du" completely overwhelms me. I don't even say anything
to Tūla about it. That's the way I remember that "neorealist" Italian
evening; you couldn't imagine a gloomier one, but still! I hold her
plaid coat—it was the first time I'd seen this one; she aims her arms
into the slippery sleeves and giggles. It's horribly biting in the street;
those same corpse-people with corpse markings on their foreheads;
we get onto an empty trolleybus, now a real glass coffin. I let you
in first... go on, Tūla, they'll nail the lid on right away. I go along
as far as the Antakalnio traffic circle; I don't even ask where you're
going, or who's waiting for you; is that important, really. I go along,
knowing that when I return I'll find the door to the Second Section
locked; no clever handle will save me; it's already late, and if the sister
on duty writes in the book that I returned with a smell, tomorrow
they'll throw me out of that sanatorium into the street again... at
night I'll fly around as a bat, but during the day? Maybe I'll come visit
you, Tūla says, her eyes lowered at the cracked sidewalk, strokes my
old jacket with her glove, and leaves so quickly I don't even have time
to ask: When, then?

I return plagued by the sweet torture I'd already forgotten—
that's the kind of guy I am! I was with her for a few hours—and
I'm happy! Only an honorable person, only a person who loves self-
lessly can do that! I headed for the home's white gates without blam-
ing myself in the least for flagrantly breaking the rules. I sobered up
quickly from the biting cold, but I chewed on some green cedar from
the hedge just in case; maybe its bitterness will suppress the bitterness of the vermouth and chrysanthemums?

I was very much in luck: the sister, who smelled the reek from the
door and was already leaning forward to write my surname into the
journal of miscreants, unexpectedly raised her eyes and briskly asked
if I wasn't... Domicėlė So and so's cousin? My eyes bugged out and I
asked: Whose? But I immediately confirmed: Aha! Domičiūtė really

is my relative, my cousin, yes! The middle-aged sister shone with little golden wrinkles: they didn't age this woman in the least—she and Domicėlė danced in the same national folk dance group in Siberia! Oh, those were the days! Exile, of course, was unjust, but when you're young... Domicėlė played music there, and sang, and what a comic! Domicėlė a comic? I thought. And why not? It's just in the long run, everything atrophied—humor turned to sarcasm, irony to malice, and so forth. Sister forgot both her infamous journal and my bad smell, reminded me again of how pretty, intelligent, and friendly Domicėlė was. But how badly things turned out for her there! Of course, no one did well, but her? She was madly in love with an Estonian, you see, this mechanic who played the accordion, but it turned out he was married and ridiculously stubborn—he wouldn't agree to divorce the wife he left off in the wilds... you know those Estonians. I didn't know this dramatic detail from my relative's life, how could I? So that's what happened! Sister nearly cried, she was so sorry for Domicėlė. Even now, after so many years! She made me swear not to let anyone see me, but when I started moaning that I badly needed a little drop, she sighed and trickled a drop of pure alcohol into a beaker, diluted it with water out of a grimy carafe, and gave it to me: Go ahead, choke! But not angrily, not angrily...

Incidentally, our senior doctor, the actor's brother with the twitching cheek, would cure the most hopeless drunks with spirits. Not all of them, of course not. Just those who were brought in already flying with the pink elephants: the sisters and veterans called them "delyricists." At first I just shrugged—those guys bore no resemblance to either degenerate lyricists, or artists of any kind. Dazed eyes, a sleepwalker's movements, and an endless struggle to get free; they'd tie them up in the tiny sixth ward, not far from the bathroom. Tie them up tightly, with sheets, wetting them down first so the knots wouldn't come loose. We, the comparatively recovering ones, would take turns watching at their deathbed, moistening the dried lips with a rag and wiping the cold sweat from their brows.

Furnished with an intravenous drip, continually poked and other-wise prodded, the delyricists either recovered or rather quickly gave up the ghost. They'd have time to rave all kinds of nonsense, some of which really would have been worth writing down. Actually, they did manage to haul some of them off to the intensive care ward in time, where they'd bid farewell in peace to seas of vodka and their drunken non-life. But to my great surprise, after a few days those who returned to this terribly imperfect and disorderly world began looking longingly again at both the woods beyond the wire fence and towards the noisy street—that's where the grayish Rytas, a store with intoxicants, stood. They don't remember anything, the orderlies and even the sisters would say, as if in their defense. So you see, it was those raving under a death sentence that the doctors used to water with pure medical spirits. With a sudden, well-practiced movement, they'd open their firmly clenched bridges of teeth and slosh in a good dollop of burning liquid, all the while holding the jawbone pressed in a way that not a drop ran out the sides. I've held one by the feet during this operation—hey, the poor guy thought they wanted to kill him, maybe strangle him? Lo and behold, most of the time this medicine would raise them from the dead; the revived patient would start demanding a second dose himself, and the doctor almost always poured him some.

One day the senior doctor called me in. A week had already gone by since the meeting on the Prospect and the visit in the café; don't tell me they'd sniffed out something? I waited all that week for Tūla to show up—she didn't come. On my way to drink tea, I'd glance at the intersection, loiter in the gateway, sit for a while on the bench next to the registry office—no, she's not coming.

The senior doctor took my blood pressure and listened to my heart. I saw how he loathed these procedures. Then he nudged me and his eye twitched, maybe even so more than usual.

"You see," he began, "my brother told me everything... well, you know, that you're... this tramp." He tried to giggle. "Forty-five days have gone by, actually even more now..."

I looked at him silently. That's how long the course of treatment takes, as determined by the specialists—forty-five days.

"I'm releasing you," the good man decided. "Tomorrow. Stay somewhere for a week, okay? Well, drink or not… whatever works out for you. It'd be better not to, of course! Then come again on Monday, I'll take you in. You can stay today."

He probably only wished me well, this neurasthenic, who, as I later discovered, was an unhappy man in his own way, but no, he wasn't omnipotent either. I used to see these types, men and women with folders and briefcases, dashing into his office, some of them waving their hands in the doorway or even wagging a finger. No, not omnipotent. Apparently even he fails to carry out some responsibilities or another, or treatment plans; maybe even the percentage of cures is too small, so there you have it, he has worries up to his ears! Maybe even serious unpleasantness. But to me he only complained that his brother still hadn't gotten his pivotal role, he'll be standing there with a halberd again, like a stuffed dummy! He tried to smile; this time he almost succeeded.

I went out into the yard, smoked a cigarette under a brown chestnut, and from a distance saw Tūla hurrying up along the gravel pathway. She ran full tilt for the horribly green office door. So, not to see me. My heart beat calmly again, my blood pressure returned to normal. Not to see me. Just to the office. I gave a shout. She turned, squinted, recognized me. Waited for me to come up to her. She looked thoroughly irritated, maybe even angry, although she spoke in a half-whisper as always. She needed some paperwork from the hospital office—wait a bit, if you want. If you want to, she emphasized again, or maybe it just seemed that way to me, suspicious and now assigning significance to everything. A possibility. What paperwork could she need there? To travel out of the country? Hardly likely! Or maybe she is going, what do I know. After all, anyone traveling beyond the cordon has to show they're not crazy: the madhouse office searches through its extensive card catalog, and if you aren't in their archive, they give out a certificate that maybe you won't do anything foolish, you can go. I waited for you for a good half-hour; coming out, you looked even more grim and angry. Not a word about paperwork. No polite questions about how I, the patient, was feeling. We quietly headed off for that same Rytas for coffee. I climbed the stairs and stood in line, while she ran into the store and said something to a woman standing in another line. It was only as I finished slurping the coffee that I suddenly realized it was Tūla's mother. I was itching to ask her why they were *both* here, what they needed in this... I barely restrained myself. Tūla was no longer in a hurry. The muscles in her face composed themselves; her lips seemed more seductively swollen than ever. The wrinkle next to her lips relaxed and straightened out. Apparently her mother had agreed to wait somewhere. Probably there was a lot I didn't know. We went out into a cool sunny day. When I suggested a smoke, she nodded vigorously: Let's go!

Maneuvering between the cars, we ran across the inhumanely broad Olandų Street. On its opposite side, comfortable two-story townhouses that had earlier belonged to Polish military officers had been completely renovated quite some time before. Their entire little gray and brown neighborhood nestled in what was once a quiet and remote area on the edge of Vilnius. The road seethed, roared, and wheezed there now; the cars, it seemed, climbed atop one another as if they were marked with the sign of death. To me, at least, they resembled those pedestrians I had seen—barely animated drunks and drowning victims just pulled out of the water.

There were no doors left anywhere. We entered a narrow corridor, then went into the former kitchen—a smashed gas stove was still parked there. I picked up the glass broken out of the air vent from the floor and raised it to the hole of the former window. The frame, you muttered, what a little beautiful frame! I immediately noticed writing in black paint on the wall, for some reason in German: *Wir sind ein okkupiertes Land!* Well, at least there in the Polish ruins. It should be photographed and sent to *Der Spiegel,* I said, and translated it: "We are an occupied country!" But it seemed occupation didn't concern you much, Tūla; you sniffed your little nose, and that was all. I even remember what we smoked then sitting on a fragrant stack of boards—it was Salem, long cigarettes smelling of menthol and packaged in Finland according to some kind of license—it was you, Tūla, who had them. You even gave me a couple of those cigarettes for a reserve; I smoked them later, thinking about this strange meeting of ours—it was completely different from the other one, in the café. It was as clear as day that she hadn't come there with her mom to visit me. But it wasn't because of that invented paperwork, either. And what of it, if after so many years I know the truth—you, Tūla, were supposed to be committed to the First Section with the milder cases and losers tormented by romantic depression. But your mom, when she found out that my sullen shadow hung around even there—you never did, after all, hide anything from her?—immediately dropped the idea. Yes, Tūla, it was only because of me that you evaded milk soup for supper, MGB in the vein, the silly interns with their psychological test folders... all that merry madhouse, when, after you left, I was there hardly a half a day longer! Maybe something else really would have happened? You know, patients are like family. Maybe something would have changed? Changed where? Well, in our relationship, maybe even our fates, what do I know? After all, the two of us, smoking fragrant Salems, mild Ronhills, or ordinary Primas, would have turned endless circles in the madmen's lanes, climbed the wooded slopes, snuggled in the cold shade, or even wandered as far as the Butterflies Cemetery. You always did want to see it at least once, I'd filled your ears talking about it. Maybe we would have laid down there ourselves?

I put an arm around your shoulders, and you didn't so much as stir. I quickly pecked your cold, bloodless cheek and for some reason jumped back, but you sat there like a stone. Only the hand with the smoking Salem cigarette slowly swung down (you blew out a column of white smoke) and up (you greedily inhaled, the cigarette shortened by nearly a centimeter). "Nothing would have turned out for us anyway, nothing at all!" you suddenly shouted, so angrily that I

cringed and slid off onto the ground; it was the first time I had heard
your voice so low and angry, Tūla; it was so different from all the
hues, nuances, and modulations I had heard up until then! "What
wouldn't have turned out?" I wanted to ask, or maybe I was already
asking, what was supposed to have *turned out*? How badly I wanted
to be disappointed in you then! Certainly all it would have taken
would have been a single glance full of scorn or disgust, or even a
carelessly thrown "drunkard!" No, no, nothing of the sort! You sat
there as before, from the little tip of your nose a clear drop dropped,
you sniffed, wiped it off with your plaid sleeve, and laughed: Do you
see, I'm crying! You should be pleased! You announced this so solemnly, so seriously, that I was astonished—you weren't putting on
an act, you weren't mocking me? I didn't even suspect what it was
that threatened you, but you already knew: from the Second City
our militant, organized family had already raised its wings to move
somewhere near the border with Belarus. But even if I had known!
Everything was already decided, as if it had been drafted with preci-
sion on a white sheet of paper. This was the plan—and I know this
now—the daughter would rest in the hospital, and when she recovered, go straight to the shelter of peaceful nature by the Belarus border. There were too many bums of all sorts in the Second City, too.
That's the story!

I was powerless, but you, Tūla, were even more so. Anyone
observing us from the side would probably have said, run as far as
you can from one another, you'll be done for! But I'm already done
for as it is, I would have said to a prognosticator like that, but what
would you have answered, Tūla? After all, you still suffered, suffered and how! But no one asked anyone anything. We crushed our
cigarette butts and went out the opening into the suddenly gloomy
street. Goodbye!

You went off without looking back even once, a gray knitted hat
pulled over your head: back then, half of Lithuania wore hats like
that. Some peevish guy who came out behind us started yelling—all
the scum that come around here!—but I silently continued to watch

you; you walked faster and faster. All I saw was a woman come out from behind the little dogwood trees—your mom; now I recognized her. You joined arms and instantly disappeared from my view. I didn't even see where the two of you turned off. And how could I foresee that the next week I'd finally fall into the hands of the bluecoats, that, after rotting in a temporary holding cell, they wouldn't release me into the sodden autumn, but instead take me straight to the Drunkard's Prison, actually called by a much more innocent name. And I didn't foresee that I wouldn't see you, Tūla, for three whole years, and that when we did see each other again, that time would really be the last. No premonition. Only an emptiness in my heart and completely normal blood pressure. All I knew then was that I wouldn't be returning here on any Monday. Or any Tuesday, either.

With this decided, I crossed roaring Olandų Street's racecourse without hurrying, and there I was stopped by a writer I knew wearing dark glasses, a white coat that reached to his ankles, and the carefully tended mustache of a walrus. That's who was actually preparing to travel past the cordon, to West Germany no less, the moneyland, as he himself said. So it was he who had gotten that bit of paper, Tūla. Even I was certain this guy wasn't going to raise a stink while he was there, that he'd know how to use both a bathroom and a fork. That type doesn't disappoint. *"Wir sind ein okkupiertes Land!"*—the writing on the wall of the Polish townhouse's kitchen came to mind.

IX

So there: once more I saw with my own two eyes that Vilnius, even though it's a long way off from the Baltic, has huge advantages in comparison to the proud capitals by the sea or the gigantic dark gray cities sprawling to infinity on the plains; we've all seen those, haven't we? It's the terrain, the sometimes startling difference in heights, that does it. Of course, I already knew, theoretically, that once you've clambered up past the tufts of poplars dotting Liepkalnis to the beginning of the road to Minsk, you immediately end up higher than St. John's Bell Tower, and it's hardly the smallest. But I really never expected that, leaning on a window sill on the fifth floor of the Drunkard's Prison, in the hall that served as both a club and a theater where the display trials of runaways and the rare concert took place, namely, that from this gloomy, sweat-soaked hall, a truly outstanding and unexpected view of the capital would open before me—a gleaming panorama from imprisonment: the Old Town in the front plane and the emerald hills of Šeškinė in what must have been the fourth. The expanse of the view wasn't even darkened by the yard of the penitentiary next door, where those you couldn't say were slaves of the bottle—the serious criminals—suffered behind heavy bars. My section chief, Captain Tchaikovsky, said about them: "There's men for you! Not like you burnouts, riffraff, weaklings!" Actually, a part of the city was blocked by the cupola of Visitation Church, but you could go over to the hall's other window, or crawl down into the little room set up behind the stage by Mogila, the ham

radio operator—another drunk, of course—and use the same occasion get a gulp of *chifir*—very strong black tea.

I didn't, understandably, come across the gleaming panorama
immediately, not at all; it was a good half-year later, when I had already
managed to gather my senses a bit, get around, come to terms with the
routine, the stink, the conveyor belt, and the constant humiliations
or open scorn. For another thing, as spring broke beyond the fence
of the Drunkard's Prison, I had already made friends of a sort. I met
men of more decency and dignity than those in so-called freedom,
beyond the high fence wound with balls of barbed wire and netting
and lit up at night by a search light. The fence wasn't much different than the one Cap'n Tchaikovsky's "eagles" patiently sat behind,
those brazen robbers, grand-theft swindlers, assaulters, murderers,
and other birds of that feather—just that there were at least six similar fences there, each more intricate than the other. I would often see
those real men through my workshop's window, or when I went out
to smoke: they raised their black-billed caps to every boss and lined
up to go to work as if they were going on parade. I would see their
faces, too—faces like faces, a lot of them young. But I simply won't
have the time to tell you much about it: neither the good men, nor
the dregs. I'll only mention to you in passing, Tūla, about the "medical procedures"—they didn't manage to think up anything very new
there either: at first they made me vomit too, just now with a harsher,
forced method, using apomorphine injections, and later, when the
torture was coming to an end, they forced me to swallow revolting
white tablets that are probably curdling my liver yet today. The medical personnel would only occasionally put on white coats; most of
the time they, like the administration, wore green Interior Ministry
Army jackets with the appropriate number of gold stars and grating
red, almost crimson stripes and caps; the faces wide and puffy, the
lexicon plain: Well now, come to me, *sinyuga*, I'll tell you something!
They called us, the patients, *sinyugi*, the blue ones, apparently because
we were dressed in blue tunics and thin blue pants, wore blue berets,
and in the winter headed to work in blue padded jackets. Or black,

whichever fell to you. Our instructors and supervisors didn't look the least bit better—after all, we were forced to live soberly, while they hit the bottle nearly every day. Actually, in the operations section, which caught the frequent runaways, you came across young, athletic jocks—when these guys caught someone, they handed it out without mercy, even to those who didn't resist at all, usually a still half-drunk runaway after he'd been surrounded in some wasteland or pulled out of some cussing slattern's bed.

You see how it is, Tūla. I don't even know why it occurred to me to reveal this stage of my life—it would be difficult to call it just an episode, although what's there to hide—I ended up where a homeless man with a persistent odor on his breath should. I'll be upfront: in many ways I actually did better there than in the Second Section. At least no one there went on and on about the disorders of the central nervous system and no one beat themselves on the chest promising to never drink again. What for? No one either demanded or asked for it. In the Drunkard's Prison, whether he cared to or not, a man opens up completely and shows himself as he really is; a similar thing probably happens only in the army, in a real prison, or on a ship far out at sea. You'd certainly not put on any pretenses there, and you wouldn't yell in anger: "I'm sick of this, drop dead all of you, I'm leaving!" Actually, you could run away from the Drunkard's Prison—whoever worked in town would up and run away at least once but rarely lasted even a whole week in "freedom." It wasn't unusual for some to return on their own: sometimes these wouldn't even get stuffed into solitary, they'd just get shaved bald and planted next to the conveyor. Before I saw that panorama from the club window, I, for one, wasn't even thinking of running. They fed me, dressed me, and the work wasn't hard, only exhaustingly boring and senseless. But half a year went by, the creeks began streaming through the snow drifts, the aspens on Rasų Street budded out and began to scent the air, and even the only tree in the zone—a pathetic mountain pine next to the former Vilnius Kapitula building—began to put on new growth. Then, late one sunny morning when I stopped by the club, I raised the black light-blocking curtain—it was designed to darken the hall during movie showings—raised it, and was amazed: lit up with gold, somewhere far off and close by, the still bare but already budding Vilnius sparkled, twinkled, and quietly hummed. I propped my chin on my fists and glued my eyes on those so newly shining spires, cornices, and window bays, at the chimneys and the barely visible weathervanes. I don't know how long I would have dawdled there, but the loudspeakers that were everywhere crackled and bellowed: You're summoned to see your crew leader! In the time I'd been in the Drunkard's Prison I had already reached the summit of the career ladder—I was the librarian, I belonged to the well-fed work brigade and could go out into town practically every day—either to subscribe to periodicals, or to order new books at the circulation desk, or whenever I found some excuse or another. It was only later that a gung-ho captain drove me out of the library, this half-educated Andeika—just where did he get a name like that? If he'd been a Nadeika or a Mandeika, but no—Andeika! After all, even looking at it self-critically, I was an entirely decent librarian; at least the contingent was happy with me. I was a rather independent person in this enclosed space too—I could even plan my day, sometimes even my night; and in the meantime I exchanged books, distributed ragged, no longer readable detective novels, bound the newspapers, and waited for spring— blossoms and freedom!

During those six months I remembered you only rarely, Tūla—I was constantly depressed, gloomy, and as cranky as a beetle with its wings pulled off. What bothered me nearly the most was that there was nowhere you could be alone: those same angry eyes would be looking out of even the most out-of-the-way corner—and just what are you doing here? And then there was the required "medical treatment"—apomorphine in the rump and a glass of vodka or wine immediately afterwards. Drinking was required—otherwise you wouldn't get very nauseated. The injection would immediately make your peter stand up, but as soon as the desire arose, it would be drowned out by dizziness and a boundless nausea; the pukers were valued highly here, too, and even had privileges—unofficially they were allowed to drink *chifir*. But when could you think, or ponder bygone times? Besides, I could tell you, without even trying to defend myself, that I didn't believe I would ever encounter you again, or even if I did... even if I did encounter you, I no longer counted on anything. I made no plans for the future, not even for myself—not until I saw the sparkling city's basin with the dark red Bernardine tiles. They stuck out as they always had, the pale new tiles shining from afar—oh enzymes, paint enzymes, Mr. Petryla, why did you die without sprinkling the tiles with your bodily fluids? I could even see birds perched on that roof. Your house, Tūla, couldn't be seen from there, nor the long cloister; they were blocked by other walls, and the terrain was such that they simply couldn't be seen. I only felt them grieving somewhere, not at all far away—after all, I could see the thick oak next to the waterside and the covered bridge; I could tell by its top, by the dried-up crown. It was that spring I wrote to you—you were all still living in the Second City, and I found the address quite easily in town, from that long-legged girl with the leggings: it was quite strange that she told me right away, poured it out from memory: rat-a-tat-tat! I couldn't go without writing anymore, since I had a desk in the corner of the library and a little cabinet with a pathetic lock—the *praporshchiki*—warrant officers—would break into it every time they checked the living quarters, but I kept putting a new one on a few days later. They weren't looking for intoxicants there; it was knives, tablets, or tea leaves, and even though they knew they wouldn't find anything, they'd break it without hesitation, with gusto. Regardless, when I became the library's chief, I became, if not an honored, then at least a necessary person, whom it was worth taking into account, to some degree at least. Of course, I was a far cry from the clothes locker or sugar distributors, or even the staff bread slicer, but I was no longer the lowest drudge. I would distribute old newspapers to the tea sellers—the place was full of them!—to pack their wares. My closest friends could rely on my support if in need of hiding some valuable object—a ring, a watch, money, or sometimes—quick, quick, quick!—to finish off a bottle. A bottle of vodka here cost barely a few rubles more than at the nearest deli in Gervėčių Street, while the difference in the price of wine was even less at first. A portion of the profits from the smuggled intoxicants went to the perpetually hungover warrant officers, or even to the section chiefs—*vse my lyudi, vse my cheloveki*—we're all men, we're all hu-men! Of course, anyone here who had some bit of strength remaining got by as best they could. Artists with degrees hammered castles and beautiful girls into metal sheets for the lower-grade officials and the medical personnel, while this Pedro, an ex-sculptor, one of those I sincerely liked, made artistic works of far more merit. No matter if it was just a fireplace grate and a set of tools for the prison chief himself, Vaidevutis Tribandis. The other VIPs picked out the best bricklayers, joiners, cement layers, carpenters for themselves... after all, a lot of urgent work was constantly turning up in the collective garden districts going up around the capital. Guys like that would spend practically the entire summer in the gardens, eating and drinking there, and would come "home" only on the weekends. Less valuable tradesmen labored in the work brigade; in their free time they made knives, penknives, handsome wood or ebonite cigarette holders, chain necklaces, fishing reels, even sets of forks and spoons! Many would have gotten along just fine if it weren't for the *shustryaki*—gangbangers—those suffering from chronic incurable alcoholism were most often brainless young men of an athletic build. Without finding the evidence to cram them into the over-filled jails, the government "bodies" played it safe by sticking them into the Drunkard's Prison—come on now, every last one of them drank! They were everyone's scourge, even the bosses'. They kept escaping, even from the guarded zone; all of them had some kind of beaten weapon; they'd frequently clobber each other savagely and terrorize not just the old men and the cripples, but anyone they didn't like or didn't please them, even the "self-government's" christened work managers and foremen. They'd run amuck in the medical personnel's quarters looking for narcotics, and feared practically nothing:

they'd only attack in a pack, with a tenfold advantage. They all knew full well that sooner or later they'd leave this Artek—that's what the neighboring recidivists named our zone, after the famous Soviet children's camp—and end up behind the other fence, so out of curiosity they scanned the penitentiary yard and quite fearlessly observed the life of hardened criminals sentenced to many years. Some, without fear of punishment, through all the fences, enclosures, and barbed wire, managed to pass over packages of some precious cargo—they'd send the recidivists knives, daggers, or shiny rings, while practically only a single type of merchandise traveled in the other direction—atominals, or whatever they're called, a particularly strong form of tranquilizers. When caught, the throwers wouldn't betray a thing; they'd calmly sit out the days in solitary in the basement of the Kapitula, and when they came out, they'd take up the same trade again—you need to live somehow! Almost all the *shustryaki* were abundantly tattooed—in the showers I even saw one whose back had the Cathedral of Basil the Blessed in Red Square with all of its onion domes—but when Pedro, who'd gotten the idea to make himself an atlas or album of tattoos, tried to sketch them in the shower, he was very forcefully warned off—we ever see you do that again, you're done for! The sluggish villagers weren't the only ones who awaited their "going-away parties" with fear: the friends would see their exiting pal off in an exemplary grand style, arranging a feast that rarely ended peacefully—of course you couldn't leave with accounts unsettled! But they needed my services, too—they liked reading little books about spies and adventures, and if a boon was needed, I would let them cut the beauties out of old magazines, never mind if they were half-naked. The *shustryaki* would pay me for the reading and the pictures with cigarettes and tea, the "real" currency. Yes, that library was truly my salvation: neither those of the liberal arts, nor the musicians, nor the former educators, nor even the petty mid-level managers (there was an ex-lawyer, a church choir director, and even a Komsomol organizer from the university in Vilnius there) got any respect. On the contrary, the "erudite" were especially hassled, excepting any kind of drummer or guitar player. These would organize concerts, compete in the prison establishment's competitions, and were, at least occasionally, patted on the head. In most cases, all the local *bon ton* demanded of the four-eyed learned ones was to be the object of public and private ridicule, hoodwinking and, if necessary, a smack on the back of the head. They always got the worst jobs and the sorriest cots, as it is everywhere, by the way. No one felt sorry when they were stolen from, no one defended them; and if they just dared to show a spark of wisdom or wit, if they appeared to be in the least bit smarter, to know something about the arts, politics or even sports, they were instantly beaten up and even forced to... well, enough of that! It's just that I had already grown accustomed to this tradition in the streets and I'd noticed a similar phenomenon in the Second Section, so it wasn't big news to me—play the fool, and don't argue with anyone!

Eventually I found yet another panorama—it opened out from the window at the end of the corridor—the blue-green of Belmontas with small cottages next to the woods, the hills of Markučių off in the distance, and in the foreground—an old depot with yard-high letters on the very top: *Slava KPSS!*—Glory to the Communist Party of the Soviet Union! My library's windows looked out in yet another direction: towards Liepkalnis, towards Rasos, towards the quiet Vitebsko and Gervėčių streets, towards the railroad rumbling hollowly somewhere down below; it rattled day and night and provoked a sense of longing, too. For some it's the nearest station, for some the Far East or Central Asia, according to the day-dreamer's temperament.

That day, I remember, I didn't go into town. I shut myself up in the library; only a little wooden partition separated it from the living "section" jammed with bunk beds. Before noon that was empty, too. That day, nearly by force tearing myself away from the window facing the stone buildings of Vilnius, I wrote the first letter from there to you, Tūla—long, frank, and... meaningless. I wrote about the view of the city, mentioned all the churches and complexes, tried to remind you of those places we had managed to visit and those we had only promised to visit. I drew an excessively cheerful picture of my life and lifestyle—buoyed up, it seemed to me, with grotesque, irony, and black humor, but the letter came out meaningless, anyway. After all, that's not the way you write from jail, from a labor camp, from an army unit or a submarine; not like that. So, finishing up, I didn't forget to write: I don't expect an answer from you, I know, after all, that you won't write, but at least let me write to you, believe me, it'll be a great help to me! Roughly like that, in that style. Is it possible to plead for an answer more plainly? Probably not. I believe I already knew how to write letters; there's people who save them even now, but that, of course, is something completely different. I was about to seal the envelope and had already stuck out my tongue to lick the narrow band of glue when it suddenly occurred to me: I'll fix you a real surprise, Tūla! I put the letter in the cabinet, thwacked the pathetic lock shut, and ran off to Pedro's studio; it was in the neighborhood. I knocked with the prearranged signal, Pedro opened the door, and I, breathless with excitement no less, demanded: Draw me! Pedro, of course, put on a front; listen, he wasn't a portrait artist, but I already knew—he drew great caricatures, and it was a caricature I needed! I stroked his ego, praised several works he'd painted in prison for his own pleasure. Apparently, I knew how to praise, too, because Pedro, mumbling something about a payment in kind, told me to sit by the window and uncorked a bottle of ink. He really did succeed with the caricature; at first I even thought of taking insult—how pathetic I looked, what a typical drunk! But thanking him, I rushed off to the library; I stuck the caricature in the envelope and this time glued it down. I knew you would appreciate my efforts, even if you didn't answer my correspondence, as I asked.

Now all that was left was to throw the letter into the mailbox. The official procedure was like this: you throw your letter into the box next to the gate in the camp's yard and a diligent censor would eagerly read it over, fix the mistakes, and send it off to wherever it needs to go. I didn't see a single fool act that way, except maybe a greenhorn or a half-wit. Earlier, when I sat by the conveyor, I'd entrust my rare letters to the ex-journalist and amateur poet Inocentas Vaclovas Venislovas, a guy particularly sensitive to injustice and violence; he constantly walked around with a black eye, or at least with the lenses of his glasses smashed—the *shustryaki* didn't take pity even on Don Quixote! *Vivere pericolosamente!*—how wonderfully this saying of the pompous Benito suited such a variety of people during the Andropov era! From a railroad policeman to a party or mafia bigwig. From a station pickpocket to a tanker captain. From the butterflies of the squares to the heads of Women's Councils.

Now I could carry my letter out myself. So, the next morning I got ready to go out into a city bursting with spring—in a padded coat, a blue beret, and heavy Russian leather shoes: I wasn't at all ashamed of this wardrobe of mine—I'd shown up in the streets dressed in worse clothes before, even ragged ones. Now I was blue all over, but tidy; even the leather shoes were shined. Well then, where are you, Domicėlė?

Just in case, I stuck the letter under my shirt—who knows what could get into the tiny little head of the warrant officer sitting in the guard shack. Actually, the *sinyugi* released into the city were rarely checked; there simply wasn't time for it; just the number of detachments they take out to suburban building sites or freight terminals every morning! But they come to their senses on the return: they weren't adverse, some of them, to feel you up; others, you look, and they're taking off your shoes. But in the evening, vodka... wine... eau de cologne will flow through the zone anyway. In a little corner of the basement you up and run across some figure with their eyes dazed from tablets, like a fly caught in a glue pot or porridge; they called them *zamurovannyy*—the walled-in.

I felt the letter under my shirt. When you go alone, it's nerve-wracking anyway; the Cerberus varies. Besides, yesterday they caught two somber denizens carrying state blankets hidden inside their clothes, no matter the blankets were filthy and unwashed. The camp authorities don't like that one bit—they shut both of them up in the "hold" under the Kapitula. I keep saying "camp"—the authorities didn't care for that, either; they would say "preventorium," or as the patients said, "eltepe." LTP, always in Russian, like all of our papers there. *Lechebno trudovoy profilaktoriy*—therapeutic forced labor rehabilitation. One scholarly Russian deciphered the abbreviation as *Lager trudovoy povinnosti*—forced labor camp service. Well, they denied him packages and visits with Marusia—if it's a camp to you, it's a camp to us! Of course, they thought up some other reason; in that respect they were truly inventive—this person, so the story went, had been bothering the young chubbies. They reported this to Marusia, too.

I got the letter out safely, of course. I threw it in the box right across from the Gates of Dawn, and I turned into the heart of the city through them, too, just on a lark, this time without any purpose in mind. I had withstood sobriety for longer than six months now; even my face had smoothed out. When I went outside, I didn't even try to drink in moderation, although there were plenty who managed, while out on the town, to drink and sober up, too. Or else they always had a fiver ready for the Cerberus—stick it under his nose and he wouldn't smell anything anymore, neither vodka nor wine. But I didn't even try; I valued my quiet little place in the library too much, and I never had enough money to cover paying for a safe return to my bed. I descended past the crumbling Philharmonic, past the Astorija being restored by our hard-working men, and suddenly I got the urge to stop at the Exhibition Hall and sit down in the same spot where I saw you for the first time and… and nothing. To sit down for a while. Drink coffee. It isn't written down anywhere yet that citizens in blue clothes can't buy coffee. True, I took the risk of running into some unpleasant acquaintances, but the Hall's coffee bar was empty—only the half-drunk Romanas Būkas sat there—pissed off, disheveled, without an audience. I laid my padded coat on the window sill, brought some coffee and a hard roll. I sat down comfortably in the spot I'd picked out and waited patiently—will Būkas turn around, or not? After all, he sees me, he knows!

"I know everything!" he bellowed without even turning around. "Everything! Everything."

Then he got up, went over in a fury to the coffee machine, and didn't return to where he'd been sitting, but to my table—he flopped down in your "spot," Tūla. Well now, I thought. The players themselves changed slightly, the scene dimmed, the play was moving quickly to an end—ripping at the seams, pouring real and fake blood, blood and wine both congealing, but the culmination had already passed by—but was there one at all? Oh, Būkas! Būkas had nothing to do with it! What's Būkas to me now, I have enough worries without him. Oho, he didn't return empty-handed—he set a full glass of brandy and some coffee in front of me. Making one more trip, he returned with some kind of roulade and, just like he did back then in the communal apartment block, ordered me:

"Drink!"

What tempted me, who tripped me up? No one. I turned it up and emptied it—the active interest in Būkas's face changed to a wide, truly sincere smile:

"Bravo! That's what I thought. A drunk is faithful only to himself!"

He could have added: "You'll never have any allies in your fight with yourself!" It would have fit the bill. I smiled, too, relaxed like a warmed-over cutlet; I even got thoroughly sweaty and unbuttoned my blue shirt. Būkas got all emotional and started to apologize about something, to justify himself, to swear—though not angrily—at our common wifey, she herself, you know... Oh Būkas, Būkas, I thought, if you only knew what worries me now! Getting drunker by the minute, I imagined you, Tūla, getting my letter, in utter amazement you carry it up to the attic, lock yourself in, and in solitude read and read, unable to tear yourself away from the text of my meandering lines, giggling quietly at Pedro's wonderful caricature, that is, my caricature. You put the entire contents back into the envelope, but after only a half-hour, or maybe less, you climb the wooden stairs again; reading everything a second time, you sigh and now you're writing, writing, writing... what's your answer, Tūla? Overflowing with righteous fury? Stern? No, more likely politely forgiving, reserved... come on now, I'll manage to sense all the nuances myself.

"Hey! What's the matter with you?" Būkas shakes me by my blue shoulder. "Have some coffee! Wait, I'll bring some more!"

He was seriously worried about me; he hadn't been born yesterday, after all, he knew what was in store for me if they were to smell it! So he poured coffee into me and repeated the same script; in the meantime, he himself was in turns knocking back brandy and that disgusting Lithuanian gin. "We all belong there!" he said. "All of us plowmen of the streets, self-styled art people... and you're the only one suffering for it!" Romanas Būkas gazed at me sadly, exaggerated my sufferings, even tried to spiritualize it. I left him all alone, but going through the door I ran into a woman with raven hair and leather pants—I saw her sit down next to the maestro and hug his shoulders. There was still gobs of time, it seemed to me, before five o'clock—that's when I had to sit at the window and start exchanging books. Būkas had given me ten rubles, that had to be cleverly hidden, too; I had enough of my own for coffee. So I drank it where I found it, but my legs on their own carried me to the little covered bridge where I'd gotten snagged by the *milítsiya* jeep six months earlier—it had dragged me off to the drunk tank to sober up, but this time didn't let me out again. There it is, the covered bridge, my old friend! I greeted several sharp-eyed crows and that graphic arts lecturer with the *Schnauzbart*. He was surprised to see my uniform, but I had already prepared an answer: I'd gotten a job in the Geological Office, so is it surprising... He laughed in disbelief and hoofed it off to his Institute with the shining windows, merely turning back to wag a long talented finger at me. For some reason this meeting put me in a cheerful mood, and I immediately calculated: I can drink five rubles away in peace, and I'll save the other fiver for the payoff! The prudence of Solomon—I downed an entire bottle of wine right there, on the little bridge, glancing at your empty windows, thinking about my letter the traveler...

But even a fiver didn't help—they grabbed me by the collar,

hustled me off to the "hold," while I was still high they plucked me clean with a dull shaver and shoved me into a stinking cell—*nakonets i etot*—at last, this one too—*bannyy intelligent nadralsja*—frigging smart one got smashed! *Tu-tu! Na Vorkutu*—toot, toot, it's off to Vorkuta!

At five o'clock in the morning, they got me up and took away the pad mattress. The bunk was chained to the wall—apparently that was the rule there. The next day, when my head stopped spinning and I badly wanted a smoke, Andeika visited me—he beamed on the other side of the bars and rubbed his hands—he was really happy to see me there, underground! He led me out into the corridor—asked about where the spare keys were, and something else. I suffocated underground for three days, then they finally let me out. Good-bye, library! Andeika's protege was already seated there, this little doofus with a big butt. And I got stuck next to the conveyor again—from morning until night. Now I could go downstairs to our building's giant basement only during dinner—that was when they brought a heap of previously checked letters. They'd throw them down on a bench and immediately a crowd of patients still communicating with the outside world would gather there—Inocentas Venislovas first of all; he actively corresponded with the Women's Prison, received scores of letters, and spent practically all his free time answering them. Yes, the booze hounds received letters already torn open and checked. This quite decent wisp of a girl who had had a taste of Lithuanian studies at the University had a position in the prison office; she might have been the only one in the administration who knew Lithuanian. Her entire job was to keep reading and reading juicy letters overflowing with love, hate, spite, longing, frustration, revenge, and emotions of that ilk. Undoubtedly they had a little list—which correspondents warranted close attention, which not so close. Even though the censor sat in a small separate room in the Kapitula's attic, and even though that reading didn't threaten her person in the least, Dangirutė (Dangerėta? I only heard her called Dangė), like the others, got a decent bonus to her pay "for dangerous conditions." The young girls or the well-fed hens toiling in the workshops didn't sense any danger, either—they worked as supervisors and inspectors; they were all enticed there only by that addition and they were all terribly afraid to lose such easy and supposedly well-paid work. Every last one of them had signed a pledge—Dangerėta, too, of course!—not just that they wouldn't have "intimate contact with any persons undergoing treatment in the preventorium," but that they wouldn't bring any vodka, wine, beer, eau de cologne, tea, tooth paste, shoe polish... lemons, cocoa, chocolate... medicines, weapons, explosives—nothing!—into the living or working quarters. They didn't, by the way, have the least intention of bringing anything. They wouldn't have brought anything even if it was allowed. What next! They held pretty strictly to their word, and if spoken to would only talk about work, output, materials... They swore magnificently—old Daszewska could have enriched her banal vocabulary quite a bit here. They were greedy for money, and even though all our workshop did was finish parts—little plastic scoops for electric meters—they still found something to take home: either gauze, or acetone, or some liquid or another that was used to wash those tiny windows, the ones you look through suspiciously at a row of even tinier numbers.

But after all, even children know that rules are made to be...

That's why promises are made, to be... And the more passionate and sincere, the faster they're forgotten. When two warrant officers, as usual poking around everywhere in the work zone, stumbled upon—*in flagrante!*—a still-young little hen being screwed by a former boxing champ, his eyes closed, in the finished products store room, no one made a big fuss—they threw the little hen out that very evening, and the boxer got sent to that "hold," the underground isolation cell, for ten days. Perhaps they wouldn't have sent him there, but the profligate managed to knock out a Cerberus and called another one a Russian, even though he actually was a real Russian from Vologda, Smirnov if I remember, so why get mad?

On top of that, when barely a few days later, in that same store room, it was *determined* (now there's a strategical term for you!) that the warrant officer Štefankovich's wife, who also worked there, was having intimate relations, the fuss started up instantly, because it was Vanda Štefankovich's best friend at work who betrayed her. The warrant officers fell over laughing: the diminutive, freckled cavalier was doing the fat broad from atop an empty box! Risking falling off, he did his duty anyway, while she, her wide thighs turned to him, continued to moan even after the detectives entered: *davai, dorogoy, ne ostanavlivaysya, tut suki khodyat*—go on, my dear, keep going, there's bitches around! Štefankovich didn't make it there in time; he probably would have killed both his wife and her partner, an electrician from Panevėžys. Incidentally, they immediately transferred the electrician to another Drunkard's Prison near Kaunas, where they held men according to a different paragraph of the penal code. It seems things went okay for him there too—the story that followed him there merely increased the electrician's status. The strumpet was out of the workshop that same day, but Štefankovich didn't go anywhere and soon turned into a real horror. A rare soul passed his inspection, and when he was on watch in the zone word went from mouth to mouth: "Watch out! Štefankovich!" He didn't object to checking the zone's most out-of-the-way places, and he particularly liked the basement; there were a bunch of small "outfits" there—a clothes dryer, showers, individual food lockers, the bedding and clothing storeroom, and the *laryok*—a stall where the patients were allowed to buy hygienic necessities and a little bit of food. Incidents would occur at the food lockers; everyone had a drawer with a number there, and those always unlocked drawers attracted the curiosity and greed of the *shustryaki*.

As I went to the basement every day to look for letters—earlier I'd only go down to the showers—I'd see Štefankovich waiting for a victim; now he always found something to object to, and the brown-haired freckled patients with a slender build suffered the most. Even when he got it in the teeth in the dark, Štefankovich didn't let up. For some reason he was decent to me; once, when he came into the library, he didn't even break the lock I'd just put on the drawer, although actually, that was before the *in flagrante*.

I waited for your letter for a week; then another week; and when it still hadn't come I wrote a second letter—maybe you hadn't gotten it? But even then I continued to walk down to the basement in vain—nothing. And it was only at the very end of April that Pedro brought me your envelope: I must have turned pale, because Pedro put the letter down and left without asking anything. Three sentences: "I got your letter. Send me that poem: "...when buggies of blue will carry the sleepwalkers out of Tula..." Stay healthy! Tūla." The place and date. That's all.

Now I wrote to you practically every day. In as much detail as possible I described the meeting with Būkas and Mr. "Schnauzbart"; I described the Vilnelė before the rain and after the rain; in a few strokes I drew the evening Bernardine landscape; I even inserted several short dialogs with Gerasim Mucha—you surely remember, Tūla, that poor doorman who shivered at his post but wouldn't take a step away from it? And only at the end did I write—one and only one time—I still love you. No reply.

In June I ran away from the camp for the first time; you see, I'd been allowed into the city again, I worked at the central warehouse. I wandered off as far as the seaside right next to the Latvian border and it was only the circumstance that I returned behind bars on my own, without being captured by the operatives, that saved me from a truly serious new term—an entire year. There were several dozen runaways; they tried us all at once. An entire truckload, guarded just for show (who was going to run now?!), rolled up to the door of the district Soviet Court. Everything went along just like at the conveyor—next, next, next! They added only three months; when I went out the courtroom door I no longer regretted running. Once again I turned one and the same little screw into one and the same bushing, that's what it seemed like, sitting at the actual conveyor. And then your second letter came, a short one too, but with a question at the end: "So what should I do?" you asked. "Why are you *there*?" Rhetorical questions! Once more I wrote and wrote to you, but it was only in the late autumn (they added another ninety days!) that your second-to-the-last letter came; it wasn't at all difficult to memorize it: "Please don't write to me. Tūla." Of course, I answered right away, but now I was walking down to the basement merely out of habit. Seniors at the end of their days, or more accurately, men who had aged prematurely—their contemporaries in "freedom" were still tickling women—were always sitting around there. If the large plaque in the yard with the sign "We are all the forgers of our own fortune!" seemed funny, the more modest banner in this basement, above the heads of the unfortunates, immediately put you in a melancholy state: "Drink Without Moderation, Die Without Procrastination!" To these nearly-dead, the camp basement was truly a home: when the loudspeakers throughout the entire zone started in announcing the drunks to be released to freedom, the poor guys would have covered their ears if they could, they so feared hearing their names! After all, where could they go from here? These disowned disowners, half-dead, homeless men who were no longer dangerous to anyone for quite some time now, neither to themselves nor others. I myself saw Šarka, an inhabitant of the village of Daugai, upon hearing of his release hide himself under the stairs in this space like a doghouse where they kept the mops and rags—he didn't go anywhere for three days, cried behind the door he'd barred from inside, threatened to kill himself to the jailers who approached, and would have done it, too, but they deceived him; they promised he could stay in the camp, as long as he came out to eat! The hungry Šarka took the bait and came out—gray, with a hollow chest and a pointy, grizzled little chin. They actually did feed him, actually gave him the two packs of Prima cigarettes they'd promised, and then hustled him out the gate. Behind him they threw his padded coat, his pack, and an envelope with thirty rubles—the amount he'd slaved for in two and a half years!—on the snow. As I remember, another similar unfortunate led Šarka away with him: he still had a shack in some neck of the woods, but there were dozens of Šarkas.

The perpetually smoky, stuffy basement: the pertpetual domino players would hang around there, and the clandestine second-hand buyers; the *shustryaki* used to mix in there, too. They were attracted by the food stall, where you could spend only small change, but they, athletes, gangsters, perpetually discontented about something, hungry, had things to do there—either take away a package, or openly rob the drawers with food. They'd pull them all open in turn, and when they found something, stuff it into a sack. Inocentas Venislovas got back at them—he poured laxatives into his abundant stewed fruit and jams, impatiently awaited his hour, and when the entire gang finally cut loose, when they realized the treachery and ran around threatening, he was already marching out the gates.

But two months later they finally let me out into the city again; this time they assigned me as a freight handler at the "Litenergosnabe," as the sizable warehouse not far from the Railroad Workers' House of Culture was called. Mostly it was sluggish villagers who worked there with me—they didn't know the city at all, didn't have any relatives there, or if they did, they were ashamed to visit them. They were serious cowards and telltales; they snitched on me for fixing black tea in the break room, well, all right, all right, it was *chifir*. They practically didn't punish for it; just a slap on the wrist, for appearances' sake; supposedly, it was stealing electricity, ruining the wiring—what bull! I frequently thought: maybe I should get a job here when I leave the preventorium? There wasn't a lot of work there, the merchandise was clean—all kinds of wires, lamps, ovens, heaters. The women in the warehouse didn't complain about me, didn't pick on me, didn't yell at me, and sometimes they even fed me sandwiches. But it was still a long way to relative freedom, I'd have time yet. I never went outside that warehouse; waiting to be sent for over the phone, I'd read a book I'd brought along, or play Sixty-Six with some "colleague." I avoided the city, particularly since hard times had arrived for other people, too: the new boss of the empire, who had just knocked a South Korean airliner out of the sky, now took on his own vassals—to him, the entire giant country seemed to be a breeding ground for idlers and freeloaders! First thing in the morning, big-shouldered green men started showing up and zooming around the beer stalls, markets, movie theaters, and other spots of "unlawful assembly." They had a lot of license; they could beat you up or drag you off to one of their ubiquitous offices, where you'd "sing a different tune." Terrible times came for the wanderers and the freeloaders, the drunks and the homeless—the clean-up went on interminably, day and night; groups competed between themselves, contended for awards and honors, and I thought: How many of them, the enforcers, are needed to make everyone work? After all, there were hundreds, thousands of them; they too got wages, "built up seniority," had the right to take time off. And our institution kept overflowing with ever new troops of asocial drunks and homeless men, whom the old-timers called *banglo*—that was a word that came from distant Bangladesh. It was easy to see they weren't all drunkards. But the plan was exceeded; the contingent was already sleeping in the club hall and on the ground—there were even a few exhausted lice-ridden men sleeping on the stage. "Temporarily, temporarily, they said!" the supervisor Tribandis fumed, "what does that 'temporary' mean!? Where will I put them?" But people no longer poured in, and construction of a new building began; there were quarters prepared for women, too, and talk went around that similar institutions were expanding rapidly all over the empire—from the Pacific to captured East Prussia.

Then your last letter came—I never got any other letters from you. You returned the picture—no, not mine. A long time before I had sent you a photograph of the view from the club window. Even though photographing things there was, of course, strictly forbidden, but everything that's forbidden is... So anyway, you returned the view from the window showing the Visitation Church in the foreground and a barely visible Bernardine complex—the picture's quality was poor. That's why you'd glued a cut-out from another picture on top. On the grounds of the church, a smiling young just-married couple were walking hand-in-hand; both of their faces seemed revolting to me. It wasn't you there, this collage was perhaps trying to tell me—leave me in peace for once! I smiled—by then I could manage to do that—and got ready to go to the showers. I wasn't very surprised to meet my still-not-outfitted acquaintance the stonemason on the stairs; he used to work in the Bernardine complex, too. "Yet another victim of the drunkards' genocide!" I shot out, and he laughed out loud. A strong, cheerful man! He wasn't in the least regretful over this "bad end," apparently, he believed he'd be out of there soon; he'd only gotten six months. He scratched at his thick beard, but I looked at his brown ski boots. That was what I begged off him first: "What do you need those for, Kaributas, you'll be sitting at the conveyor anyway!" He took them off then and there: "Take 'em!" In the evening I took him to meet Pedro and introduced them. We drank tea, then the quiet Pedro applied himself to hammering a sheet of copper—his talent couldn't restrain itself, and a ruble was useful to everyone there. The newcomer and I got into conversation. After so much time, I finally met someone who knew something about you, Tūla! I pretended I didn't really care and got ready to listen closely, but Kaributas had already told me all he knew: you were living strangely, avoiding people completely... yes, you were already there, in Bibelarus. Shutting yourself up in the garden apartment and not letting anyone in, not even your family. Actually, Kaributas hadn't seen you himself; he had spoken with your brother. Yes, he'd been to Bibelarus! An excellent, solid farmstead, a fence, gates, a dog! He told me the name of the little town, too, but of course he didn't know the address... oh, that insatiable need of mine to write to you!

But that was the one and only news I had of you.

Just before the evening count, I went to the musicians' room. The saxophonist Giedrius N., when I asked very nicely, sighed and agreed to play "The Criminal Tango." He smiled before putting the mouthpiece to his lips, but later he slowly got into it, took off as if he'd risen and flown off with the sentimental but dramatic melody— just what I needed today, just what fit the bill in that place: something to make the legs tremble and the disturbed soul cry. Let it be.

The evening count took a particularly long time that night— Štefankovich, on purpose, was in no kind of hurry; he kept ordering the count be done over, while we, some fifteen hundred unfortunates in our worn-out padded coats, froze in an enclosed fenced yard. I looked at the dimly twinkling stars, at the low shreds of clouds passing overhead at a breakneck speed, and thought: You've gone to bed already, Tūla, you've settled in your cot, you can't see either the stars or those scattered shreds through the basement windows... is there really only emptiness inside your little head? And: Maybe someone will yet forward my letters to you from the Second City; there would be so many of them, a whole bundle... maybe some day you'll up and write another short sentence to me: "Please write to me! Tūla."

Well, at last! They finally got the count, the clipboard with the final sum was given to the officer on duty, the prisoners scattered through the yard, the little flames of cigarettes flared up. Like every night. But you go ahead and sleep there, sleep and don't let anyone in. I'll be back, after all, I'll steal you out of there... I'll pay a huge ransom... forty camels piled with gold and jewels, will that be enough?

X

To the north of Dnepropetrovsk, the line of pyramidal poplars began to thin very slowly. No, there's still plenty of them, the poplars continue going along the roadside, along the yellowed horizon of the steppe, dividing a village from a village, but they thin out all the same, because after who knows how many days of travel you suddenly miss them—those boring, tall, identical pyramidal poplars that I know should be called aspens, but there's aspens in Lithuania, on estates and on Rasų Street—old aspens with rotten trunks, whose fluff the neighbors, sometimes even the omniscient radio, get into arguments over: some contend that only the aspens purify the city's dense air, others yell that those cotton fluffs that get absolutely everywhere cause terrible diseases of the lungs; well, let them be aspen in the north, and here, on the steppe, in Crimea and elsewhere, pyramidal poplars, in Slavic tongues it almost sounds like a prayer—*piramidalnyye topoli!*

The weather to the north of Dnepropetrovsk gets cooler only gradually, too. You could say that it doesn't even get cooler; it's just that all the edges slowly enclose themselves in a gray film, in a fog that drives you to despair, that will spurt no breeze, no thin rain. Though when all you're wearing is a plaid shirt, thin brown pants, and light shoes, when your empty belly growls, and heavy, warm corn stalks rush by the cab's window, rain is no friend of yours anyway. But who's a friend of yours now? Maybe no one.

There is truly nothing more hideous than cities of millions in warm countries. They aren't redeemed by the pyramidal poplars, nor by the parks, squares, or plazas given the most resounding names, with their hideous cement fountains and crumbling sculptures— no, this is no Athens! You'll find dirt and poverty everywhere, of course, even in the most prosperous countries, as much as you like in our dear greenish-gray homeland, too; it's just that in the South, the bleakness and disorder is even more terrible. Those cities of millions there should simply be closed: evacuate people to some village or *khutora*, or at least plant the entire country up with those sad-smelling poplars, not necessarily pyramidal ones. But then, where would the wheat, corn, and sunflowers rustle? The people here would shell them and shell them forever. No, it's difficult to even imagine something drearier than a city of a million; sickly from the heat, coated in dust, hungry, angry, rude to the traveler! Perhaps some like living there, but even the expanse of the Dnieper looked horrible to me. On its banks, on its lagoons and limans—I don't even know what to call them—these rusty poles held up even more rusty ghostly-looking cabins made of tin, and broiled in the sun. At first I thought people lived there too. No, the driver smiled wryly, no, those are shelters for cutters and motorboats, they keep boats there. So that's what they are! You couldn't see an end to those shelters—they looked like a neglected cemetery on the water, like a city of the dead, gloomy despite the blinding sun.

So you see, Tūla, I made it as far as the former Yekaterinoslav. A colossus on both sides of the Dnieper. A giant railroad station. A threatening football team. And buildings, buildings, buildings. The driver let me out next to those jetties, those cemeteries above the river. Without a word about payment; he could see for himself— what are you going to get from someone like that? Lord, I thought, heading down a small impoverished suburban lane, it's my third day on the road, and I've only gotten as far as this unending city in the searing heat! How much farther do I have to go? Not a cent in my pocket: only a reddish passport, returned to me when I was released from the preventorium, and a brown sports bag, also empty. Now I'll

have to interrogate every passerby about how to get to the Kiev highway. In that heat in Zaporizhia, I didn't ask around; I wandered off
in completely the wrong direction, and what a mistake! I ended up in
a metallurgy district, not far from the famous Zaporizhstal smelting
works. Horrors! True, there were roads there; buses inched along,
people read newspapers and drank beer first thing in the morning,
but I say it again—horrors! The Zaporozhian Cossacks, come to life
again, would take off without writing any letters to the Sultan. How
can they live there!? As far as you can see, flames rise and flicker,
smoke gushes, and sparks fly out of pipes, chimneys, and furnaces.
The roar is out of this world, too.

Yekaterinoslav doesn't have a hell like that, that's true. Over
there they have tramways, an entire host of them. Thin grass, rust,
and a sign: *Liniya vremenno ne rabotayet*—Line temporarily out of service! But despite that, an empty beer bottle lies next to the tracks; a
yard further on, a second. I see another neck sticking out of a garbage
bin. That's something already. I run around for an entire hour before
I get to the center of the chimera-city. So, where's that Kiev highway? My, the citizens there are really helpful; they take to explaining immediately. While a bald man explains his version, three others
seem to agree with him, but as soon as he finishes, all three start
explaining it completely differently and make a fool of the old man.
Then they argue, nearly grab each other by the lapels. I slowly walk
away; they've forgotten me already.

There it is, the Kiev highway, the road to the heart, the liver, the
kidneys of this country of steppes! Covered in asphalt, wide, divided
into six lanes, growling from a distance like an apocalyptic beast. The
highway is a workman, as they say in this country, as they do in ours.
Just that I'm so beaten down, for the time being I don't even stop
those cars. I get into some suburban rattle-trap bus; as far as possible from here, as quickly as you can! What a miserable city, Yekaterinoslav! Although I found five empty bottles there, successfully
exchanged them at a stall by the station, and bought myself a lemonade and a large soft bun, still warm. I exchanged the lemonade bottle

again and got three tokens, but they weren't enough: there were double rates everywhere. Some woman sighed and paid for me—did I really look so destitute? Now I'll get someone to stop! Some small car with a soft seat. It's still early afternoon; if all goes well, I'll zip through at least a couple hundred kilometers. If it goes well! Skidding a bit, a little Zhiguli the color of coffee with cream stopped next to me. The driver, a chocolate blonde, with not much hidden. A forty-year-old Amazon. Thanks, I say for the Marlboro, thanks, for a gulp of Narzan mineral water. But her attention abates immediately when she sees my peeling skin, eyes red from sleeplessness, and the shoes barely holding on my feet. She quiets down before she even gets going. All the better. I'll be calmly quiet in her luxurious shade.

Tūla! Should I tell you how I got to this land of pyramidal poplars? Well, very simply. After all, it made no difference to me where I went. When I got to Minsk, I was even happy. I hoped I would forget it all: you, and the dim sky above drunken Rasų Street, all that muck; I even hoped that the scourge that had gnawed at my nerves and guts would finally calm down and maybe I'd grab onto some outcrop of life, or climb into some crack. Not a chance! I forgot nothing, not a bit of it. Maybe I didn't even try very hard, since I could see a long way off it was no more than a naïve illusion. At least when you're sitting behind a barbed-wire fence you can console yourself, weave dreams, create intoxicating plans; when you leave there, they fade instantly— quietly, soundlessly, painlessly, like a punctured rubber ball; barely hissing, the air goes out, and it's all over. I'll be frank, Tūla, even though you don't need this. Listen! The constant orders coming from the loudspeakers, those chatterboxes hanging in the preventorium's smallest spaces—even in the toilets!—so and so, summoned here or there! To the section chief! To the operations office! To the medical section! Sometimes they would broadcast an excessively optimistic Vilnius radio program, too. Returning from the "pukery," curled up on my second level mattress, I would listen, whether I wanted to or not, to some program for the Pioneer Youth. You couldn't shut that thing up when you wanted; it was turned off only at bedtime, at the same moment all over the institution, after they'd read off the punishments and new work assignments. News reached me while I was at the clothes dryer; I had carried my mattress and work clothes down there. The register book for pediculosis—so you'll know, an infestation of lice!—was filled in diligently; the personnel had no desire to get overrun with them. The pale little creatures weren't very common, actually, but they weren't a rarity, either. I didn't really have to take my mattress down, but a good opportunity arose—this puny soul who lay next to me moved out. In the year he spent there he never did figure out where the showers were. So, waiting until they took the clothes off the hooks and threw back my hot, disinfected mattress, I heard through the loudspeaker: A large art show from our brotherly Belarus has been brought to Vilnius... aside from this, that and the other, you can see Marina Pechul's tapestries as well as... there the broadcast cut off, the speaker crackled, shrieked, and the "pukery's" doctor, in a smoked-out bass, started naming her clients, who were required, without delay, to... That hell was a bygone stage for me by then—I was counting my last days in the drunkard's boat. I just realized: if the bass had started barking an instant earlier, I would never have ended up in Feodosiya, nor in Dnepropetrovsk, soaking in a bloody swelter. When I heard about those tapestries of Marina Pechul, I even gave a start—that's the same Marina! Everything fit: the Belarusian show, tapestries, and Marina! We had corresponded a long time before, when I was serving in the air force: I'd come across her poetry in the Belarusian cultural newspaper *Literatura i mastactva*: there was a photograph, a couple of lines about the author, and a batch of poems. I wrote then to the personnel department—Marina had just graduated from the Institute and was working as an artist at a textile factory. Later she even unexpectedly visited me in the army. For half a day we wandered through the garrison's pine woods, but Lord knows nothing more. Especially since Lavinija had already arrived to visit me—she was waiting in a cottage in the village when

Petya Guskov ran up to me out of breath: someone's come to see you! I told Lavinija that I'd been suddenly ordered to the weather station. In a second it all came back: the military airport at Machulishi, tiny, wan Marina Pechul, the dreadful racket of the long-range bombers taking off, our weather station right next to the runway where the takeoffs and landings took place, and Marina's frail little hand, waving to me through the window of the electric train. We wrote each other for a long time still after that visit, "expanded each other's horizons," and then suddenly everything broke off; I was demobilized. I hadn't heard anything of Marina Pechul for fifteen years, and there now: that frail little hand wove and tied tapestries of a sort that they even brought them to Vilnius, announced it on the radio, and thanks to a happy—but unhappy, after all!—coincidence I heard about it.

That very evening I wrote Marina a letter and only then started puzzling over where I should send it. In the end I wrote to the address of the Artists' Union of that other republic; if she was that famous already, she should belong to it. And I was simply astonished— an answer came a couple of days later. And what an answer! Full of enthusiasm, exclamation points, interjections, pleasant double meanings! Marina was living alone, raising eight-year-old Maksim, lecturing, creating, writing... she was dying to see my dear face, which, you know, she had never forgotten. Now that's a new one! I wrote her everything then; not everything, of course, but I admitted where I was and what I was doing. This time, too, the letter from Minsk came without delay—now full of heartfelt sympathy, understanding, pity... how much I missed all that!

We wrote to each other so intensively that when I returned from the shop, I already knew I'd find a fat envelope from Marina on my bed again. The helpful Juozukas, who worked as a *shnyr*, that is, a cleaner, and wandered around the building all day, used to bring them for me. From the abundance of letters it became clear that Marina, like me, was very lonely, that I would suit her even being a prisoner in an institution of that sort, although of course, she hoped that... In practically every letter she would weave in some terrible incident from her surroundings: a drunk neighbor burned up in bed, another neighbor stabbed his dear wife's eyeball with a corkscrew, two sauced young men drowned, and where? In a little puddle! Marina knew how to write up all of it colorfully, without being boring, it was just that I'd heard my fill of similar stories on both sides of the fence—up to my ears! See, the day before yesterday, unable to stand the threats, a quite young man from Kupiškis strung himself up in the toilet. We had worked together. Another one, a runaway, they found on the banks of the Kaunas reservoir: feet on shore, head in the water...

After she found out that my "treatment" was coming to an end, that they would soon release me, Marina wrote straightforwardly: We'll see how it'll turn out, but as soon as you get out, come see me in Minsk! From there we'll all three—so with Maksim too—go to Abrikosovka, it's not far from Feodosiya, the former Caffa; her close relatives live there, they ran away to Crimea right after the war, now they've done quite well there. Marina, apparently, was an educated person: to her, Lithuania looked like the "cultured West," where people—sober and smiling!—walked on sidewalks, drank coffee, and didn't spit on the lawn. So as if she were justifying herself, she wrote to me that it wasn't for the good living that her aunt and uncle took over land the Tatars had lived on; the Fascists had burned their house down to the ground. With that opportunity she even mentioned Khatyn, because she surely had never even heard of Katyn. After the historical digression, she again shyly reminded me where a drunkard's path led, where it ended, and truly painfully described her latest visit to her home village near Volkovysk: her father and stepmother drink non-stop... the potatoes are rotting, the cabbage chewed up by worms, and the two of them as drunk as skunks first thing in the morning... eyes covered in fog, her father didn't even recognize her at first... Her half-brother, actually, had just returned from the same kind of preventorium where I'm still confined, but what of it; he'd already lost his job to the bottle, now he drinks every day like a

beast... he goes out, supposedly to fish, and drinks, drinks, drinks...
She didn't write directly: Don't drink! She wrote from afar: See!

Going out the iron gates, I got two hundred eighty-four rubles,
that's how much I'd garnered in almost two years. Since they paid
in fivers, the bundle of banknotes looked almost decent. Greenish,
worn, and nearly new currency symbols fell one upon the other; in
my thoughts I counted them together with the teller, and the devil
hiding in me counted too: a bottle, a bottle, yet another bottle...

But for now, no: I kept a hundred rubles, and the rest—for the
first time in my life!—I put into a savings account. And sober, pale,
with a box of water colors for Maksim, I boarded the trademark train
Chayka, "The Seagull," running between four capital cities.

I forgot to mention one rather important thing: Marina was a
cripple. How she gave birth to that huge tyke with a nearly square
head, I just can't imagine! She said herself: Cesarean section. I
remember with shame how disappointed I was the first time I saw
her—back then, in the army—and she'd come such a long way, from
Baranovichi. An angelic face, pretty hands, a full bosom, and... a
hunchback, a real hunchback, like a young dromedary. At the time
Marina was barely going on twenty-two. Pechul was sincere, cheerful, and open, like most Slavs of an artistic nature, although as much
as I tried to convince her that her ancestors spoke only Lithuanian,
doubtlessly with a Dzūkian accent, and it was only later... She just
smiled, and once she told her story too: no, she wasn't born a hunchback, it was father... Daddy came home one time furious, drunk,
and threw everyone off the stove, that's where they slept. Her spine
was bent, this hunchback grew. And today she brings gifts from the
city to this Daddy—shirts, cigarettes—and cries when she sees him
continuing to drink.

So there, Tūla, what do you say, now that you've heard this story?

Marina had already bought tickets to distant Feodosiya, actually, to Simferopol—other relatives of hers, a cousin and her husband
who were our age, were supposed to pick us up there.

I've already said that I got to the railroad station sober, bought a ticket to Minsk and the latest newspapers, but, twenty minutes before departure, I slipped: I bought a liter bottle of Hungarian vermouth at the canteen, overpaying by almost three rubles; see, I couldn't hold out. The same vermouth, Tūla, that we drank then in the "Yuppi Du" café, do you still remember? I'll bring a gift, I said to myself, stuffing the bottle into my bag, but just past Shumsk I tore off the tin cap, drank a gulp, and screwed it back on. After a smoke in the vestibule, I drank some more—I gave some to the guy sitting next to me, a middle-aged guy coated in dandruff. He glanced over so sadly that my heart melted: here, my man, pour this on your embers, drown them, I can see how unpleasant you find this life, this stinking train, and probably the home you're rattling off to with half a bag of grain...

When she saw me, Marina just sighed and fell upon my neck, the way they do in Russian films about the war. I hugged her slim waist with one arm, and with the other arm that hunchback—in fifteen years it had neither shrunk, nor grown. It was night already—she hadn't woken little Maksim. She fried up some eggs and even pulled out a half a bottle of wine, apparently left over from some party, maybe even New Year's. "But tomorrow!" She stood up and put her tiny palms forward seriously, "not a drop!" I quickly nodded, "*Da, da!*" But in the morning when I went to the store for bread—Marina and Maksim lived on the edge of the oversized village of Minsk, on a swampy plain not far from the airport—I grabbed a couple bottles of beer, too. One I drank down right there, in a filthy yard; the other three I brought home—beer is beer. My protectress—who else?—gave me a reproachful look, but didn't say anything. You see, Maksim, a homely and enormously friendly boy, at just the right moment started showing me his pictures and little sculptures made out of plasticine, what was she going to say then? Marina looked at me just as reproachfully on the train, somewhere past Kharkiv, when, overcome by the unbearable boredom of travel, I staggered through the hideously shaking couplings to the restaurant car and there, in one go, downed two glasses of dessert wine: a horrible sludge, even to an unfussy drinker. Barely breathing the reserved coach's stuffy air, we approached sunny Crimea surrounded by snoozing or snacking Soviet people. They splayed out or moved about half-naked, wearing no more than thin blue sweatpants—women as well as men. Marina had already stocked clothing like that for me and Maksim, of course. After finishing the chicken and hard-boiled eggs they'd packed, the future vacationers were now munching still-warm corn on the cob—they sold these out of baskets at the stations, or straight through the windows from the platform. The pyramidal poplars showed up along with the corn on the cob—looking through the train's windows, it was practically the only distinguishing feature testifying that we really were rolling to the South; it had been hot already leaving Minsk. A small peninsula awaited us all, in which, by some miraculous means, hundreds of thousands of people from all the nooks and crannies and great centers of the empire cram themselves. Space turned up as well for the isolated villas of emperors and aristocrats, protected by alert guards. In Simferopol, as soon as we got off the train, we were met by a huge sign with a promising slogan: *KRYM: ZDRAVNITSA STRANY*—Crimea: The Sanatorium of the Country! Marina's relatives with their beat-up Moskvitch were already waiting. We sped through the humid night to Abrikosovka, a dreary settlement next to Feodosiya. After a while, I stopped paying attention to those fruit and vegetable place names: *Grushevka*—Pearville, *Vinogradovka*—Grapeville, *Cibuliovka*—Onionville, *Vishniovka*—Cherryville; returning through expansive Ukraine, I got used to a different style: *Pyatichatki*—Fiveton, *Shistichatki*—Sixton, *Semichatki*—Seventon, *Vismichatki*—Eighton... In Abrikosovka, even though it was already nighttime, they had arranged a real welcome for us—all they knew about me was *khoroshiy paren iz Litvi*—a nice guy from Lithuania—that was enough. Marina's extensive family and some Muscovites—Yasha Leichman and his young girlfriend— waited for us around a loaded table. "Marysh!" shouted Yasha, sauced from the chacha brandy, "Hey, Marysh? We're all good people here, eh? This is no Yalta!" Marina didn't even try to restrain me: everyone was drinking there, everyone was singing; her aunt was the first to crash. I have no idea how I ended up in that aunt's yard; maybe the uncle dragged me there? But it was aunt Niura—or maybe it was Shura?—who woke me. She poked me in the neck with a cold bottle of cider and put her big, hardened farm worker's hand on my bare stomach: Get up! We sat together in the yard under a roof of grape vines; if you stretched out your hand, you could pick a ripened peach. Yes, my first impressions of the South were simply wonderful. It was just that Marina kept glancing at me in an immensely serious and searching way. And wanted me non-stop: I constantly felt her cheery look—inviting and questioning—when? What are you waiting for? I tried the best I could; as soon as little Maksim would run off with the kids or fall asleep, we'd immediately fall together in her aunt's room. Marina would get aroused just waiting; she'd put her little palm over her mouth to avoid screaming, and after a little while that searching look again—when? She wasn't, apparently, very picky; she just badly wanted to have a steady man, to fuss over him, to be jealous of him—when her aunt put her hand on my belly, Marina immediately pushed her aside and poured me some foaming cider herself: it was manufactured in Abrikosovka at a thriving collective. They grew a lot of tobacco, too—it was already drying, hung on special frames; I'd never seen such a mass of tobacco leaves.

I drank that cider, picked peaches, chewed mild garlic and spicy pepper pods, and in the mornings, at least in the beginning, we'd ride into Caffa, that is, Feodosiya, with Marina and Maksim, where those who longed for art gathered at dawn in a line at the Aivazovsky gallery—it didn't thin out even in the afternoon—priority was given to foreigners and the local notables. On the bus, always cramped, always overcrowded with people nearly panting, Marina would press up so tightly against me, get herself so aroused, that when we got out at the seaside she would be furious—if only the bushes here would be more like bushes! Or there'd at least be some little hollow! She calmly admitted: a fellow tapestry artist had fixed her up with Maksim: at dusk, he pushed her over in the thickets next to the railroad tracks, pulled up her sarafan, and a few months later that big-headed child first stirred in her belly. She liked to talk to me about similar things; she would get aroused remembering details and try to infect me with that arousal, although she was, without question, a decent mother, an unhappy woman, and, it seems to me, an exceptional artist. She wrote poems in Belarusian about the village, an old woman with cataracts, the hay in the fog... but, unabashed by her hunchback, she would immediately throw off her thin clothes as soon as we were left alone. Even when we trekked off to Azov with the family and Yasha and Marysh. When we set up the tent on the bare steppe—only Yasha and Marysh had a small two-man tent—she couldn't even wait for the children and her gentle cousin, the giant Mila, to fall asleep. She never asked if I loved her; she only asked if I liked her, if it was good for me with her. I asked her nothing. But when Marina quite calmly mentioned she had inquired about a job as a night guard for me in Minsk, of course, I said nothing, but inside I reared up: No, no way! I'll do no guarding in Minsk!

Once we went to Caffa by ourselves, stopped at a café, and looked over the antique vases at the ethnography museum; there was no line there. White wine was still cheap; she sipped a bit herself. And started thinking aloud: she could stand anything, if only I wouldn't drink! Oh yes, she said proudly, they offer good money for her tapestries, so there would be enough for us, but... She spoke sincerely, without any cunning, and only on the way home did I realize—so she thinks I'm such a loser, such a wreck, that I'd agree to whatever she offered and accept all of it as salvation, as a gift of destiny!

After a while we practically stopped traveling to Caffa; we didn't even go to nearby smoldering Staryi Krym, where Grinevičius or Grinevski, a Lithuanian noble, probably some Grinius—the dreamer Grin, offspring of revolutionaries, known and beloved throughout Russia—had died. Only once did we have a chance to get off to the mountains; there, drunk, with Mila's half-witted husband and tiny Yasha Leichman we pumped lead from a small-caliber rifle into empty cans and bottles and drank chacha in the wearisome heat.

Just then tanks started shooting in the valley; there was a military tank base there, too. Yasha mocked my poor aim; he himself fired away like a real sniper. He kept teasing me, how do I, you know, even manage to hit Marina's hole? Oh, Yasha!

Leichman, who was staying at Marina's aunt's, barely a street away in an identical little house that got whitewashed every spring, didn't leave his significantly younger Marysh for a moment; that's why he took her with him to this isolated village, so she wouldn't catch anyone's eye. God, who bestowed Marysh with a perfect body and bearing, got stingy only with her little face: it was somehow too small and freckled, the lips pale and thin; at least her eyes—with unfailing astonishment constantly looking not just at the clearly balding Jakova, but at me, too—were pretty. I kept meeting them more and more often, but I'd turn mine down; was that what I'd trekked here for, to enrage my benefactress? Why do you need that hunchback? Marysh asked wordlessly. But I felt Marina getting more attached to me; she kept snuggling up to me tighter, and I also felt that I couldn't manage to satisfy her irrepressible desire anymore: I nearly started to believe the superstition that cripples are particularly insatiable. Disappointed, more and more often she just sighs, pulls out her pastels, and draws my portrait, my torso; me sitting, lying down, peeling potatoes in the yard, lounging next to a giant bottle of cider, and all of those sketches, portraits, drawings were titled the same: "*On*"—"He" in Russian. Without any mockery. It was just that I felt neither pride nor the ordinary self-satisfaction a person who's been successfully drawn feels, seeing themselves handsomer, nobler, looking entirely tolerable.

Mila, the cousin, celebrated her birthday—this time Yasha crashed first. Even though he was a Jew, he was an insane drinker; apparently, he was one of the Moscow bohemians, he bragged that he even knew Vysotsky—he'd partied with him somewhere, that's the kind of acquaintance it was. Marina took Maksim home, and I didn't even feel it when Marysh's hand landed on my thigh and slid upward... or maybe my hand landed on her rosy thigh? I don't know anymore how we suddenly ended up in the brambles next to the pen, I just remember that aunt Niusha's sheep bleated the whole time right next to us. Just what I needed there—Marysh! Not for the soul, not for discussions about about the vanity of the world, not to watch the sun set—it gets dark fast in the South!—but for the body. God didn't short her on talent in the realms of love, either; Marysh did everything so naturally, it was as if she were sucking on a ripe peach or mouthing a wrinkled pepper pod. Even drunk, I felt that naturalness, I was thankful to her and didn't say a word when she slid away from me like a weasel and disappeared, and when she reappeared at the table didn't even glance in my direction. And how I looked for an opportunity! I felt that Marysh was looking for one, too, but no more opportunities ever did turn up. Maybe Mila whispered something to Yasha, maybe he started sensing something himself—oh, that Yasha! But he started giving me dirty looks, and it wasn't just that he wouldn't leave Marysh's side; he started holding her hand all the time, until even aunt Niuta made fun of him: lock her to you with a chain, why don't you, but make sure it's a gold one! That's the way it was, actually—Yasha pulled out Swiss chocolate and American cigarettes, bought expensive wines, bought and chopped up chickens—he was prepared to sacrifice everything for that waist, bust, long legs, and the burning heat between them.

I forgot you there, Tūla; there simply wasn't time to torment myself, irritate my imagination, and grieve my spirit. I'd fall asleep quickly, sleep like a log, and wake up covered in sticky sweat. With the blanket kicked off, I'd grope around, looking for the sour grape wine I'd put aside for the night. In the daytime I could no longer look at Marysh calmly, although I suspected that left alone with her for half an hour, we wouldn't have anything to talk about. There were still almost two weeks left to stew in Abrikosovka, but both Marina and Leichman had already started scrambling over tickets to the Great Land—that was what they called their dear home. Of course, before September it was always a trial to return from the *zdravnits*— the sanatoriums. Marina's uncle was pulled into the fray, but neither his medals nor awards helped; there were a lot of those there. Then, for some reason, Yasha called on Marina—listen, let's go together to Feodosiya—he's a Muscovite, she's an artist, maybe it would be easier? I think he was putting all his hopes on Marina's hunchback; surely they would sell them to someone like her! The two of them rushed off first thing in the morning, and a half hour later Marysh and I were already trembling with impatience, meeting next to the ponds on the peach plantation—they call them *vstavki*—insets. We were hidden only by occasional little peach trees, dry, coarse grass, and a tiresome fog—it was already muggy. After we jumped into the green water thick with silt we recovered a bit, and everything started all over again. We never did say a single word. I don't know how long this took; Marina found us half-naked, collapsed in some pathetic shade. I lifted my head. Marina turned around and left. Marysh didn't even see her. Yasha, it turned out, was a real strategist—he'd sent Marina home, saying he'd get those tickets himself somehow. And that was it. Too bad.

Marina didn't betray us; Yakov, soused, returned in the evening with the tickets, but I no longer needed a ticket—Marina and I had agreed—it would be better if I left on my own, hitchhiking. That night she laid down next to me anyway, sobbed a bit: *durak ty, durak*— fool, you fool! Listen, it's because of nymphets like that Marysh that men drink themselves to death! That's quite possible, isn't it, Aurelita Bonopartovna? It's just that the gods themselves want it that way, not just Cupid or Eros; all the rest of them, too.

Living on other's generosity, I slowly spent my hard-earned money as well. There wasn't a lot left, but not a little, either: sixteen rubles. I was so looking forward to my trip through Ukraine that I agreed to all of Marina's reasonings about good, evil, and decency. She packed me some sandwiches and pears: now go! No one was surprised I was leaving; I don't think anyone even noticed me go. Although all of Abrikosovka saw me heading through the apricot grove to the two-story village store, buying two bottles of wine, and, accompanied by the pyramidal poplars, heading down the dusty road to the highway—farewell! Marysh didn't even show up at the window; evidently, Leichman really had tied her to himself with a chain. When I got to the asphalt, I immediately hitched a ride in a Gaz jeep to Simferopol: no one even thought of getting money off me. Encouraged by this success, in Simferopol I immediately headed into a cool wine bar. It was afternoon already by the time I got back on the *trassa*—the road. Well, then it started; all those towns named Shack-, Strut- or Smelt-something. No, I wasn't the least bit sorry to leave either ancient Caffa or the peaches in Aunt Nata's orchard. I felt great for the first two days, until I left Zaporizhia with all its hellish flames and smoke and suddenly felt sober, hungry, irritable, and so half-dead that I couldn't even manage to stop a car. I would sit down on the side of the road with my bag, and that was it—stop, if you care to.

All of these confused impressions, maybe not even in that order, came up and stirred me now, sitting in the Zhiguli next to that passably young lady who stopped being interested in me as soon as she saw my shoes. When she found out I was from Lithuania—it's doubtful she believed me at all—she just tilted her head, shook her curls, and offered me another Marlboro. Thank you for that, too. So there she was, already getting ready to let me off—there were only a few kilometers left to "her" crossroads—when a truck with a trailer passed our Zhiguli. Both the truck body and the trailer were crammed with shiny black tires. I even jerked, and stuck my head out the open window: Lithuanian license plates! The trailer was marked LŠČ, the body, LI! Lord, my heart pounded, if only I could luck out and stop one like that! We zoomed around far ahead of those tires, getting out I thanked the Megaera, and now I was waiting for just that vehicle, that one alone! If only it would stop! If it stops, then it'll take me, get me home, my nights lying on the floor in stinking stations will be over, I won't be seeing the sullen *milítsiya* officers looking to find fault while inspecting my reddish passport, questioning why I was traveling alone, was I really traveling, and so on. The passport would nevertheless dispel their suspicions, since in it—I knew!—there's intentionally mixed marks and little numbers, things an ordinary mortal couldn't perceive, indicating I hadn't sinned against the government and that the passport is genuine. My sides already hurt from those wooden Ministry of Transport benches and floors covered in intricate designs; they weren't in the least bit softer than cement. All those stations would make excellent sets for a horror film. Spires from the outside: the Chernigov *vokzal* alone was worth a fortune. On the inside, the same Muromets, Shiskins, and Surikovs, not to mention the travelers themselves! The entire station was soaked in shellac and urine; the smell went right through the brick and cement, even granite and metal—the instantly recognizable smell of the imperial greatness—*ot Moskvy, do samych, do okrain*—from Moscow, to one end to the other—more like from the Pacific to captured Königsberg.

There he is, there he is! The tires, black from afar, were rocking and shaking. Now I'll stop it! Still from a good ways away, I started to wave, swing, squat, stand up; I nearly ended up in the middle of the wide road and shouted something senseless, too. He stopped! I rushed through the dust to the cab: *"Labą diena, labą!"* I made my greetings in Lithuanian; the middle-aged driver, as gray as the cab body, in reply growled *"Privet!"* A cap with a bill in front and a button behind, tightly pressed lips, squinting gray eyes. Steel, not a man! I immediately realized I wasn't going to get anywhere. Yes, he was going to Vilnius. I said right off: "I don't have a cent!" But I then pulled my savings book out of my bag: "Here! When we get there, we can go there first, I'll take out the money and pay you. As much as a hundred." He took the book in his strong hands, looked at the total entered—one hundred eighty. *"Ne gusto!"*—not a lot—he said then. And shook his head: *"Bez deneg ne povezu"*—I'm not taking you without money. I grabbed his sleeve: "Don't leave me!" Humiliating myself as best I could, I was even prepared to give him a kiss on that hardened hand, if only he would take me. But no; he shoved me off,—not hard actually, without anger—slammed the door and drove off, rocking from side to side. On that door I saw some Latin letters I hadn't seen in a long time: *Komunaras*, from the tool factory in Vilnius. Scream, if it makes you feel better. Not so much as a cigarette butt left. I picked up the one he threw out on the road, blew on it, and smoked it until the burning ash scorched my lip.

I dragged myself along the highway without even turning to look at the cars passing me; it was still light out. But one stopped on its own: a new truck, IFA, a German one. How beautifully the guy at the wheel spoke! He practically sang his Ukrainian; it was a pleasure to hear. He offered cigarettes, opened a bottle of warm beer for me, told a joke. I believed in the existence of a law of compensation. Next to us, huts covered in yellow straw, as bright as they could be, flew by, and it was only when the truck slowed down a bit that I determined they were for real and not stage sets for the movie *Taras Bulba* under the open skies. Shortly it became clear that the guy would take me about seventy kilometers, where he would turn off to some coal mine; there were signs for mines everywhere there. But don't be discouraged, he said, the city's not far now; you'll make it before dark. As he was talking, we unexpectedly slowed down—in front a backup of cars and people could be seen, and a *milítsiya* jeep somehow or another got around us. It's an accident, sighed the driver, but he was in a hurry and just looked for a way to squeeze through this traffic jam. He adroitly turned onto the steppe, but I still managed to see a bit of it. My innards froze; my heart stopped—on the other side of the highway I saw a gray cab turned upside down and black tires rolled away on the flat-as-a-pancake steppe. I imagined I saw them still rolling off in the distance... "Hey, what's the matter with you?" The Ukrainian shook me. "How come you've turned so white?" I just shook my head; I still couldn't manage to get a word out.

To this day I don't know, Tūla, if that man of steel was killed, or just injured. Or maybe he made it through without a scratch; after all, we didn't even stop. The Ukrainian was in a hurry to get to the mine. But even now, whenever I remember that highway to the north of Dnepropetrovsk, something always stirs inside: a hideous, slimy

fear, what else. Experts say that the instinct of self-preservation in the
instant before a catastrophe frequently saves the driver, so maybe that
guy survived too? But that's why, the experts say, the passenger sitting next to him almost always dies; that's the rule. And I had already
nearly set foot inside his cab; I had already seen myself zooming
alongside the flat steppe... the forested Belarusian expanses... On
the other hand, remembering those tires rolling across the plain—
were they really still rolling?—I feel easier. It's easier to wave your
hand at it all—a human being is just a pathetic bug! But it's one thing
to read about that in the writings of the wise and something else
entirely to experience it with your own hide. Which, once again, was
left in one piece, just more horrified than ever.

That night at the railroad station I had a long chat with a drifter
well past his youth. He called himself that, *brodyaga,* although to look
at, he seemed a typical inhabitant of a large station. From Petersburg.
I told him about those tires. I expected surprise at least, a pat on the
shoulder, a *povyazalo tebya starik*—you got lucky, old man—but he
just raised an eyebrow: Yes, yes, it happens, he muttered, and started
telling stories about a night next to Lake Baikal, the heat in Kushk,
the heartless Afghan border guards, and the cholera hotbeds next to
the border with India. What was I to that? I was ashamed, actually.
The drifter gave me some great advice—to hell with the *trassa,* go
ahead and get on the electric trains and travel that way. You've got a
passport, he said; well, they'll throw you off the train, big deal! When
you get off, wait for another, there's loads of them here! But no one
will throw you off, I tell you!

Towards morning he took off to the South and I in the other
direction. He poured me half a pocketful of roasted sunflower seeds,
nodded, and that was all I saw of him. He'd been in Lithuania too, by
the way, and not just anywhere—at the Šiluva Festival of the Virgin
Birth! A rare bird, or at least he seemed that way to me.

But I got caught anyway. In the town of Smela—not much
smaller in size than Dnepropetrovsk!—they held me in the *milítsiya*
station for nearly half a day and didn't give me anything to eat. You

see, they caught me without a ticket after all, and weren't too lazy to take me to the station; it wasn't far. No, they didn't beat me, didn't even yell at me, I just needed to wait for some chief who would decide what to do with me—let me go, or let me stew some more. That chief turned out to be a gentle guy; he came, greeted me, looked through my passport, nodded, and said: Go on! As I was walking through the door he remembered: You don't have any money, do you? I shook my head—no-o. Sighing, he gave me a tenner and confessed his secret: *Zhenka moya litovochka… byla*—my little wife is Lithuanian… was! I never did find out if his Lithuanian wife was good to him or not; did she leave him, or pass away. When I left, I headed back to the same *trassa*. This time I was in luck; I was taken in by an ensign with a green shirt and no epaulettes, he told me himself what he was; he was proud of his service. If I had needed to go to Moscow, he would have taken me right to Marysh—I had her address on a crumpled, stained piece of paper in my shirt pocket. But I didn't have to go there; I was happy just because I wouldn't have to get through another monster, Kiev, the biggest city in the Lithuanian Grand Duchy! I was the only passenger in his pickup; the entire back end was stuffed with the bounty of the South and he kept stopping to buy things from the women at the side of the road; here plums, there pears again. He told me to help myself, don't be shy, and I wasn't. The serviceman had never been to Lithuania, but he knew everything: he had seen *Nobody Wanted to Die* at least a couple of times. A first-class film, he said sincerely. I agreed, there was one like that, yes. We discussed the cinematic work from top to bottom: from the realistic staging and the excellent acting, we turned to history. The ensign kept comparing our forest brothers, first to the Basmachis, then to the Bandera rebels; he even mentioned Father Makhno. He happened to be a well-educated driver, you can't deny it. We crawled around Kiev at night; crawled, because for some three hours, at the pace of a turtle, we passed a giant caravan of military vehicles. I'd never seen such a mess of them before. Any other driver would have cursed and fumed over such a waste of time, but my ensign turned to me several times in pride: *Krasnaya armiya dvinuvshey! A vy tam?*—The Red Army's on the move! And you there? And like an experienced lecturer—maybe he was one?—he started a lesson on what would have been left of Lithuanian if not for the *Krasnaya*. That to this day we'd be wearing clogs, dressed in rags and burning oil lamps. I'd heard this more than once before, but the lecturer expanded my horizons: the Lithuanians, it turns out, would have died of hunger. The Latvians and Estonians maybe not; in his opinion, the Latvians would probably have survived, but every last Lithuanian would have died! I didn't contradict him: he was driving me through the endless night-time Kiev with its barely glimmering lazy summertime lights and the brilliantly-lit Mother Motherland on the hill, with laurel branches, a sword, a coat of arms, and what-not, seemed to agree with his lecture on the fate of nations. We snoozed in a hay rick next to an alder grove and at daybreak returned to the road. After about a hundred kilometers, the ensign started in again: How come those Lithuanians are always unhappy about something? Other people are people, we all suffer together, but we don't moan and groan, just the Lithuanians do. Tell me, what do they want? Freedom! I unguardedly sighed, and he got pissed. Barely stopping, he suddenly leaned over, opened the door, and shoved me so hard I fell out backwards. *Svoloch*—scum! My bag flew out after me. He could have shot me, I thought, rubbing my elbows and rubbing spit on my scraped knees. Or drive me off somewhere. It was a good thing dawn was breaking—turning cloudy, gray, more and more northern, but daylight.

Even now I sometimes see myself there, on the *trassa:* by now chilled, half-dead, and no smokes. Dump trucks, vans, logging trucks, tankers whiz by. And no one is intending to stop. Maybe it's too remote a spot? Hitchhikers, the ones who have something to pay for the ride, usually hang around at the city boundaries. But now, after so many years, that trip seems better and better to me, more symbolic, even though I know very well that it was perilous. Even those tires rolling on the steppe finally stop, wobble, and fall over without a sound; nothing so terrible, huh? After all, you forgave me,

Tūla, because it was only when they started rolling that I remembered you, shuddered, and, even though I was never fond of, and indeed, hated vows, I swore to myself: When I get back, I'll find you, see you if only from a distance, wave so you'll recognize me, and that's all! This vow seemed sacred to me then and I didn't forget it on my return to Vilnius: I found the city too, scraggly from the rain, foreign and rude as well, but all the same not like Yekaterinoslav or Zaporizhia with its chimneys. I cursed the entire world, but toads didn't fall from my mouth. You hadn't been in Vilnius for quite some time already, Tūla, and maybe, to me, you weren't anywhere anymore; neither you, nor a ray of sun between Užupis's low clouds. I glanced at my grizzled face in the mirrors of puddles and beer mugs, and I didn't know what to do next: to live, or not to live. But when you don't force yourself to do anything, when you go with the flow, quite a bit of time shows up to look around at the river banks. I floated into a tiny cove; just in time, because winter was coming and the rivers were getting ready to freeze over. A cove: a room with a cable radio speaker—this time without that screaming, that squawking!— outside of town, in a giant factory's worker vacation facility. My title: guard for the winter season. The contract will end in the spring; I'll have to quietly get lost. That's what was agreed. A quiet corner and eighty rubles a month. Through May. A few duties and complete independence. That's where I spent the winter, Tūla, still thinking about you. Ever less often... less and less often. Watching the bird feeder, I noticed one little titmouse, I named it Tūla. When it flew in, I chased the crows and those noisemaking jays from the feeder, but it was a silly lonely game. After all, I rarely went into town, even though it wasn't far—I just needed to transfer to the trolleybus at the traffic circle. I no longer wrote letters to anyone, not even to you. Instead I delved into books—I had the key to the facility's library. I even read Gorky's *The Life of Klim Samgin*. I paged through old journal collections, solved old crossword puzzles, and made strong black tea. I almost got unaccustomed to drink, but I knew: spring will gust a bit, the ice will melt on the rivers, and I'll have to float downstream again. And so on, without end—what could be more boring? When I awoke in the night, I'd frequently not fall asleep again—my eyes got as red from reading as they do from drinking. They'd check on me sometimes—the phone would chirp, but only deer would wander by the window—no one was interested in these buildings in the winter, neither the homeless nor the burglars. In the spring, I said to myself, in the spring I'll find her for sure, I'll dig her out from underground, whatever it may cost me. I had no idea, of course, that this would happen at some point; how could I? The melting drops from the slate roof played an accompaniment for these daydreams: real-ly, real-ly, real... I'd toast bread and make tea on the electric stove—real-ly... I managed not to even think about spring, but it was true to itself—it roared in like a dragon, tore up the pines and willows around the summer house overnight, and was even ready to flood the basement of the object of my guarding. But in any event, it didn't flood; workers arrived to cut up the fallen trees, and when some cheerful foul-mouthed women painters showed up shortly after, I clearly understood my nice little days were over, hello, muddled world, once more I hurry to your suffocating, tiresome embrace! With my eyes wide open too, but with such thick skin that you couldn't very well penetrate it, even with an awl. You could make shoes for a drifter out of skin like that, but I still had need for it myself, and later it turned out to not be so thick... not so thick at all.

XI

It's possible, probably, to come to terms with everything by degrees: with the sky falling on your head, with your own shadow getting more and more perverse; even with the fact that when you pinch yourself as hard as you can, you no longer feel pain. You need more severe sensations, a more brutal everyday, to find the strength to shake your head in horror: This is me? It's not a dream? That towards morning, bloody, beaten, your head ringing, you crack open a swollen eye in the Butterflies Cemetery—not a dream? No! That gray thing over there's the Vilnius Burial Palace, that's where you're crawling to, isn't it? Yes, yes, that's where, you mutter to yourself, where else? Still alive, and so still crawling... and not to die yet, to live a while yet. What for? The butterflies are already fluttering above your head; when you stop to rest and turn over on your back, they literally perch on your face—what do they feel perching there? Nothing. Absolutely nothing... June. It's June already! Where did you get to in the winter, where did you wander off to? Maybe they would want to ask. "Little gray bee, where did you get the honey?" Honey? Oh, okay, not honey... Crawl, crawl, you green shit! Over there, in a little meadow, not far from the building, military officers stand in parade uniforms the color of steel alloy. Of course: they're burying their dead. Let the dead bury their dead... *Wir sind ein okkupiertes Land!* ... what of it? Crawl, blathering nonsense, crawl, maybe you'll at least recover a bit... wash your face, the clots of dried blood, in a puddle, the water here's clean... you see—on the bottom, a green frog on a leaf ? It won't perch just anywhere… *Wir sind ein okkupiertes Land!* For words like that… do you know what you'd get for words like that? What? An eternal… an eternal bed in a madhouse! A life sentence… a death sentence. Nothing, nothing! Those officers aren't… let them stand there! *Vivere pericolosamente! Rodina slyshit, Rodina znayet*—the Motherland hears, the Motherland knows… There's thirty grenadiers with carbines over there. They're going to shoot, apparently, while burying one of their own. *Svoyak*—brother-in-arms—is what they call them. Their *svoyak*… Crawl, lick the dew with your parched lips! There's no dew anymore, the sun's been broiling since first thing in the morning… like on the steppe! Not the slightest cloud, like in Caffa! *Poshyol ty na okhotu*—go stick your thumb up your bum!—that's one steel alloy to another. And how the sun is cooking! *Sobre toda España so cielo despejado*—over all of Spain, the sky is clear! So we'll begin the assault of the Burial Palace… Ready, get set, go! After all, there, under the high vaults, next to the No. 3 funeral hall, your friend sits and tirelessly letters memorial banners. He writes in the three European languages—Lithuanian, Polish, Russian! "For Dear Uncle, Brutally Tortured in the Hospital! Rest in Peace." No, you can't do that anymore, there's a list of approved sayings, pick whichever your heart desires… but no torture, no abuse! Three of those calligraphers sit in a stinking little room and labor from morning to night without straightening up—they write with a smelly black paint that's mixed with some chemical so the thieves in the cemetery can't tear the banners off the wreaths, wash them, and sell them again. You know everything here, you're a *svojak* here… Go! *Sobre toda Espana…*

You don't, after all, remember anymore how you got to the Butterflies Cemetery, who kicked you and beat you like a green apple. Although actually, you do see, like through a fog… you wallowed through blooming sedge for a long time with someone, blathering about something, arguing… and that's all; you don't remember anything else anymore, and now here you are, crawling like some bug to the Burial Palace. You even try to stand up when you see your friend the calligrapher at the door, you wave to him, wave... Oh, he saw you! You're quiet as he leads you, holding on to you, down the asphalt, shoves you in some door (you manage still to see the steel uniforms shaking ashes into the wind and watching all of this), pushes you into the dark, and says: Wait, I'll be back in a second! To shiver in the dark, even though there's so much sun outside!—you shake like a leaf. He returns, returns with a half-quart of a cloudy liquid, opens your mouth just like that doctor with the tic in his cheek, and pours the burning stench down your maw. He knows, after all, what needs to be done. A stench? Come on, you don't smell anything anymore—neither that drink, nor your friend reeking of corpse paint, with whom you once—it seems so long ago!—spent the fall cooling your heels in the Second Section. Colleagues! But the stench slams into you; tears just as cloudy run from your eyes, a lump rises in your throat, bitter as befits such lumps, the roof of your mouth stings, but everything immediately recedes. You hiccup and try to hold onto the wall. So this is a coffin warehouse!? So, what of it, growls the calligrapher, isn't it all the same to you? You won't find a quieter little spot anywhere, believe me. You'll rest; here's the bottle, I don't even know why I care, well, I'm going, there's clients waiting, they'll be pissed—I've got to earn my bread, you know: two kids: Jean-Christophe and Francesca! What Czesca? you mutter, and he pats you on the only healthy jaw: Down, down, wait, I'll help you. Leaning over, he sets a coffin on the ground, lifts you like a piece of firewood, and lies you down on a pillow smelling of resin—you can smell now! And he throws over you... no, not a wreath, more like some gravedigger's coat. Rest in peace! *Sobre toda Espana...*

For a long time when you wake up you don't know where you are. It's quiet; it smells of resin; it's neither hot nor cold. You just badly want a smoke. You hear a man snoring not far away. Hey, you say loudly, who's got a smoke? Snoring and rattling. Yow—the lamps light up painfully—the calligrapher smiles widely, cleans the lenses of his glasses, aha, so there's where you've gotten to! Into a house of death! You get up out of a pine coffin, grab your colleague's warm hand—rise, Lazarus! Three men rest in two other coffins; they weren't here before, were they? Two of them, hugging each other, sleep in one; the third, his legs spread wide, his feet raised up and set on the floor, lies alone. "Gravediggers!" The calligrapher mutters scornfully. "They've been done in since first thing in the morning! They buried a colonel."

So it's early evening already! We're going down that same threateningly growling Olandų Street—past the triangulation tower on the summit of the hill, past the "Polish" Architecture Polytechnic—straight to the immortal Rytas, whose name means morning even though it's evening there now too. A damp drizzle; where did that clear sky above all of Spain get to?

We take a taxi; why not take a taxi, if the three-ruble pieces for memorial banners fall like big, lush green burdock leaves—for the flawless calligraphy, for the quick work. You cracked like an oak in the forest, my dear... so and so! Rest now in peace! S.P.—*Święte pamięć*— In holy memory—*Requiescat in Pace! Skoropostizhno skonchalsya nash komandir, no... No*—an unexpected death for our commander, but... But! The calligrapher is quiet; we zoom past bridges, viaducts, cloverleaves; now we're outside the city and we're still zooming, somewhere past Jeruzalė, past Cedronas?

You can come to terms with everything... that I am a small gray clod of dirt, that it will never get any better, that the shadow of your body falls longer and blacker all the time, though the day is even longer than the night. You thank—no, not fate—the calligrapher, for a corner in his wood shed, which he calls his workshop. It really does smell of paint, thinner, must, and carpenter's glue; there's chickens cackling down below and in the rafter pigeons coo, coo, or maybe broo, broo? You even resign yourself to the fact that despite twirling the ancient little VEF radio in that wood shed, you just can't find the Prague radio station anymore, the one that from time immemorial broadcast concert requests for the Italian and Turkish workers *in Germania Occidentale*, "Quando a primavera," "La Fisarmonica," and so forth. What day is it today? How many nights since... What time is it? Everything worries you again as soon as you feel a bit better, even in a wood shed. So what's to be done now? Well, nothing! Water the calligrapher's father-in-law's cucumbers and tomatoes, carry water from a shallow well to three metal barrels, avoid speaking Lithuanian too loudly, because... no, nothing, but you know, they... they don't like it very much, anything can happen here! They do give you clabbered milk, don't they? They do. And fried potatoes too, sometimes even homemade meat pies, so why irritate them? And... and Jean-Christophe and Francesca, I ask, how do they talk? Oh, the calligrapher frowns, what's it to you? Truly, to hold your tongue is to love God! So, no. Go on, eat, eat. Everyone knows invalids have quite the appetite! So I was sick? You were delirious, the artist says seriously, I thought it was all over for you, really. Now you'll have to look after yourself, fend for yourself, this will kill you, you know! In the evening he makes tea as black as tar for himself and me, we smoke in the meager garden, chew on half-ripened gooseberries, and he quietly dreams of opening his own exhibit... two exhibits, three... to stun, to shock that worthless city with his work. And then? I ask, quietly too. What then? Then nothing. Then you can soak your feet in the lake and fish, what's your problem? So that's how it is: three exhibits, a shocked city, and amen. Really, what is my problem? I don't dream of anything myself; I've already forgotten my vow to find Tūla too. But I didn't forget. It's only art that keeps me going still, the calligrapher says, perfectly seriously. I turn my eyes aside so I won't giggle at that seriousness and throw my cigarette butt into the bushes. The father-in-law's mutt sitting there just growls; he doesn't bark at me anymore. Jean-Christophe doesn't run to hide from me anymore, either, like he did at first—oh those bruises, those swollen eyes! And in a fragment of mirror I see for myself: the face has thinned, the wounds healed, the bruises yellowed, soon they'll disappear completely. Neither my back nor my rear hurt anymore, a person can live! What day is it today? Wednesday? Woden's day, says my hostess, seeming to smile, and gives me my last task in this house: to

wash and haul out the empty bottles in the wood shed! Either they
don't take them, or *czasu nie ma*—there's no time, the old lady says
as if justifying herself, listen, they've been gathering here some five
years maybe. The calligrapher just smiles, aha! I wash, shine, stack,
and sort bottles, pull out dried-up corks with a thin wire, while my
colleague smokes next to a stack of firewood and starts remembering old times. He tells me about how he drank earlier... how he tried
to kill himself, cut his veins... it wasn't just the entire house he had
jumping, but all of Jeruzalė! He tells it all in great detail—openly and
methodically. You know, he says, I had sworn not to drink at home,
so I made myself a hiding place in the wood pile—I pull out a couple
of sticks, put a bottle in, cover it again with a log, and start in like I'm
running to the outhouse—one swig after another! How much my
Manusia suffered! It used to be I'd come home... Listen, I interrupt
him, how am I going to haul out all these bottles, how will I carry
them? After all, there's... Oh, he says, that's not a problem!

And really, a silver hearse arrives, we pile the bags with the bottles onto the platform made for the coffin, climb in ourselves, and
drive through all of Vilnius to the Rytas deli, where else! So there
you have it: I'm slicked up, maybe even recovered, tanned, wearing a
green Indian shirt, canvas pants, with brand-new four-ruble sandals
and cracked sunglasses, a linen bag in my hand, bathed, and almost
cheerful. Goodbye to the Jeruzalė health resort, goodbye to Cedronas, hello, midsummer in the city!

Now then, says the calligrapher by the dogwood next to the
underground toilet at the Olandų Street traffic circle, you think
about it! He even gives me a short sermon, constantly reminding
me that here he's gone two years without! You get it? How could
I not! Go on your way, guardian angel, thanks for everything! He
rustles the red banknotes gotten for packing up the woodshed and
grandly presents me the larger part of it: Take it, you earned it! But!
But remember—I won't help you out again, you know!

I set off for the bridge. I'll go along the Neris, on foot. In the
yard of the fire station I hear an unseen firefighter learning to play

the accordion. *Ekh, yablochko, kuda ty katishsya? Kuda, kuda*—Hey little apple, where are you rolling? Where, where? I answer in my thoughts, *gde mozhno bez truda*—wherever the wind blows. I'm out walking, after all, arisen from my deathbed! "The plans of the Party are the plans of"—a drunk! For every drunk—A soft deathbed! Beds of that sort, of course, reek of pathology. Along the Neris, along the Neris... this footpath isn't fit for dogs, but at least there's no cars rushing by. It's a rare, nearly indescribable state—an elated sadness. Fragments of conversation drift by: let's take a kilo of sugar, a spoon of lemon juice... Here's the graffiti-covered bridge abutment—oh, it's much easier for them now, they have all kinds of sprayers and neon paints, not like me, the fool who once scrawled Tūla's name on the wall of the Bernardine with a giant paintbrush! It's too bad I don't have a fancy thing like a sprayer. I'd gladly spray some stirring word or even a phrase next to the Tatar swear words and names of rock stars. If only "Cacato = Shit!" Or: "*Stronzo cacato per forte!*" Without the translation: shit, squeezed out by force! In the old days, our forefathers went to great pains to carve their name, or someone else's, on the bark of a willow, and now, just push a button! There's progress everywhere, and the dear sun glares in your eyes so harshly, the not very white steamer, for forty summers now cruising against the current, hoots so sadly, it's so green and fresh about that even the bleak Slušků Palace and the penitentiary cells on the very edge of the bank don't ruin the mood of a holiday Wednesday. That steamer is still struggling... It's the *Tashkent*! Soon I'll eat some ice cream, drink some coffee, and smoke a cigarette, crumbling a crust of bread for the sparrows.

Why on earth did I say all that? Who do I think I'm fooling? Come on, it's all going to end with a splitting head, puffy cheeks, and trembling hands again! Drunkard's tales should, no doubt, be classified together with animal tales—they all start with a cheerful neighing, yapping, or meowing, and end with bleating, the ground splitting open, the most disgusting smell, the gnashing of teeth and the flames of hell. *Caput mortuum*, yes, a skull; the skull of a drunken beast. But animal tales are a favorite of children. Happy people live happily and tell tales about horrible things—why? It'd be better to tell miraculous ones, Arabian or Caucasian ones, they always end happily and cheerfully: the two of them crawled under the covers, snuffed the candle, and reached the limits of all their desires—there's a formula for you! But when they crawled under the covers didn't they drink wine? Arabs? Wine? Bah.

Piove a catinelle—rain pouring in buckets! Like in the Prague radio's song for Turkish workmen, heard so long ago. Has the time for "Yuppi Du" come to an end, too? Probably. I manage to run without getting wet to the Rotonda at the foot of Castle Hill. *Piove!* Cramming Italian phrases from a conversational dictionary while I was in the army, *ot nechrena delat*—with nothing else to do—didn't go entirely to waste, I still remember everything! The amount of sitting, prattling, and spewing of fire that has gone on under this "mushroom" structure! Ugh, it's almost dry. Better no one I know gets underfoot! I'm not used to them, not for some time now. Even if almost all of the people I know are from the same species of unfortunates, they're nevertheless more energetic, capable, tenacious, and forceful. And richer: with a scarf on darkly tanned neck—that fashion had returned briefly in the summer of 1985. No, glory to Allah, they're all strangers, at least for the time being. Even if, from the little faces, from the expressions, from the pants and the little skirts, the bags and the shoes, from the occasional word reaching me, I instantly sense they're drifters! Trash, vagabonds, *brodyagi*, post-hippies, minstrels of all sorts and social situations who aren't abashed about either their lice or their shitty undies—is it a protest against totalitarianism? Like the frisbees in the square next to Aleksandr Sergeyevich, braids tied with shoelaces, army boots in midsummer?

No, not everyone here's that way. What did you say? Oh, coffee and ice cream. Cake and a pack of Prima. That's all. Now, just take a seat. A wet newspaper on a metal chair. A slender girl with a white belly at the next table, alone… no, there's no need. Over there, in the corner. Almost in the dark. Well, like I said, not everyone here's like that. There! Remigijus Oskaras Birža—a bearded poet from the sociology and egghead circles—is here, too. You see, it's not just trash, not just *brodyagi*. *La piove*—the rain. *La Fisarmonica*—the accordion. All right. More coffee. And everyone else is *tutti-frutti*. Next to Oskaras Birža sits a familiar-looking little woman of Samogitian origin, from the world of culture and art. A touch of Bohemianism and memories of youth—coffee at the Rotonda! A *mise en scène* of the everyday theater, how can I put it better? I knew her once upon a time—as modest as a Mother Superior, nothing came off for me then... yes, sixteen years ago. High morals, like Cecilia Perelstein once upon a time. Or like Frau Fogel, the faculty laboratory assistant, grandly explaining to every freshman: phonetics is the science of the world of sounds! There's still one more person at that same table of prominents; a translator of all the Germanic languages, Bernardas Malonė. He sees me. He recognizes me, too. But he neither sees me, nor recognizes me, get it? How stout he's gotten! And quite bald already. And he was such a beanpole when he played Krivių Krivaitis, the pagan high priest, in the courtyard theater! A tall, thin beanpole. He knows everything, understands everything, even back then no one could get enough of Bernardas Malonė! The lecturers, the directors, the girls would hold him up as an example. The unlearned envied him; those who clung to him weren't unfamiliar with Kafka, Hugo von Hofmannsthal, and Maeterlinck. Bernardas Malonė wrote sonnets, plays, acted and directed, and he'd tell me back then already: My dream is to be in my own room, wrapped in a robe, translating Thomas Mann, smoking Tallins, and drinking real coffee. He's doing all of that now, I guess, but he doesn't look particularly happy. Even eggheads that are particularly moderate about their drinking go bald. Aha, how does it go? *Si possono occupare i posti liberi*—is there a free spot? I would ask on approaching them. But all the places there—even the free ones!—are taken, and my Italian vocabulary's too limited. But: *non piove piu*—it's stopped raining.

It stopped raining, and here ends my sober irony, all my malice

for the eggheads, even for Bernardas Malonė; after all, I could have
been like that, or at least close! I no longer envy the cheerful flighty
creatures, the post-*brodyagi*, the inhabitants of the art world, the
Samogitian Madonnas. Everything around me vanishes and melts
into the air, because over there on the wet gravel footpath, carrying her sandals in her hand and wading through the puddles, comes
Tūla! Good Lord, it's her, it's her! Tūla, whom I never did forget; she
was the only one I would think about, turning and driving the clock
of that distant March week backwards and forwards over and over
again—white hands on a black clock face, the kind parents buy for
their little ones; they turn the hands around themselves, faster and
faster, and constantly ask the child, turning into an egghead right
before their eyes: Well? What time is it now? Now? Now? *Che ora è
piccina*—what time is it, Tūla, my little one?

I stand up in my dark corner and sit down again, I've seen this
done in movies many times. In life and in the movies. Tūla! I recognize her from afar, a thousand days and nights unseen, irritated,
wet, in a different but still green skirt, a sleeveless sweater with a high
collar—who's been kissing you all over, Tūla? She doesn't see anything; she heads straight to my corner, sits down facing backwards,
and suddenly turns as if overcome with horror: You? Yooou?!!

It's me, me, melted like a block of ice, grinning from ear to ear,
as sober as rain, my cracked sunglasses set down next to the wet
newspaper, me, saved from death not just on the steppes of Yekaterinoslav, but in the Butterflies Cemetery, me, raised from an open coffin in the Burial Palace, me, me, me! You, she says, her lips still seeming swollen, they always made me shiver, shiver with desire... clean,
sad, dark-skinned, her feet already slipped into her sandals as if she's
hurrying somewhere, even though I haven't said a word yet. Listen, she says slowly, talking just like she did seven years ago... seven
years ago already? Yes, yes. You wait, she giggles shyly, I'll just... She
takes my hand, then the other, probably like she'd pick up the glasses
lying on the table and that newspaper, if it were dry—takes them
and blows on them, puts them down. I'll be back in a minute, okay?

She leaves her brown leather bag buttoned with a copper button and an umbrella with a broken spoke and runs off down the same path where the Samogitian Madonna, Oskaras Birža, and even Bernardas Malonė himself are hurrying—the city's underground "terminals" are down there.

So what do I do *now*? Tie her up, carry her off with me to the hills beyond the Vilnelė, and look, look at her? Tell her that all those years I didn't just remember her, didn't just drive that black toy clock face with white hands back and forth—*che ora è, piccina?*—but also... But also? Maybe she'll figure out for herself how I live? From my eyes the color of beer, the rainbow circles under them? Hardly. How can I tell her, is it worth it? Spew out some fairytale... do you know, Tūla? I've slept in a coffin, I've slept in a heating tunnel next to a drifter who died during the night, polluted myself with strangers' blood in street fights, looked straight at a good friend who had hung himself kneeling on the knot of a birch tree, drunk of course, and now I'm sitting and tapping on the damp Rotonda cement with new sandals—what can I say to you, Tūla?

"Now I'm free!" says Tūla when she gets back from the "terminals." Like the wind? She takes my hand, looks at it, and puts it back on the table. Hello, Capricorn. I won't say anything; she sees it all, knows it all. My elated sadness, how much longer will it last? From madhouses, hospitals, treatment centers, and foreign cities I wrote her dozens of letters and postcards. From Rasų and Vitebsko streets. From Simferopol, Caffa and Brest. From Kapčiamiestis and Sudvajai. What time is it, my child? She answered decently only once: I'd like to get that poem, the one "when buggies of blue will carry the sleepwalkers out of Tula" and "in the promised quarter, with white lilies between her breasts, all green as a plant, you sit naked on the window sill." That's all. The last letter: "please don't write me." All of her purism, salubrity, stubbornness, her sacred and naive renunciation, lay hidden in that one sentence. And in that collage, actually.

It's no longer raining, I say; a warm steam rises from the chestnuts and the grass around the Rotonda. The eggheads and drifters have fallen to the wayside, to return here in half an hour. Where did you come from, Tūla? What angel flew you here? Unspoken questions. That's what, incidentally, one of Malonė's poems to Doña Clara, or somebody, is titled. She announces herself: I'm only here for the day, briefly. So what do I say? What about, "in the promised quarter?" I ask. "With white lilies between her breasts?" Tūla laughs and blushes, "So you remember?" Then she gets so serious that even my once-injured knee twinges. I'm going nowhere, she says all of a sudden, nowhere... Be good, don't ask me anything. Not a thing. Are we going?

Fate shakes my hand and waves a blooming nettle. As if the wounded Socrates, flustered, flashes in the window. She remembers everything, and I thought! I don't ask about anything and I don't explain anything. To hold your tongue is to love God! *Vivere pericolosamente!* Every little step of ours is dangerous, isn't it? Who knows, what if I had given her a good shake then, if, rather than playing the clown, babbling on about nothing and cussing, I would have started ripping those crusted bandages off myself? No, no, what am I going on about!? I wouldn't even have had the time, for she took my hand again, clutched it, clutched it with both of her hands even, pressed her naked shoulder up against me, and I finally felt the nakedness I had thought about that other March. So why? Unless it's to sit down sometime on a mound in the woods, take your heavy head in your hands like a figure of the grieving Christ, and up and ask yourself: so why? And I had long since pounded it into my head anyway: that week was a gift of fate. What would it have turned into, if... but then, and I wouldn't have... no, this is impossible! But who will deny it? Happy people who separated in peace? Probably. Like the two of us this afternoon, searching for dry grass on the other side of the Vilnelė—to sit down, and to sit for a while! It rarely happens, after all, that formerly close people, with seven years gone by... And I was the disappointed one anyway, feeling nothing but doggish thankfulness for a meager petting, but I wasn't ashamed before her, sitting on a wet aspen stump and then sliding down the slippery path to the valley—I'm not going anywhere! Then: Of course, you've had a bunch of women? Without waiting for an answer: Oh, I would have been a ball and chain to you! But the laugh didn't come off, as hard as she tried. I hugged Tūla, she pressed up against me with her entire body, immediately pulled back and pointed to the cement bridge below: We'll go there in the evening? A wave of warmth flowed down to my toes. I took her short-haired little head in my palms and embraced it: My own, my own.

We marched through town, sometimes holding hands, sometimes letting go, as if we'd met for the first time, even though we both knew it was just for this evening. The evening and maybe the night. At least I thought so. What she was thinking I do not know. Fate shakes my hand! The vagabonds and *brodyagi* shake my hands, rock me by the shoulder, crush my bones, thrust tattooed fists under my nose, and others—their relatives and the blue coats—chase me out of the stairways. They threaten to call whom and where needed, promise to stuff me into a windowless cell, but I'm still alive, I'm walking with Tūla and I spit at your furnished apartments with a bidet and life-sized stuffed animals! From the highest roof in Vilnius! Shall we take the steamer, Tūla? I see the *Tashkent* is going! Let's take it! You promised, after all! What? That we'd take it. I promised, I promised you everything without even promising—in my letters I just turned and turned the white hands around the clock face—what time is it now, my child? Three-thirty! That's what I said, glancing at my tiny, yellowed and blackened watch, let's take it, let's take it! And maybe, Tūla? Maybe? Let's fix ourselves a feast? I tremble; if only she'll agree, if only she won't go behind the dogwood like she did then, when we came out of that Polish townhouse. Do you still? Ask me that, Tūla, ask me, I'll answer you. Why don't you ask? Self-defensive armor, silly jokes—let's have a feast? Kill the golden goose? Or maybe? Maybe we'll stop by a church first? It's on the way, isn't it? All right... There's your fingers, your finger bones on the wide, flat forehead of the devil on the door to St. Anne's. Do you know I wrote your name in meter-high letters... in green oil paint? On the

Bernardine? On the Bernardine! Hey... maybe you still remember Jurgis with the beard? So maybe let's go hopping through the pits of memory a bit? What else do you remember? Huh? Baldassarre Cossa? Jundziłł? Borowski? Hebert von Karajan? Oh, I don't know anything about conducting, but... But? But it always impressed me: the old man flew alone in his private plane to conduct concerts! That's something, isn't it? What, really? Yes, a conductor at the helm. Tūla, Tūla, keep your fingers on the devil's forehead for a bit still, rub his metal horns, both of them? Shall we go in?

Drat, but we won't make it back, you know? It's the last steamer. I know, Tūla, I feel, I hope, I believe—we won't make it back! We'll come back on foot, crawling home along the shoreline, along the footpaths of fishermen and dogs, we'll shake the dew off around the rye fields... around all of Vilnius! Listen, Tūla, let's buy some wine, I don't remember anymore when... all right? All right... I've got some money. No, take it anyway! Dutch treat? With. And cheese? Lots of cheese!

Why does your lip tremble, Tūla? What do I know... don't look. So how much of that wine should we take? Take as much as you want, I'm not your ball and chain! But then what are you to me? Red wine, Hungarian. Do you have Hungarian? You have it, you have it, I see. How much will fit in my linen bag? And cheese, half a round. A cup from the soda water machine? How are your folks? What folks? Well, those at the Rotonda. Oh... Well, okay, I'll take it myself, don't get upset. Hey, come closer, what will I tell you... Well? I, after all, you... I know where you were and what you did, I know all about it! Let's go. Here's the glass. We'll wash it later, those color-less bacteria die off fast by themselves! So you see, I know. But even I don't know everything about myself, Tūla... sometimes I hear these things about myself I never dreamed of! You know, we'll build a fire there? Let's go. Kiss me. Now? Now. And on the steamer. Getting on and getting off. And in the cabin... does it have one? Listen! People even have their picture taken on these occasions! After all, it's like we two... Like? No, nothing.

Unfortunately, there's not a single photographer in the square. It's always crawling with them, and here Tūla arrives—and not a one. Still a good half-hour before the steamer. A deserted city, not like that other fall of All Saint's Eve, but nevertheless. Some guy's smashing the soda water machine with his fists... finally! We were the ones who swiped the glass, and he's trying to stick his green hat under the little stream. Idiot! Empty bottles in the smashed telephone booths; now I don't need them. And Bernardas Malonė, the already fleshy sage, heading through the square with a jacket, a tie, and a leather briefcase, even in summer. Who is he, really? A poet, an actor, a Caesar, or simply an infiltrator? Bah, what's the difference? Hey! What, Tūla? I want some Tokay... if it's okay. It's all right, we'll still make it. You wait here...

The last *Tashkent*! Tūla, where are you? Quick, let's get on board! You've got matches? We'll have to walk quite a ways there! Let's go, let's go! Kiss me!

On the deck, then inside the saloon. Warm, quiet rain. Lean on me and take a nap, we'll puff along for a while yet. No... So this is a boat? I told you, it's the *Tashkent*! You see, you're dozing off already. I'm not sleeping! I'm just thinking... Better not say what you're thinking... It's like we were to take a boat like this every day to go visiting, or on a picnic, or to work. A linen bag full of goodies at our feet. Hey, Tūla? No, she really did doze off. A dragonfly, a moth, a butterfly. A warm, tawny, spotted dragonfly with a khaki skirt, a high-necked sleeveless... a neck that hasn't been kissed all over. An arm behind my back. It hasn't gotten pins and needles yet? No, no... There's so few travelers. No one's swimming. They're afraid, the water's polluted. Everything here's polluted, everything... And it's evening now, too. Drizzling. The deck is completely empty. Not empty. Look, it's Petryla sitting there! Tristan and Radames... already pickled! Yes, he does look like him, but to me it's not funny. Let's go into the other saloon, there's two of them here! Saloons? These are saloons? Then you're a salon-lion! Well... cabins, maybe. Wardrooms. The *Tashkent's chajhana*—its teahouse.

A white whirlpool behind the little steamboat's propeller. The
first bridge—see what's written there? On the underside? The second bridge... these aren't our bridges, Tūla. But still. Let's open a
bottle, how many are there, twelve? What, are you nuts? How many?
It'll be enough for us, really, after all, today's... What's today? Nothing. Do you drink there, in your villa? In my villa? Yes, every day!
I drink every day! You don't believe me? I lock myself in, barricade
myself in and drink... well, did you believe me? I told you not to ask
me anything. We live a strange life there now, we always did live a
strange life... maybe it's too proper, too old-fashioned... what do I
know. Drink some more, Tūla, I know everything too! I shut myself
up in my room... sometimes I really do drink wine... I keep drawing the same tree outside the window... the same crow... or another
crow in the ornithology atlas. So you shut yourself up and? And? And
nothing; they knock, deliver monologues, and I don't let them in...
three days, four, five, not more. When I see, no, when I feel there's no
strangers in the house, then I go out myself. What strangers? Well,
you know... They desperately want to marry me off! To the frog
prince, of course? Oh, if only it was a frog prince! They invite suitors for me; book them, order them out of a catalog, you should see
them! Bricks! A long way from you! Well-mannered bachelors with
college diplomas... brown, black, bald. An entire century older, of
course. Like wine. Some of them would come in response to a classified ad, my family did that too! A girl with an artistic nature from
a cultured Lithuanian family would like... What would she like? To
meet some old wheezer? No! She'd like entertainment! Wine! You!
She'd like to sail this panting pig-trough to Constantinople! Hey, I'm
probably drunk already? So there you have it. There's not so many of
them now; apparently they've told one another: don't set foot there,
they'll just laugh at you! At first it really was entertaining... all the
ceremony, all the lies! I'd even look forward to it, at least it was something different. *Cyrk na drucie!*—A circus on a wire. No, my dear,
wait. Later, if you want... Dear? Dear, dear, dear, dear, you're my all:
today, tomorrow, and never! Cigarette? Give me one. What smoke.

Whiter than the water behind the propeller. White water. White…
like? Snow? Nothing? Salt? Like cambric! What's that? A kind of fabric, smooth, white… So you knew Begbis? Uh-huh. Listen! Well.
You know what? In Russian cities… and Ukrainian ones, big cities
next to the big rivers, there's water taxis, they take you wherever you
want. You don't believe me? No, I didn't see it in a movie, I was there
myself… the other summer. Yekaterinoslav, for example. Put your
arm here. And those suitors of yours?… They had horses? Horses,
horses! Even borrowed ones, one guy even had a stolen Volkswagen!
What a laugh! But I got tired of it really quick… really. All of them
so serious, in dark suits, scented up… as boring as death. You think
death is boring? It's bleak… maybe only one came by that was a wanderer like you… but my parents drove him out right away. Like me?
No, not exactly—literally, they showed him the door, and the door
goes straight to the lake. A lagoon? A lagoon. Plop?

I remember even this silly talk, even her skinned knee—she just
barely skinned it on the gravel as we descended to the city from the
hill. I leaned over then and licked that sore, salty and hot. And felt
her lips on the back of my neck. I put my head on her lap—I felt her
stomach rising and falling, I felt her hands on the back of my head.
Her hands on the back of my head… The hollow in my stomach
started to ache. Aren't both cannibals and drifters sentimental? And
there was the wine, too.

The dock on the outskirts—a pontoon—has already gotten dark,
too. A few retirees—former interrogators, 16th Division politruks
and the bosses' chauffeurs—with straw hats, baskets, and grandchildren, shuffled off to their private villas. The pilot (who maybe was
the captain, too?) watched us blankly from the boat's glass booth.
A burned-out man with the face of a toughened drunk. An eagle.
He watched us kissing; he saw everything! He saw us drinking and
smoking; he saw Tūla lying on the bench and putting her little round
dragonfly head on my knees. A half-hour goes by. The boat's empty;
no one's sailing back to the city? It rains. It stops raining. It spits, driz-
zles. A quiet evening. An evening on the lake of the Four Cantons?

What else? An evening with a post-pseudo-hippie. Have we already gone on shore, or are we still sailing? Hey! Well, maybe?

"Hey!" shouts the "skipper," or whatever he is. "Don't be stupid, let's go back! *Tut bandy khodyat*—there's gangs around!" Well, true. Gangs. Again? *Nobody Wanted to Die?* Gangs, gangs. Chains and brass knuckles. A clever pilot, a true Charon ferryman. A black eye! He sees we still have plenty of wine, so... I carry my dragonfly-for-the-day into the boat; in her hand she still holds onto the bag with the wine for our night-to-be—and anyway, Tūla wanted to say it, too: Let's sail back to Constantinople! I set her and the wine on the deck, take a bottle to Charon: "You're welcome!" He acts disappointed—dry, red... but waves a thick wrist: "*Chare! Poplyli!*—Okay! Let's make sail!"

Wine is the friend of imagination and the companion of the dark. She chirrs quietly, her head on my shoulder, while I... I clearly see the matchmaking at the little country manor by the woods. The suitors attracted by the classified ad knock at the gates of Tūla's parents' yard... Somewhere on the border of Lithuania... between Petersburg and Warsaw? To where the swift Merkys carries its silver waters? There, or somewhere... The suitor smiles shyly; pleasant greetings from both sides. The bride—Tūla!—watches from a crack in the curtains as the polished car rolls in through the wide-open gates; this one's really not borrowed! Father shows where best to park it so the sun won't overheat it or the rain fall on it, depending on the time of day and the weather forecast... are you still looking, Tūla?

"Why are you smiling so strangely?" she murmurs. And lays her head on my shoulder again. A scene from the movie picture *One Summer of Happiness.* Or: *The Camp Followers?* There's a lot of those movies. Wine is the friend of the imagination...

Let's continue! There now; another suitor. This one with a shifty friend, and he's no fool himself—there's a Ford in the yard. Talks to the dog, unloads gifts from the car; what has he brought you, Tūla? Polite talk about the weather, the early potatoes, concerned questions about the trip, exaggerated praise for the beautiful

scenery, and dignified gratitude for the graciousness to drive over—
such a long way! An invitation to the table... you've gotten hungry
and thirsty! She'll be here any minute now! But, you don't show
up; you've already assessed the suitor from afar. You're sorry for
that seemingly decent man, you don't have the slightest intention
of insulting him. Behold: the suitor, warmed up by now, gives his
short biography as awkwardly as if he were at an entrance examina-
tion: interested in technology since childhood... if there was a screw
somewhere, I'd always have to unscrew it! Everyone tries to laugh,
and he continues more boldly: Well, I finished high school, served
in the army, in a technical field again. I wanted, you know, to study
acting, yes, yes! But I was half a grade short. The arts, you know, I'm
very, very... Then I entered... So you graduated? Father worries. I
graduated! The Agricultural Academy, and now—he makes a meaningful pause—now I'm studying economics part-time! Excuse me,
may I smoke? Please, go ahead! You know, our daughter is an artist...
maybe's she's not such a... Oh, I understand, I understand, that's
very good, very... What, excuse me, is her specialty? And where is
she? Aha! Why are you hiding, Tūla? You'll sit down with your eyes
lowered, drink some champagne, try not to snort when the suitor
describes his wealth and conspicuously smokes an American cigarette, you'll excuse yourself... leave and not return... you'll slip off
into your attic like a weasel. "So what is it you want, child?" Your
mother will ask sadly; your father will shake his gray head as the car,
angrily squealing, roars out of the yard. "What do you want, you little
fool?" the neighbor will ask too—she's been recruited to help out, so
she'll occasionally whisper: "That's enough silliness from you!"

Why do all of those men—so mature, so serious, dressed in
suits—those physician's assistants, mechanics, engineers—fail to
see that you're not at all interested in marrying them? Why are they
all two or even three times older than you? Why didn't they marry
when it was the time for it? They're all ex-athletes, amateur actors on
the local stage; they've all tasted life as bachelors—in the ad it clearly
said: "Divorcés and adventure-seekers needn't bother!"

Two fishermen, anchored, straining in the current, their fishing lines cast. We're moving so slowly, practically without a wake, that their skiff barely sways as the *Tashkent* chugs by. Listen, Tūla, what would we have done if we'd married? Who knows what... what everyone does. Climbed under the covers, snuffed out the light, and reached the limits of our desires. Or perhaps we would never have gotten out of bed, and told each other our dreams or imaginary stories? Or paged and paged through that tattered album of reproductions? Do you hear what I'm saying? You know, Tūla, once I knew this dashing married couple. At the time, they were still very young, much younger than we are now. Are you listening? So, now listen carefully, they both wanted to be writers, and not just any old ones! They both worked hard during the day in a canning factory and in the evenings studied too—she history, he journalism, so it was only late at night, after they'd gone to bed, that they found time for their creations, yes! They'd undress, hug each other, maybe even kiss, and start whispering the plots of their future creations in each other's ears! A girl lived on a farm, she whispers. A lonely, unhappy dreamer... continues the man in the shell of her ear, because, on the other side of the thin plywood wall, the landlords are partying. "Unexpectedly, a friend came to visit with her husband... That husband was an invalid!" she murmurs, "He loses his heart to the farm owner... She liked the guest, too... she tortured herself... But... but... that friend—her guest?—understands it all and secretly goes home, and those two?" "Killed themselves!" the man cries, "They turned on the gas and..." "No!" she shouts and sits up naked in bed, "The hell they killed themselves, you ass! They torment themselves, understand?! Their conscience gnaws and eats at them, and they start torturing one another, eh? Maybe we should leave it at that; I'll write it down tomorrow before our shift starts?" Not a bit; they don't leave it; they go on all night long—kill them again, revive them, tear them apart—the authors get so carried away they don't even notice the night go by, they don't realize they're shouting louder than their partying neighbors! They create a whole pile of these stories; you couldn't say they were ordinary—they're sensitive, touchy idealists, brimming with imagination and creative energy! But the editorial offices and publishers kept mockingly returning all their creations, and the two of them would fight like cats and dogs; you shouldn't laugh, Tūla. Well now, he continued as he was, a working man. And she? You know, she… much later of course, wrote an excellent novel about those sleepless nights of creativity. She was merciless—even to herself!—she laid it all out! The way her fellow author, you know, went nuts over the slightest little erotic scenes; how she would patiently explain to him that it wasn't possible to do without! How, in bed, she used to quote Freud to him and from a brochure translated from English—"*Tekhnika sovremennogo seksa*—Techniques of Contemporary Sex." How she had explained to him, as if he were a small child, what ejaculation, libido, perversion are. You understand, Tūla, she wrote a book about their real life and published it. And he… He killed her? No, not a bit! How could he kill her, a worm like that! She was probably physically stronger than that little husband of hers. He, of course, read that novel; he read it several times, getting more and more pissed off. After all, she had written about him, showed him larger than life, as they say, naked, shallow, perpetually drunk… he probably did get that way later! And he took his revenge; it wasn't for nothing he'd been famous for his imagination! He begged this powder, a white one, from his chemist friend… And poisoned her? Wait, let me finish the story! He wrote her a note, put on some rubber gloves, and sprinkled that powder into the envelope, sprinkled it on the letter, too—he wrote that he'd read the novel and wanted to see her. They'd been divorced a long time ago, after all! The novelist worked in a fur factory; she edited the copy on the tags. When she opened the envelope, some kind of powder fell out; the writer snorted, rubbed her dry palms, recognized the handwriting, and was in the mood to read it. Her fellow author wrote, you know, that it was very painful that she had… he'd have never believed… And the powder? Wait, wait! She'd barely finished reading and lit a cigarette, when she immediately noticed some kind of extremely unpleasant smell. She sniffed her nose a few times and answered a telephone call. A colleague in the doorway yelled: damn, what reeks so bad in here!? She hurried to the bathroom, scrubbed her hands thoroughly—with soap, her palms even sizzled!—and when she returned to the office, the stench was already unbearable—the windows thrown open in mid-winter didn't help at all! The telephone rang again—her former husband asked, had she gotten his letter already? Yes, she hissed, what did you put in there? It smells worse than a latrine! It'll pass, the villain promised, in just two weeks! Put up with it! She was opening her mouth to tell him he'd rot in jail, but he'd hung up already. The writer rushed home—she smelled so bad that no one could stand to be near her. In the middle of the night, she flew to that filthy communal apartment block next to the Belmontas woods, do you remember, we were there once? He was already waiting—alone. Everything turned out like it does in bad novels or fairy tales—she rushed over determined to poke his eyes out, to pin him to the wall with a dagger, but as soon as she walked into the modest room she broke out into such a wail that her former fellow author was sorry for her—he sprinkled some other powder—yellow—on her palms. There were horns, and now they're gone!

When we got off the boat, the "skipper" didn't so much as poke his nose out of his pilot house. We weren't his concern. Even if we were the only passengers on the *Tashkent*.

The city that evening—or maybe night?—was warm, even if it was overcast. Not a shadow of that other dreary one, when we had met and stopped at the "Yuppi Du" café, is that what it was called? Well, what of it, if it wasn't. I hugged you, my seven-year love—so, you pushed all the suitors away, not even thinking of marrying me! I didn't push anyone away, but I remained much closer to you, closer to the moon and the morning stars than to those women—exuding heat, urine, and cats. Much closer to you—to the gloom, to a perpetual irritant, to quiet hydrophobia; come on, didn't you, down there in Lithuania's prettiest spot, grasp anything at all? You felt nothing? Nothing, I would sit down in the basement a week at a time, even two... In the basement? Didn't you say in the attic? I said so? Oh, it got to be unsafe in the attic—when I'd fall asleep, they figured out how to open the latch, there was no lock there. I'd sit in the basement, I told you... You got confused about something. Probably. In the basement, in the basement, why not?

I turned around. The pilot house of our steamer barely protruded above the bank. Half-empty trolleybuses rolled by, not at all resembling either glass coffins or display windows with mannequins; they clattered their way down the rough-hewn stone street past the Vrublevskio Library, past the "philosophical egg," the sculpture whose creator, I remember, was prepared to philosophize here on moonlit nights. Past the Temperance Society, the Theater Association, and the half-empty Literati's Salon, where they wouldn't let us in—we're closed, that's it! Inside conceited, insolent-looking people we didn't know—neither you, nor I!—raised a din; you took me by the hand and led me the way wives lead drunken husbands away from a get-together, a restaurant, or a lost competition. You led me—the drunken calf—to Malūnų Street; we tromped through the empty Cathedral Square; only a few couples and some drowsy *milítsiya* sat on a bench next to the Interior Ministry. A warm, empty, soft summer city, as unfelt as a shirt. We drank soda water across from the circular flowerbed—"the parterre!" you giggled. White, barely hissing, lukewarm water—the automat growled like an old person's guts. I was the one who immediately swiped the glass, the same kind, faceted. The vein of a blue jeep flashed past my eyes—you didn't even glance at it, while I involuntarily shuddered... no, it clattered down the black clinker brick pavement—to hell!

We still had wine; we had cheese, cigarettes, rolls, and marmalade in tiny "silver" boxes. Now I gently tugged at your sleeve—we'll go down Šiltadaržio Lane, Tūla. It seemed to me that you nodded. A branchy old chestnut tree across from the yellowish czarist brick building, the still-warm red pavers, the high fence of the printing press, and the smell of dust flattened by the rain. Hey, look! What? A man. What's he doing there? There's a briefcase on the sidewalk, between his feet, do you see? I see. Listen, he's drawing! Drawing! Drunk, huh? It looks that way... He's standing next to the wall and drawing... painting, even. And quietly, quietly giggling... Of course he's drunk, what else? Would a sober person, and an old one, too... A gray ostrich; he doesn't see or hear anything! Wait, Tūla, it's... really! It's him! It's that dear old guy, the chemistry professor, it's him, it's him! What's gotten into him? We're standing just a few steps away, and he goes on working; he's pulled out a bottle of red paint, dips a paint brush into it, the tip of his tongue sticking out... now he's painting letters! Oh, a maestro! I always thought only teenagers did that, well, brainless jocks up to twenty-five, and here—a *professore!* Tūla, just don't snort, let the man finish! But the old man's heard us now; he quickly turns around, throws down the brush and bottle— real, live evidence!—grabs his briefcase and darts off like a little rabbit down dimly-lit Šiltadaržio Lane. Here's the bottle, here's the paint brush—I pick up the *corpus delicti.* Let's go, Tūla shoves me, let's go, next they'll think we... No, no, I need to see what the *professore* drew on that ancient wall. Tūla stretches out her thin neck, too. Oh my, oh my! *Bravissimo, professore!* On two not very uniform, nearly oval circles stands a cannon; the stubby, barely raised end of the "barrel" is raised—soon to shoot? Pretty? In red paint! And unfinished lettering: GORBY IS A DIC... We interrupted him!

Actually, the paint and the work tool are in my hands—maybe I should finish? There's not much left to do. Tūla rolls in laughter, but drags me down the Šiltadaržio clinker bricks past the Olizar Palace, past its honeycomb wall, still giggling pushes me around the corner into a little cross street of Pilies, and by now almost completely seriously says: listen, what if they were to catch him? What then? Amen, I say, the madhouse, guaranteed! And it won't be great for the family, either, that's a fact. At these words, out of the gateway above which gold letters in the marble announce that Adam Mickiewicz once lived here, the no-good-nik artist appears smiling; the man's smiling from ear to ear; well, of course, he's barely standing on his feet! Pleasantly, even ceremoniously, he asks for a cigarette, and when he gets it expresses another wish: would you be so kind as to accompany him for a little way? If you would be so good, young people! He lives in Užupis, past the bridge, tip-tap and he'll be home already, that's the only place he'll be safe! I know, I know—I start to say, but bite my tongue—why? You've tired of giggling by now and the *professore* wants to take us by the arms, but the yellow briefcase gets in the way—there's something rattling inside, it's obvious what! He reluctantly hands me his precious burden, clings between the two of us like an oversized child—it's not far from here at all! A short man wearing a hat even in summer, a completely extraordinary old guy, and we're leading him, leading him. Just think: an enemy of the system, Gorby's profaner, the defacer of Old Town! What a laugh. But after all, I think, holding his heavy body with both hands, you need to make careful arrangements for a job like that; think everything through while you're still sober and only then set out for town, get drunk in some bar so all the fear evaporates, and undertake the intended mission—and anyway, that drawing, whatever you say, it's a creation! Wait a minute, the animator artist asks when we reach the Vilnelė, let's go sit down, over there, on the bench by the oak, I'll treat you two, inside the briefcase there's… come on!

Back in the day, the Latin language teacher in the thick blue wool coat, cheap sandals, and a beret—the same one who showed us the Bernardine bridge—told us about this oak too. The oldest senior of the profaned Bernardine garden. Since the Latinist's telling it had aged a bit, another quarter of a century. Enclosed in a crude little fence, it loomed next to the covered bridge and rustled. "The old oak!" the *professore* shouts. He really feels much better and safer here than in Šiltadaržio Lane. A chemist, exhibitionist, and amateur art-ist in one person. And a bacchanalian, too, it turns out! "We'll drink under it, my young friends!" The *professore* sits in the middle, tries to hug us but can't manage it anymore; his little arms are too short, anyway. Then he presses his restless, talented hands between his knees, glances at us a bit insulted, and, rummaging in his briefcase,

pulls out an opened bottle and a little silver shot glass, pours some
for himself, and downs it with relish. Then he pours for Tūla, and
she downs it! Brandy apparently, not vodka. I'll drink some, too. The
professore has his mouth open to tell a story about how when he was
a young student—but he suddenly shuts it. All three of us, on cue,
turn our heads towards the depths of the park and see: along the
little pathway next to the Vilnelė comes a tall, sturdy woman, leaning lightly on a long bamboo cane, with a green canvas bag thrown
over her shoulder—a ghost? What ghost? Her eyes, it's true, are tired,
but she's almost sober; her glance is clear. She's upon us now; I see
a red cross sewed on her bag. She puts out a bony hand in greet-
ing, introduces herself military style: Lieutenant Lyubov Grazhdanskaya, Morality Police! No, not a ghost at any rate; just a madwoman,
apparently only slightly crazy. Morality policewoman Grazhdanskaya speaks Lithuanian fluently, with a noticeable Polish-Russian
accent. "Maryjan?" she taps the *professore* with the tip of her cane.
"You're Maryjan, the honorable professor, aren't you? I've been looking for you!" And just look! Instead of roughly chasing her off, the
professore merely nods his head, his little eyes darting about; putting
faith in her intercession, he clutches at Tūla, but now Grazhdanskaya
is poking the bamboo cane right at the knot of his tie and angrily
asking: Last name? After all, you, Maryjan, *sukin ty syn,*—you son
of a bitch—you've painted up all of Užupis—here she tosses out a
seriously amoral, truthful word!—Tell me your last name! "You go
you know where, you witch," Maryjan grumbles quietly. Scram!
"Then give me something to drink!" Citizen Grazhdanskaya crows
in an entirely different voice, "I can see you have some, Maryjan
Mikuilovich!" "Here," the *professore* says, and, with some difficulty,
gives her the finger. And has cause to regret it immediately: the moralist so cheerfully and so accurately smacks his hand with her light
but painful cane that Maryjan yelps and whimpers like a true Užupis
mutt, and starts sucking on his paw, "you fool, you fool!" In the
meantime, Tūla pours Lyubov some wine into our glass—pours it
full; Citizen Grazhdanskaya stands up straight, clicks her heels, with

a single motion empties the glass, returns it to Tūla, salutes, and...
raising her feet up and pounding them down, marches off towards
the Orthodox Church: tramp, tromp, tramp, tromp! Professor Mari-
jonas Mikulionis drinks, but in his anger chokes and coughs so hard
that we pound on his back until he waves his little hands: "Enough,
enough!" And suddenly he comes undone: "But I drew it anyway,
damn you! I drew it and I'll keep on drawing! Screw you! I know, I
know," he shouts, as if forestalling me, "the madhouse, guaranteed!
Shit! Scram, all of you, scram! Go on, shout, snitch on me to the
Russians, to the KGB—I was the one who drew it, it was me!"

I give him back the little bottle with the remains of the paint and
the brush; now his little eyes get so big that it seems they really will
jump out of their orbits and fall out on his lap. But no, it's nothing.
He calmly puts his work tools back into his briefcase, waves a hand
and toddles off over the covered bridge, although it's doubtful that's
the shortest way, very doubtful...

XII

Tūla, my love… how are you? Alive? Still in one piece? Alive, still in one piece…

Let's go? Where? You know yourself… And give me some more of our wine, today to me everything's possible, everything's allowed, never mind the idiots, perverts, and self-proclaimed morality police! Everything? Everything, everything!

So… let's go? Let's go. By this bridge? This one, this one… and not far…

So now that's everything.

A night of burdocks, a night of sleeping dragonflies, a night of homeless cats and unhappy madcaps! The dark fans of burdock above my face, above your face, Tūla, from time to time the blinding night stars flash and sparkle through the gaps and breaks in the leaves, or maybe it's just sparks flying from my eyes; they burn through your green skirt, all of the scanty clothing you were wearing today when you so unexpectedly wandered into the Rotunda… was that only today? Sob, Tūla; writhe, cry, lie to me, poison me, until that cement cloud from Bekešo Hill finally slinks over, until the coins raised by the whirlwind spill from the sky—thalers, ducats, and groats; until all the coffins open up and call us all to the Last Judgement—me, you… Lavinija with Romanas Būkas, all of your disappointed suitors… the lithographer with white eyelashes, the *professore* and even citizen Grazhdanskaya… all of Užupis will howl and thunder when we arise! And now with my body I'll shield you, as long as you still feel my thighs on yours, here, between the burdock, knot-grass, nettles, catmint, valerian, thistle, dill, goose-foot, as long as you still whisper to me—press me, press me deeper into the earth—press as hard as you can! And I feel myself plunging ever deeper; some kind of spring breaks through under you, Tūla, what's that gushing in the dark—blood, silt, rusty spring water? Let's roll away, but let's not let go, don't let go under any circumstances—hang on to me with your nails, feet, and arms; after all, we've broken through to an underground spring with our bodies, when we get up from here a fountain will probably gush up in a jet to the very skies—we'll see how yet! Tūla, my true one, my patient Tūla! Why are you moaning? You're crying, Tūla? Your face is smudged, my dear, muddy now with fingers that have plunged into this gruel, the fingers you try to brace yourself with, to push yourself away, you're straddling me now, your fingers sinking deeper and deeper, you sob like a child being beaten, even though no one wants to hurt you, don't you be afraid, Tūla, dance, it's truly our last dance... pour wine on my face, wash it off, then I'll wash off yours... Don't shout, don't yell so loud, don't shriek, I beg you, we don't need evil spirits to hear us, we don't need good ones to hear us either; breathe into my green as a burdock ear, poke me with your pointy breasts, fall on me exhausted, all your strength gone, wait! Wait a bit yet, don't fall!

Burdock on your thighs, on your quivery breasts, on your belly overgrown with shadows—like moss, like grass roots; why did we pick this spot in particular, what knocked us over here, laid us down on this blocked spring, no, not blocked, just overgrown with grass? Now I'm afraid to slide over, it really will spurt out, gush to the skies, outgrow the hills and towers, tell me, Tūla, why are we making love here? Now you press me into the ground, Tūla, press me... Why are you pressing my mouth with a palm splattered in thin mud, I'll suffocate! It just seems to you that I'm talking, that I'm screaming, I'm quiet, quiet, quiet! Why do you just brush against my face with that same slippery palm and a black elbow and whisper—it's cleansing... What cleansing, cripes, now I'm drowning, I'm sinking! All right, if

it's cleansing, then why are you crying, Tūla? Are you really crying?
Go ahead, cry, cry, trample on me, Tūla, trample me into this dirt,
this mud, press me with your brown bottom, that's all I'm worth,
press me with your hands, mouth, nipples, all of your beloved flat
body, here, on this slope, in this sludge pit a bit below the Užupis garbage dump, below broken double bed frames, rusty baby carriages,
mattresses, tires that keep on rolling here too—they lie at the bottom,
next to cradles in which neither our nor anyone's children will cry,
below the potato peels, cat shit, and rotting stalks... tell me, Tūla,
confirm it for me... is this mud where we're wallowing, tortured by a
burning passion as if we were trying to make up for seven long years,
is it really cleaner than our entire lives, than the lives of the shadows
watching us, than our deaths to come and everything that will happen afterwards? Repeat it to me, comfort me and beat me, Tūla, turn
your face to the dark sky so at least your nostrils won't fill with mud,
be careful of your nostrils, Tūla, at least while we're making love,
while the giant burdock leaves rustle above our heads: their under-
sides are silver, pale, coarse... lie down on me, rest for a minute...
who would have thought that underneath this tangle of grass such
a hideous mire billows and a spring bursts... you're lying down? Lie
down, rest, Tūla, until they come to take us away—it doesn't matter
where—to heaven or to hell... or until Užupis's veterans and decrepit
aristocrats in silk robes and fringed slippers hurry over; until out of
the basements and attics, rubbing their eyes, people not of art, of love
or not of love, crawl out; until the first satiated crows fly in to peck out
our eyes; but it's not their time yet, Tūla! Only then does love attain
its purpose, when it ends with death, said the executioner, and cut off
both their heads, where's that from? I don't know, Tūla... Love me
when you're dreaming too, quietly chirring on my limp body, dream
while loving me, rest, Tūla. Rest some more, until the cloud on
Bekešo Hill rushes over, killing everything in its path; we'll undoubtedly finish saying everything to one another, so few words remain.
We'll sit whimpering, splattering mud with stalks of grass and roots
and flowing blood on the barbed wire, the sharp mattress springs

emerging from the ground; who will wash and bandage us then, Tūla? Who will drown us and pull us out—no longer needed by anyone anymore—not even each other!—naked, squeaking like the rats mating over by the sheds, oh... what do we have left anymore? Only to love, to whimper, to cuddle, to moan, to spit black blood through clenched teeth, love's blood, the blood of a mad dog, the juice of the moon, to rub burdock liquid on our already marked foreheads... you rub my forehead too, rub it—it's so refreshing, even if it's revoltingly unappetizing, that juice of burdock and goose-foot... hey, Tūla, do you still hear me, through one little ear at least? Do you realize you're lying on me, your legs astraddle, that in the green moonlight only your little bottom shines dimly? Do you see me, splattered with dirt, memories, spittle, and tears, do you feel my rod arisen anew in your groin, are you riding with me to hell via a damned and beaten path, to hell, whose red glow over there is already shining beyond those hills, from the direction of the Butterflies Cemetery, from the Polocko road, Filaretų Street and Belmontas—why are you quiet!? Why don't you say anything to me, why are you spitting blood too? Why did you lock me up by the legs and arms so I can't even budge? Where do you get the strength, my puny one? Who told you these herbs are poisonous? Nonsense! They merely bring on an even greater desire to make love, they drive you out of your mind, actually—chew it, suck its juices, pull them out by the roots, yank at my hair, you crazy woman, you Medusa, you traitor, strangle me to death because there is no longer any other way out, don't tell me you don't hear me, my smudged, beloved, inebriated Tūla, or maybe I've gone deaf and blind myself? What did you yell at me? I don't hear anything anymore! Whaaat? Don't scream! Or else scream, howl, fall over on me again, grab onto the rocks so you won't lose your balance, let's lock ourselves together again like beasts, splattered with dirt and blood, beasts grinding their teeth, that's what's been made of us, that's what the world has nurtured—raw meat and the luminescence of your ribs, which I can see even through a layer of dirt—hit me as hard as you can, Tūla, my love, I beg you... so that then I could smack you too, nibble at your sallow weasel-like breast; stab me with the rusty kitchen knife groped in the grass because I never managed, back then, to love you so that your howl would echo above these slopes and hills, so the echo would resound in everyone's ears, so everyone would understand that you are mine alone and no one would dare to stand in our way anymore, stab me, that I didn't manage to do it, that I didn't resolve to steal you, tie you up and take you away with me to my wilderness, to turn you into a slave, into a drifter just like me, because I didn't, in the end, pay forty sheep and camels for you, as is accepted in your conceited Second City... kill me because I'm drunk, because there's only wine flowing and oozing through my open pores, not even blood anymore, strike me and put me down! There's neither life nor death for me without you, anyway... I'll never tell you anything anymore... well? At least hit me if you don't dare kill me, knock out my front teeth, they're all that's left—as long as I live, I'll suck burdock juice with my gums and love you... Tūla!

Burdock, that's *varnalėšos*, "crow feed" in Lithuanian; huge, green, worthless banknotes, money for the eye-feeding crows' patience. Listen, Tūla, can one night like this really take the place of seven years—entire years of famine, never mind that... Let me scold you to my heart's content, you scold me too, if you've got the urge; scold me and whip me with a lash of roots... then I'll dress you and throw you into the creek... you'll float along like the mad Ophelia, singing... What will you sing to me? "Yuppi Du?" Or "Una paloma blanca"? I'll pull you out, I'll scrub you with all your little clothes, I'll wash your silly little head and you yourself—green from the burdock, red from love, sallow from the morning, and black from despair... I'll scour your little pink hollow, the shells of your ears, your neck splattered in mud, your breasts trembling like waves, your belly, and once again—your little pink hollow... I'll scrub you and lay you out on the covered bridge, covered in green burdock leaves— as green as an emerald, as a broken beer bottle...

I'll do no such thing! Thrive! I'll accompany you down the path next to the Vilnelė up to your cloister, to Petryla's former windows, to the remains of Sigismund Augustus's water pipes, I'll accompany you, so that neither the perverted *professore* Maryjan, nor the morality policewoman Lyubov Grazhdanskaya, nor your rejected suitors will frighten you... did you really reject them, Tūla?

Well? Let's lie here for a while yet, in this mud, in this plopping and gurgling puddle, with the stars fading, the fountain gushing... let the poets darting by on the other bank, putting the squeeze on their credulous readers over the damp benches, laugh, let them! Tūla! Why don't you say anything? Absolutely nothing? You won't say anything anymore? Open your mouth—I'll splash you some wine, wake up, sit up, I'll take you in my arms and carry you to the water... sit, perch on my palms, exhausted dragonfly, shine so my eyes hurt, and fly away humming quietly... The two of us are back here again, on the bank across from the Bernardine, across from the long cloister next to the house with the apse, across from crumbling houses that will maybe rise from the dead again, maybe... Kneel, sit down... I'll drag you by the legs into the cool water, the muddy, blackened water, I'll lay you down on a flat rock... lie down, lie down for a while... the flowing muddy, burbling water will get even blacker from the dirt, the dirt from our bodies floating downstream, always downstream, there, from where nothing ever returns. Open at least one eye under this burdock sky, are you waking now, Tūla?

I told you, sit yourself down on the rock, hold on to me! I told you, after all, I told you this is the way it was and will be until... let me talk! There, I'll float you like a log to the creek's mouth, to the first crow of the morning, seeking its feed in the burdock—a still-shimmering summer crow, the kind you used to draw outside your window—to a solitary crow, as solitary as we two, as solitary as Bekešo Hill and that cloister... Give me both your hands, Tūla, I'll wash them, just don't remind me of anything anymore, never ever... I'll wash your feet, too. You'll be as white as the Orthodox Church... and don't remind me of the coming winter when, perched on a branch, I'll look through your window. Will you draw me then, Tūla? I promise to perch there very quietly and for a long time... as long as you need.

XIII

I never saw Tūla again—neither alive, nor dead. For a long time I didn't even sense she was gone, and later I didn't know where her grave was.

I remember once spending a long time watching some still-young people, probably students, digging out the remains of that water pipe not far from Tūla's former house, Petryla's house, Aunt Lydija's cloister, not far from those stairs my father climbed just after returning from serving as a laborer for the Reich. The rumors that Grand Dukes were buried there had just faded (later it was plague victims, later still, monks from the Bernardine monastery); the ranks of the curious gathering around the pit immediately thinned out. Who was interested now in some kind of dug-up stones, hollowed-out tree trunks, and crumbling bricks? No one, almost no one. People are interested in bones, skulls, coffins—that at least stimulates the imagination, not necessarily a morbid one!—jewelry, money, treasures... or at least fragments of some kind. But there weren't even basements there; just the remains of walls, huge carrot-colored bricks. Carrots pulled out of the basement: pale yellowish, darkened things, rotten... Carrots and a pit of water, that's all. A little blaze of piled-up scraps of lumber burned next to Tūla's house; the diggers would climb out to get warm, perhaps toss off a little drink and puff a smoke. From time to time they glanced at me; I was standing leaning on the board fence. But they didn't say anything to me. I didn't want to be spoken to. I just wanted to watch them scrape the bricks, scooping and sifting the debris, the entire so-called cultural layer, through a fine sieve—straw, dust, particles of former objects and bodies. Oh! A guy with glasses at the very bottom of the pit hollowly cried out once—in his palm lay a large greenish coin. The others stirred, bustled, began digging and sifting more eagerly, but soon cooled. In any event, it seemed to me that they were unearthing and defiling a large grave— waking the dead, their voices, not allowing someone to sleep and rest—by any chance were you there too, Tūla? Without question I understood they were doing good and necessary work; even if they didn't find anything, it would be worth only respect and thanks. But they had found things already: stones, lumber, the remains of the water pipe. A long-since buried existence crawled out from under the earth: I seemed to once more hear laughter, quarrels, laments, the crash of breaking dishes; at any second, submerged gases will erupt, spaces buried for the ages will open up, and blood, wine, water will gush out... Isn't there too much of everything there, between those two bridges? Turning away from the pit, I sipped some wine, strong, fortified, from a flask. By then no one was living in your house anymore, Tūla, and Petryla rested in some suburban cemetery. Taking another gulp, I turned through the "minefield" towards the blue mailbox anyway, through piles of trash and smoky brick fragments, tripping on rusty wire and lumber bristling with nails—how much even poor people accumulate!

How many years had already gone by since the "night of the burdocks"? I don't know—maybe three, or maybe five. Does it matter? I stepped through the door; a starving cat darted by. It reeked of urine, damp plaster, and scorched rags. In the kitchen of the former enzyme worker, I lifted that same giant enameled pot from the floor, the same one with the two horse's heads. They were still perfectly visible, almost like they were back then. It was the one Tūla had mixed her paints in, to Petryla's enormous, but feigned, frustration. I forgot to take it back then. I'll take it now, just clean up the dirt a bit, I won't even scour it, let it be. I'll throw small copper coins of all the nations and empires into it, and after accumulating several kilos of copper, well, we'll see what I'll do then; but now I have to go—now it's gotten completely dark. There I go with a two-liter enameled pot, rattling several kopeks I'd thrown in myself; finally I throw it into my canvas bag—a different bag, a different one. Then I seat myself in a mustard-colored bus. Several stops later, I get out; after all, they're surely following me again, or if they're not... Who's following me, who? Of course, those shadows, those drinkers of wine and water from the pit, plump, squinting women, the guards—they won't succeed! No one will succeed in anything, now that...

Tūla burned up in a bath house on the bank of a forest stream. I found out after six months had slipped by since the accident or murder, and a year after the last time I had visited the house with an apse. Only a few copper coins gleamed on the bottom of the pot, and Tūla was no more; she had burned up. And here I had already decided to melt the gathered copper and give it to some copper engraver to engrave her portrait—and there you go! Burned up. Gone.

But the plumber I visited—I never did manage to figure out his exact relation to Tūla, it was so distant and slight—well, that plumber knew *everything!* He confirmed it: Well, yeah, she burned up, but there's nothing that's still unclear about it! He nodded once more, and in a business-like manner, as if he was changing a bathtub faucet, added: But the funeral now! The funeral, apparently, was strange too. It wasn't just that it was extremely modest—see, there wasn't much to bury: a handful of ashes and a little heap of bones. You know, said this cheerful and seemingly decent guy, she wasn't alone in that bath house! I think: Of course. Everyone apparently escaped, while she blazed like a piece of pine kindling. "So who else was there?" I asked, but the plumber unexpectedly got irritated: I don't know! Like I said, her dentist identified her from the fillings... well, it's a clean death, isn't it? And you shouldn't meddle either, don't delve into it, it'll be better if you don't. A clean death... really! No autopsy behind windows painted exactly halfway... no rotting in the ground, a perfect pagan death! So where did they bury her? You know, he put two freckled fists on the table, if you're really all that terribly worried about it, why don't you go there, find Jutoka

Japaka... What, who's she? Well, her friend; a neighbor, if she tells you anything, then she'll tell you. Don't ask me anything more about it. I've already...

The plumber and I sat in his "sophisticated, comfortable" furnished (not much said—furnished!) apartment in a decent quarter of the Second City and drank beer, snacking on cheese. A lot of good beer, a mountain of excellent cheese. The toilet glittered, the kidneys functioned too—just the thing for drinking beer! No dripping, no gurgling. Like in Philadelphia. I only asked him to turn off the tape player: I can't stand yowlers, and the plumber, of course, didn't have a recording of "Yuppi Du." Physically, I felt great. At least beer, in any event, is an intoxicant. He handed me a lighter:

"Don't get upset. It's a complicated story. They could have raised a scandal if they'd wanted. They saw her with some visitors, tourists maybe, but winos for sure... you know how it is when five men and one woman end up in the woods. So! But no one raised a scandal. They buried her quietly and peacefully."

We were still drinking beer, even though his wife, some kind of technical graduate student, didn't just cough and bang the dishes in the kitchen, but openly glared at me. And I remembered her as a small freckled girl with braids wound around her head and a broad gap; her milk teeth had just fallen out. Now those teeth were gold. They didn't just glitter blindingly, but angrily, too. Then her husband openly pulled out a bottle of vodka—not out of any great generosity, but merely to show whose word came last and was decisive in this house. So that's the way it is!

"Go visit Jutoka, if you're that interested. She's heard plenty about you. Though what you'll get out of it... Well, no, I understand, don't get me wrong! Maybe it's tough on you: the number of men she went through! She just teased all of them. What it was like for her parents, for the neighbors... you know, everyone sees everything there."

This plumber was a great moralist, like the majority of not particularly saintly good family men. I didn't say anything more to him, nothing at all...

The plumber described what Juta the Japanese looked like perfectly; Jutoka Japaka was what they called her there. After getting
off the train in the little town, I recognized her immediately. She
was standing in the bookstore wearing a blue jacket, black pants,
and rubber boots, chatting with the storekeeper while I stood a few
feet away, supposedly absorbed in Verba's book of poetry, *Ugnies ūgis*
(The Height of Flames). Flames leapt from the stanzas and curls of
black smoke writhed as Juta told the storekeeper: I don't remember when I fell asleep—I don't even remember whether I undressed
myself or someone else undressed me... ha... I wake up, the windows are open, I'm all by myself!

Who knows whether she really looked all that Japanese? Hair like
a crow's, petite, eyes somewhat slanted. Maybe more like a Kazakh?

I followed her down the little town's main street; she looked
back several times and then stopped next to the pine woods. She
stuffed her hands into her jacket pockets and stood there. I had no
idea what to say to someone like that; I was going to pass by, but she
herself grabbed me by the sleeve. Hey! You're looking for me, aren't
you? Come on, I know *everything*!

Well now. Yet another know-it-all. I had already come across
people like that, know-it-alls. Where? On the road of life, where
else. One scribbler, when he was still drinking pretty heavily, would
sometimes invite me to his pad. Actually, he did all the talking himself, I would just nod. He knew *everything* too, he'd tell me *everything*! Why the salt disappeared. Who killed the film cameraman
in Žirmūnai. How to cure trichomoniasis quickly and effectively.
When the Kremlin would fall, and so forth. The salt, apparently,
was wearing away in a warehouse, and they don't bring any more
from the mine in Wieliczka. The fags killed the cameraman because
he had betrayed their "clan," and the Kremlin will fall only around
2002. He spoke like the chief of a general staff or a long-distance sailing captain. Oh, if only he had written that way!

I secretly hoped that maybe Juta would deny the plumber's words.
Maybe Tūla didn't sleep around with everyone—although did that

matter? She didn't just confirm it; she embellished it with undeniably realistic details. In the beginning, Tūla wandered along the creeks alone... later, she herself had seen when... another time, when she came home unexpectedly... they would both go visit... She was nearly going out of her mind over some mafioso. Well, what of it... small towns, small minds... those who don't go to bed early... And by the way: this Jutoka was Tūla's best friend? But why on earth not?

She made tea, sliced some bread, cut some smoked bacon, and thumped down a bottle: just don't imagine that we're beggars here! She drank and smoked like a real drunk—she kept up with me. Shot for shot, cigarette for cigarette, did I say that correctly? Articulate. She laughed often and for no reason; her teeth were sturdy, white, and beautiful; clearly, she knew it herself. Half Kazakh. From her father's side; her father hung himself to dry on a branch when suffering through a hangover without vodka. A librarian, with an unfinished degree. Like mine, I nodded, unfinished... She went on and on about you, after a while, I told her not to, I got tired of it. So that's what you're like! I put my hands on her hard breasts, but she adroitly slipped away, sat down on the other side of the table, and flashed the whites of her eyes: Got a condom? Well, well, all right, I'll be quiet!

I woke up in the night. No dogs barking, no roosters crowing. Just the Japanese quietly sawing logs next to the wall. Jutoka Japaka. Put my feet down on a cold floor. More to drink would have been great. I cringed: oh, Jutoka turned over, and the entire cottage shook—her little bed was well worn! Hey, I heard you, how come you're not sleeping? Come on over, come on... A cat's voice, as soft as fur. I took her like a soldier on leave; quickly, quietly, with no caresses. She sighed, put her ashtray on my chest, smoked a cigarette. She reeked of vodka.

"I'm moving to Kazakhstan," Jutoka told me. "How many times I kept telling her: Let's both get out of here! I almost had her talked into it... afterwards, you know yourself... Hey! Just don't get the idea that I turned her into a slut... no! She kept asking me to beat off

those suitors of hers, I did the best I could! I loved her, you know? I
hated you, the way she went on about you! She kept babbling about
some steamboat and the Butterflies Cemetery… she was a goose, I'm
telling you straight! She didn't know how to do anything, or how to
have fun either; she bumbled everything. Actually, she was good at
drawing; nothing but crows, what a laugh! How many times I asked
her to draw me! The answer was always no. Listen… could you manage one more time… I just got an itch… huh?"

Later, later, I murmured, tell me some more…

"Oh, so you're nuts, too! Obviously. Maybe the two of you could
have… you're both nuts! What can I tell you? Well, when she first
showed up here, it was awesome! We went everywhere together.
We'd get on the train, get off somewhere in the middle of the woods,
and run around all night! We were friends to the death! Well… then
her mommy started suspecting something, that I was some kind
of… come on, Good Lord, I tell you, there was nothing! Then they
started in with those ads… jokers! Oh, I didn't envy her! You know,
when city folk come crashing out to the sticks for no good reason,
nothing good comes of it!"

Jutoka was a real provincial egghead, maybe in the best sense. She
was on the ball! A lively little speck of Asia in the sands of Bibelarus!

"She should have lived back in the nineteenth century, maybe
then. You think she enjoyed doing it with those hicks? No way! It
was pure lunacy, that's all!"

Jutoka sighed again and glanced at the window. Dawn was breaking.

We had breakfast late. Jutoka decided not to go to her library at
all that day: listen, no one comes there, anyway! Now we're drinking
wine; she ran to the store. "So, do you know where Tūla is buried?"
I finally got out the question I'd come here to ask. She sighed completely differently; the air hissed as it forced its way out of her lungs.

"They did one more stupid idiocy… they buried those ashes in
the woods. Hardly anyone knows where. Well, not far from that little bath house. They put them into this round tin. I got it from the

movie theater operator, and they said: It's an urn! There's no grave-
stone there, nothing; just a rock standing there, so it's next to the
rock…"

"You'll take me there?"

XIV

"My penurious boy, lean on my arm, and I'll pitch you out the window!" That's what a young villain in an old Lithuanian film says to a pale proletariat poet, also young. But he only threatened him; he didn't pitch him. The truck driver, however, really did pitch me out of his cab the moment I admitted I didn't have a cent. It wasn't like that in Ukraine! Well actually, I guess that particularly patriotic ensign I met there behaved the same way, but he had already taken me way beyond Kiev, and besides... I hadn't even mentioned any-thing about freedom to this one—one of my own, a Lithuanian! I must have looked like a wimp; he didn't kick me, or yell at me, he just pushed me out, that's all. I slammed backwards into the soft grass by the side of the road; spitting on my palms, I rubbed my cheek and threw a piece of gravel after him. He couldn't see me anymore, anyway!

Limping, I turned into the depths of a spruce forest, lay down and stuck my backpack under my head. I don't remember when I slept so soundly. Despite that, when I woke up, the early afternoon sun was still shining; thrushes whistled, dragonflies dived in the heat of the sun. It was summer again, the time of lizards and dragonflies.

The asphalt melted in the heat, the air shimmered a cloudy green like the dusty roadside pines.

Would I find the spot? After all, yet another year had gone by since I and Juta the Japanese... Aha! There it is! You couldn't mis-take it—the roadside "rest area," the roof full of holes, the scorched and excessively scrawled-over shelter with scattered warped benches sculpted from old dried-out trees—I'll smoke a cigarette too. The graffiti here is more primitive, but then there's a really aggressive one: "What wasn't done by fascist tanks, will get done by Ūdrija's punks!" War-like Ūdrija! Your sons and daughters have been even here! Well, all right, there isn't time. This is the place, for sure, this is it! I turn into the forest.

I marched down a path through heat-sapped pine woods to Tūla's grave. A single hawk in the sky and perpetually restless jays between the branches. The belly of a pale, dried-up stream flashed by a couple of times now, as it should; I'm going the right way. It was here, it seems, that Jutoka and I sat down to snack and... oh, how long ago that was!

Fly-agarics again, withered russulas with chewed-up edges, white bird's bones in the moss, jays again, and an open space; a bright, desolate place; at another time it would have driven me into real despair. No romance: identical, half-dry little birches, already reddened aspens, low, flat sand dunes, clean and white like at the seaside, a completely thin or sometimes thicker white moss. Lots of moths and butterflies, a mass of tiny insects, maybe even some rare ones. At least the heroes of the stories of Chateaubriand or Tieck would have something to do down by the creek: it's darker there between the spruce, there's more dampness, shadows, whispers, real or imaginary secrets that both loners and murderers like so much. Who killed you, Tūla, who burned you up alive, or maybe already dead? Already dead... for some reason I don't doubt that in the least now, even though it's nothing more than my guess, just a guess and an evil imagination.

I trod the soft, warm, not at all dusty sand of the woods. Round, practically shapeless footprints would remain behind in it; who would give them a thought? There was no reason for me to hide, either; even if I did come across someone, neither they nor I would be surprised, even if it's not the season for picking mushrooms. A man with a backpack on a path through the woods? He's going to some farm, a forest farmstead next to the creek, there's a lot of them around. Or maybe they shot her first? Then burned that bath house and... Whatever happened, her soul still managed to flutter out of her poor body.

Look, look! A small, half-starved dog ran across the path. A dog? A dog, or maybe a raccoon, or a naturalized raccoon dog; wolves are afraid of people now, except maybe for a rabid one.

Now I'm already headed along the creek itself, next to the black alders, the parched junipers setting on berries, the short little pines. A few more bends, the spring, a spruce fallen across the current: everything fits!

There's that rock where Jutoka Japaka brought me last year, there it is! You'd never know, you've never suspect, that next to the rock, a good meter down (a meter and a half at most! Juta assured me), lies a buried movie tin with Tūla's ashes. Maybe fishermen build themselves fires here, hunters? Lay out their jackets, lie down, have a party? And nothing, of course, nothing. The black alders next to the creek rustle; a bit further on there's spruce trees, diving turtle doves, and above the woods the watchful forest cleaners, the vultures, turning in circles. And I should have a bite, too. Have a bite to eat, sip on a little straight vodka, and snooze a bit in the juniper grove, or at least try to... after all, there's work waiting: I'll dig you up, Tūla! Why else did I trek out here, march through the forest? For you! That's why there's a military spade in my backpack; lightweight, comfortable, sharp. Practically new; the green paint on the handle hasn't peeled off yet.

The rowan berries are already turning red. That same carrot and brick color. Carrots pulled out of the root cellar in the spring, bricks dug up after centuries... I'll dig you up and carry you out of this forest, and you thought I'd forgotten you, betrayed you, buried you? No. You're still mine, and now you'll be mine forever more, at least now, when no one needs you anymore, left in the middle of the forest... No one needs to know about it; after all, a lot of people are merely tormented by knowledge, it causes them a lot of terrible troubles. Don't be angry, Tūla, that I'm only just now doing it. I've thought everything through, foreseen everything! Here's the ashes from this crackling little bonfire, mixed with charred bird bones, that I'll sprinkle into that movie tin, and I'll take you out with me— every last little bit! What are those two bags in my backpack for—one of canvas, the other of plastic? You'll fit, Tūla: once more I'll hug you, carefully lift you up on my shoulders, and, via the same path, march back to the highway. You're not heavy anymore now, and you never were; do you remember how I carried you on board the *Tashkent*, onto the only boat we really did sail?

Intruder in the Dust: Faulkner! No, not at all, I'm no intruder, not at all. Remnants of sense, remnants of conscience? Perhaps, perhaps. But just no fulfillment, no relief! But anyway, there's no need to get carried away; I don't need to drink everything I've brought along—I could still need it, oh yes, I could still need it badly! And I did, after all, have some money, an entire red ten-note; I could have paid that driver, but was it the first time I was riding on a thank you? Some whistle, some shrug or spit, others refuse it anyway. That was the first time that's happened… no, never mind! The important thing now is to fall asleep, dig up Tūla after it's already dark, fill up the hole—and along the stream we go; the stream leads straight to the train station. That's all we need, Tūla, we'll return together.

I walked against the weak current a bit, picked out a pretty little meadow right next to the water, took off my shoes and soaked my feet in the water. I sat that way, doing nothing. My head was empty, overheated by the oppressive sun. Like that dog or fox skull, hung by someone high up on a dry spruce branch. Now, I need to nap… how many times can I repeat that and talk myself into it? A grass snake slithered by right next to me, quietly hissing, as if giving warning that someone was approaching. I saw it dive down the bank and swim off, disappear. I took a good pull from the bottle and afterwards didn't know anymore whether I slept or just snoozed, whether I heard or dreamed of people's voices; half asleep, stupefied by the swelter, by the vodka I'd drunk, by the cumulous clouds gathered at the edges of the sky and the monotonously swaying birch fallen into the current. But at last dusk fell; fell and landed. I returned to the rock next to Tūla's grave and pulled out the little spade; the moon glanced through the spruce trees like a comforting light, an entirely different moon than the one over the Butterflies Cemetery.

Digging was easy—even if the dirt had settled, the ground was soft, fine stream-side sand with practically no roots. A little bit of damp gravel; one or two slightly bigger rocks. Completely ordinary night-shift work, for which a premium is paid. It occurred to me that death has no secrets—it knows everything. It's only the living who, later, after death has gone on to reap others, blanket it with secrets and suspicions. I didn't get by cheaply either: a wildly beating heart and a keened sense of hearing, even if it wasn't a treasure I was digging up—just a handful of dust. *Intruder in the Dust!* Alone, at night, secretly…

I was already down past my waist in the hole when the spade finally hit metal—there! That liar Jutoka; they didn't dig a meter and a half deep; I would have been worn out. Barely over a meter. I scrambled out of the pit, stole off under a juniper, and, hiding the glow in my palm, smoked a cigarette. Soon, Tūla, soon, we'll head for home… be patient for a little while yet. I looked about carefully; it would be too bad to be scared off by some brash boar or a moose. No, it's as quiet as a cemetery. *Stille nacht, heilige Nacht!* Even if it's not Christmas. That's it; I stub out the cigarette. Now I need to lift it out—there. The cover's screwed on with pliers, the wire already rusted, snap! Now all that's left is to break the rusty… how's it called, a valve? Maybe valve. Where's my lighter?

A handful of ashes, crumbs, little coals. Tūla! Don't let a single grain of you spill over the sides! You're damp, Tūla, I feel the dampness; all right. A whitish little bone—that goes in the bag, that too! That's the way. That's all, now that's really all of it. I've thoughtfully brought over those other, fake ashes; I pour them into the movie tin, turn, tighten that rusty wire—thwang! Now all that's left is to bury it, and it's no longer you, Tūla, just ordinary ashes from my fire, maybe it wasn't even worth it? They hadn't put in even a token, but I put in a plaque I'd brought along, a copper one. With the words: "Here rests Tūla, God knows her real name."

A bright summer night; by the time I'd tidied everything up, smoothed it out, and tamped down the grave, dawn was already breaking, although it was a long way yet to morning. No, I won't go along the stream, the stream's so winding I don't know when I'd get to the station. Better head back along the same road.

I gave a careful last look around the rock next to the junipers where you had rested, Tūla; of course, a blind man would notice the earth had been disturbed, but what would they care? Fall, winter; in the spring, when the snow melts, even the best tracker wouldn't notice anything. Let's go, Tūla! Sorry, I woke you up... let's go. It's fun walking at night; my feet are rested, the load is light, the road is familiar now. Wet sand sticks to my feet, that's nothing...

Gunshots! Far way, perhaps miles away, but I hear it clearly— gunshots! Do they allow hunting boar in the summer? Perhaps the locals are short of fresh meat? When there's live hams walking through the forest... Boy, they're really pouring it on thick! Is this any of my business? Not mine. Besides, those shots are far away, and there, you can't hear them anymore. Bam—another one! And again. Boar, of course. But hey, that's an automatic! A short burst from an automatic! You can imagine all sorts of things when you're out walking. Remember bygone days; the forest brothers... No, it's not them, of course. But a burst like that makes the knees knock! How are you doing there, Tūla, in the backpack? You're quiet. See! A signal rocket, no less. Green. It's maneuvers. Military exercises. Combat troops positioned in a "forested location" and a special assignment to "penetrate" to the railroad tracks and occupy station N... hold it... hold it until I get there with you?

The more questions, the more answers, going back to the Holocene itself. The glaciers have only just retreated and the question instantly arises: why did it come here? And so on...

There's a familiar clearing already. A bit further is a dense pine

grove, good for a paratrooper to hide in, or maybe to lie in wait inside
a hunter's blind; things are bad only for Mr. Boar. A single rustle and
branches crackling. If you'd walk around more at night, you'd experience more of everything! You'd make countless conclusions that
could come in handy sometime…

"Stop!"

Well now. A Lithuanian *milítsiya* climbed out of that little pine
grove and boldly pointed his barrel at me: Stop! I stop. Two more
climbed out. Aha, there's their jeep over there; it's got a blue vein
through a yellow belly too, you can see it even at night. It's been
parked on the shoulder; there's figures stirring inside as well. The
situation: a *milítsiya* patrol on a forest road at night. Somewhere single
shots are still popping. Varied bursts; they keep getting shorter. Rat-
tat-tat, rat-tat-tat. It's maneuvers? The trio has surrounded me now;
two of them look me over in front, one looms behind my back—
that's particularly unpleasant. Two sergeants. Sturdy, yellow teeth;
I can tell they're yellow even when they're not in moonlight. In the
car, of course, a walkie-talkie. Maybe a radio telephone, too.

"It's some bum!" Sergeant No. 1 turns towards the car. "What
should we do, Captain?"

"Wait!" Apparently, the captain is transmitting or taking tactical
instructions. Ever since the Holocene. The post-ice age man barely
shows up and immediately starts solving tactical problems. There's
only one strategy—to survive! I've got the urge to survive, too. So
little left to the goal. Everything has worked so perfectly; Tūla's in
the backpack, and it's four hours until the train leaves. And there
you have it—a night patrol. Rembrandt's motif; only the spears and
swords are missing. There's a shield and sword on the stripes of the
captain who's come over; aha, see what we're dealing with here! This
is something more serious, much more serious. Where have I seen
him before, that captain?

Since I've run into ordinary *milítsiya* more than once, I behave,
it seems to me, sensibly: I'm not surprised at anything, don't
ask any questions, don't explain anything myself, and—most

importantly—don't get angry at being held. You should never try to dodge bullets; they'll come after you and catch up with you anyway! I see this is irritating them. It would be enough to show the slightest dissatisfaction and then they'd know what to do with me! The captain looks me over very carefully, shines a flashlight right in my eyes, and returns to the car. He's talking with Central. *"Priyem—*Do you read me?!" he shouts, *"Priyem!"* Tat-tat-tat! Rat-tat-tat, rat-tat-tat. Rat-tat-tat. Of course, maneuvers!

The captain approaches again. Shines the light again. Quietly swears to himself. Where have I seen him before?

"So, what are you doing here at night?" he asks. "You were out catching worms. Right?"

A nearly friendly voice. But I tremble—I'm not mistaken? It's a good thing it's still pretty dark. So, where? Where were you? No, probably not even his official fantasy could approach the truth; he's not up to guessing why I'm gallivanting out here. And I'm just itching, itching badly—is he really the same guy? That little head, glued on to the powerful torso, in Tūla's attic in the Second City? I did know who he is, after all, that rescuer of our town's drowning people! It's him, it really is him! Don't tell me he doesn't recognize me? Actually, a lot of summers have passed.

"You live in Vilnius?" he asked almost intimately, using the informal. "Yes?"

"Everywhere a bit." I try to match his tone.

"So, did you dig yourself some worms? You were digging worms?"

Now he's taunting me. Despite it all, taunting me. Probably out of deathly boredom. He didn't get any instructions; it's quiet about, so he taunts me.

"No," I say. "Iron ore. It's not at all deep here!"

The captain laughs. No, he doesn't laugh—he quietly rumbles from inside, as if grunting. Then he gets serious.

"No one's allowed in here now. Maybe you stopped by Šimas? At his farmhouse?"

True. Maestro Šimas has a farmhouse somewhere out here. A mutual acquaintance? Why does he ask? Wants to help me out? After all, it's really easy to find out if I've been there or not!

"I was at Šimas's," I say, "But I didn't find anyone home. We hadn't talked beforehand."

"Yesss... Šimas is in Finland. Men!" The captain unexpectedly shouts and gets up—we'd even sat down, we were smoking. "Men! Take this guy to the station and get back here quick, *yasno*—get it?" Then he turns to me again: "Don't let me see you here again, understand? Or else it won't be just ore I'll knock out of you... too bad... there's no time."

So, in other words, he recognized me. As I did him. That torso with the glued-on head. With shields and swords on his stripes.

They shove me into the car. It's been a long time since I've been in one like that.

"And back here quick!" This to his men again.

As the green train thunders off to the northeast, that long-unseen wordsmith, the author of "Sepijos" and other stories and novels, says to me, "Do you know..." We're sitting across from one another, hands on the table like believers at a pew. Do you know, he says, as if he were a clairvoyant, the king of information, or at the very least the father of nuclear physics, who was out hunting last night in our deep dark forests? He carelessly waves a little manicured hand at the pine woods peacefully flickering outside the window. Then a pause, during which the writer gulps from a flat bottle of good brandy, while I toss off cheap vodka from my flask, the last drop. Then he announces: Two friends! The defense minister and the NKVD chief, you know! The chief, of course, was one of ours, a local, as they say. Well, then! Everything timed to the second, he calmly continues, as if giving a speech at the General staff—but whose? From a personnel airplane to a helicopter, from the helicopter to a car, and—straight to the lion's den. Two hundred trained beaters. Then—kapow! They say the entire forest was surrounded, posts on all the roads... Actually, there were, but I didn't say anything to him. You're quiet, too, Tūla. Quiet inside my backpack. I didn't say anything. He knows everything himself. What kind of country is this, I thought, shut up in the toilet with my backpack on my shoulders and later puffing on a cig in the car's vestibule—what kind of country is this, if even ink slingers know, to a minute's accuracy, the itinerary of birds of that feather!? Maybe someone let him know in advance? Watch, I'll go back to the car, he'll tell me who shot what.

They shot nine boar, he says as soon as I sit down, and deer... they were firing like it was a military exercise! Maybe you heard them?

I heard them, of course I did.

XV

So maybe I should end my notes on Tūla like this? There I go again, past the still-under-restoration Bernardine, through the fallen maple and poplar leaves, along the asphalt and the clinker bricks towards the house with the apse from the Orthodox Church side; I stop by one of the little bridges, lean on the railing, smoke, and gaze at the damp buildings on the other side of the creek: at the long cloister, where my aunt Lydija and my American cousins lived, where, in the fall of 1945, as soon as he returned from the destroyed Reich, my father knocked; I look at the barely standing sheds, at the still open pit with the remains of the water conduit, and I believe I really am tied via visible and invisible connections to that other shore, and to the cloud hanging above the Bekešo tower, and to the ever-expanding burdock plantation. The connection changes, but at the same time grows closer; I don't know how else I could describe it. I know I'll still come here often, that will do. I must admit, reluctantly, that there's a certain amount of mysticism in this attraction, and self-induced fatuity, and maybe even inverted snobbery—you see the kind of person I am. As it is—yes, it's my territory now, marked by a drifter's footsteps, peed over like dogs do trees, confirmed by events, turning points, traumas of the head and feet, blows to the gut and kicks to the ribs. So these notes could be nothing more than a documentary confirmation of my pretensions, even if it has no legal or other power.

Standing, let's say, on the covered bridge, I see a slender dark-haired girl appear out of the brick archway—it's Aurelita Bonopartovna's daughter Ewa Lota; I see *professore* Maryjan trudging along the little footpath right next to the Vilnelė, only even more hunched over, his leather briefcase even more worn. No, Morality Police-woman Lyubov Grazhdanskaya won't show up; she died last year in a mental hospital. There's a lot of people who will never show up here again, even though my two American cousins still have an entirely real possibility of stopping at the gallery and, carefully wiping their feet on the rag laid down at the door, to glance inside... but will they use that possibility? In any case, God help them all! Over there a scorched striped mattress floats by; the current rocks it and spins it around, but still doesn't manage to turn it over—a true water dragon with protruding springs.

Maybe that's how I should end these rather confused notes about my feelings, the cement cloud still flying at me and at us from the Butterflies Cemetery and Bekešo Hill... Maybe?

But no ending is the real ending anyway; not even the last job I've thought up, which I'll take care of today in the evening... first drinking brownish ersatz coffee in the old Institute's corridor next to the Bernardine's refectory, the former one, of course, the former one. A gangly young man and his girl with short-cropped hair remarkably similar to Tūla will be sitting in the perspective of the vault; is that the ending? I'll walk by them with my faded backpack, wearing a green canvas jacket and an exactly matching cap with a peak, and they won't even notice me. It looks like that young man won't turn into an egghead; that girl won't let him, and that's already something.

Well, I'll go now. Past the old oak once honored by our grand-parents, where we'd sat with the *professore* the animalist—or maybe fecalist?—as it got dark on the Night of the Burdocks; slink across the covered bridge to visit the somewhat aged Herbert Stein, the lithographer and adherent of empirical cognition—as always, when he's needed, he's not at home. So I pass through the high arch straight to the real, live, Užupis, and, stopping at the Apotheca, I determine that the demand among the inhabitants of Užupis for *tinctura Valerianae officinalis* hasn't fallen, but grown instead. I buy a couple of little bottles myself too, for dire situations; they don't, unfortunately,

sell more. My pack's roomy; they'll fit, along with the two bottles of
vodka I promised Antoni Kurechko, construction craftsman. I pass
through the low, filthy door into the intoxicant "monopoly"; yes,
there's vodka piled up right to the smoky ceiling, buy as much as
your heart desires! I take three bottles; more and more often I have
money now, and it gives me less and less pleasure—a general rule?

Yes, Antoni Kurechko earned my thanks; he deserves more.
But on the other hand, he won't need to do anything anyway—just
drink vodka, while I... while I lay Tūla's remains to rest. Yes. That's
why! I'll finally get rid of those ashes, which haven't given me peace
for several years now! Now, when a fast, energetic restoration and
a thorough remodeling has begun on the house with the apse, I've
decided to bury her there, as I've wanted to do from the very beginning. Here, in the place where her maidenly cot once emerged from
the shadows under the arch where I'd hang for long nights... yes. In
my pack there's a small urn, soldered shut, with the same inscription left in the forest: "Here lies Tūla, God knows her real name." I
poked around for a long time; I kept looking about, sniffing out how
it would be best to bury her, who I could talk to about it. I singled
out the always phlegmatic and always drunk Antoni Kurechko. They
had torn up the floor; mold, a horrible rot that spared nothing, had
set in. A layer of cement, then linoleum, Antoni explained to me, a
craftsman barely older than I; he was the boss there, I chose well! My
road to Antoni Kurechko's heart was paved with cans of everyone's
favorite, sprats in tomato sauce, and liberally sprinkled with wine;
Calvados, no less. In spite of everything, the Poles are not just religious, not just horribly sentimental, but decent people; without considering it long, Kurechko agreed, even though I only told him half
the truth: "I lived here, you know, a long time; I want to leave a letter
for the descendants." "*Dobrze*—okay!" Kurechko waved it off, "*rób co
chcesz*—do as you please! As long as it's not a bomb! Just remember, I
didn't see or hear anything!" Drinking *Senasis Ąžuolas*—Old Oak—
brandy, Kurechko even approved of my idea to thank my old lodg-
ings, it would be, you know, something like a votive, well, maybe

not entirely, but... I told him about the red brick set in the asphalt across from St. Anne's Church; while filming the flaming gothic there once a film operator fell from a "basket" raised up high and died. Kurechko and I spent many evenings in that same "chamber" where once... no, I've already told everything; I need to do my job and finish these notes, that's enough!

So today there I am. Everything's ready. Kurechko has no idea that under the two black clinker bricks I'll seal an urn with Tūla; why should he know? Knowledge merely makes things difficult. There's mortar prepared at the end of the trough, covered with a film so it wouldn't harden before evening. The pit itself—what pit!—is covered with boards. Kurechko would most likely be shocked, but he has enough worries of his own; when he finishes this "project" he'll get a real apartment himself. The two black clinkers are also lying there well camouflaged; anyone could swipe them. Those two pavers are from Didžioji Street; I didn't neglect to take them home when they tore up the street. You don't even need to have a particularly good imagination: starting in 1938, they've been trampled by thousands of decent people, thousands of indecent ones—children, priests, street women, soldiers, soldiers again, still other soldiers, refugees, returnees... deputies, blacks, celebrities, drifters, beggars, dandies... now they won't be tramping on them anymore! They'll be covered by green or brown linoleum; thick rolls of it are standing over there in the corner already. The clinker brick is a thing that withstands time, nearly forever in this climate. Very strong, resistant to frost: a ceramic tile baked in acid. Three quarters limestone, one quarter clay—that's all.

There, that's everything. Evening, a thaw. March. When I come in, Kurechko stands up, slaps his knees, winks. We drink a mouthful, smoke, talk about events in town. Then he nods: Go on, you can start. There's the urn—a sturdy copper one, not some tin can for film. I know you won't be angry, Tūla. A bare lightbulb glares; Kurechko wasn't stingy, he screwed it in. Then everything went very quickly, or maybe it just seemed that way to me?

I dribble some cement into that little pit in the floor, carefully press the urn into the still wet mush, cover it with a paver... This is the hardest part; the paver has to lie next to the floor so evenly it won't trip anyone up, in either the literal or figurative sense. I had already attempted this operation, just without the urn and the cement. Now then! Expertly! That's all. Now that really is all of it! Amen. Rest, Tūla. *Requiscant.*

Kurechko ostensibly pages through a newspaper. *Życie Warszawy* or *Czerwony Sztandar?* Same difference. From a distance I see Chernenko's head outlined in a black frame. Let the dead bury their dead... their own corpses...

"You see," says Antoni Kurechko, pleased, "you're fast! You could work for us!" He stands on the clinker bricks, stands up on you, Tūla, stands in the same place where we... where your low cot cooled, the dim lamp hanging on the wall shone, and under the vault, lying on our stomachs, we paged through that tattered album of reproductions and giggled and giggled over that picture—a man in a red shirt with an accordion sits in a square, and a buxom beauty cuddles next to him...

"You've thought this out carefully," Kurechko, already stewed, shakes his head, "yes, carefully! But for what?"

Was it really carefully done? If only that black clinker doesn't trip anyone up, if only that cement would dry as quickly as possible! Maybe some bigwig will order it torn out? No, not likely, thank God; they're not preparing this apartment for some art commissar, this is for students, a studio. And a small black secret wouldn't bother people of an artistic nature, more likely just the opposite; maybe they'll puzzle over it, shrug their shoulders, and in the long run get used to it and no longer pay attention to that black patch on the floor. Yes, it would be better to not even cover it with linoleum. On the other hand...

Bam! The big bulb burned out. And suddenly I heard—something flew by, brushing me with its wings; flew by and touched my feverish forehead; I clearly felt the brushing of a wing. Maybe some electric charge? No, that can't be. No, of course not. There, now it's light again. Aha, then where was it I stopped? They'll get used to it and no longer pay any attention to those two tiles? That would be best. But then others will show up. Or the time will come to change the linoleum. Well, I'll be wandering by often...

I shake the senior craftsman's hand, wish him good luck. And via the cement bridge, the ordinary one, I head for Old Town. Water trickled from the roofs, and above my head a bat flashed by. A real, true one...

1991

Notes on the translation

As the reader will readily observe, Vilnius is truly a salad of nationalities. Walking down Gedimino Prospect today, a visitor can expect to overhear more languages than perhaps even the narrator in *Tūla* did. And the narrator, our guide to the city, loves languages, pulling words and phrases from Italian, Latin, and German as well as Polish, Belarussian, and Ukrainian, along with the Russian that is so much part of his experience. Where the meaning is not obvious from the context, the translation follows immediately, usually set off with *brūksnai*—dashes.

Personal names in the narrative present a problem that requires explanation. Lithuanian publishing of the Soviet time period and afterward conformed to the same principle as those larger, far more dominant languages, Russian and English, and spelled all foreign names according to its own alphabet. In addition to assisting in the reader's pronunciation, it is also necessary for Lithuania's complex inflectional system. However, Lithuanian readers would instantly recognize, despite the Lithuanian spelling, which names were Russian, German, Polish, Jewish, etc. To provide the English reader with an equivalent experience, non-Lithuanian names are spelled according to contemporary standards, i.e., as close to the spelling and alphabet of the original language as possible. By this rule, Hansas becomes Hans, Bžostovska becomes Brzostowska, Herbertas Šteinas becomes Herbert Stein, etc. But the Lithuanian names are spelled in Lithuanian, even if the playful "von" the narrator inserts into his fellow German student Teodoras Četras's name remains.

Russian, Belarussian, and Ukrainian in the text compromise an exception, as one cannot reasonable expect an English reader to make sense of the Cyrillic alphabet. Transliterations are made using a simplified version of the BGN/PCCN system, excepting those names or words that already have an accepted English spelling. Place names present another set of challenges, not the least that any given geographic feature in the area been christened many times, depending on the political and cultural winds. At the time Jurgis Kunčinas published this novel in 1993, many streets had been renamed from their Soviet incarnations, but he uses names appropriate to their time period, which explains how Maksimo Gorkio Street (now Pilies Street) got in there. For geographic features, the Lithuanian names (Vilnius, not Vilna or Wilno) are used, and if necessary, the features' translation appear (*Polocko gatvė,* literally "Polockas's street," becomes Polocko Street). Since these are the current official names, readers who wish to take a tour of the city, whether virtually or in reality, will find these spellings useful.

Lithuanian spices the translated text in a number of other place names, but there are exceptions. When a place name was obviously of Kunčinas's creation and the name had some metaphorical or narrative meaning, the Lithuanian name comes first, and then a translation; further on, only the translation is used. A notable example of this is *Drugelių kapai*—The Butterflies' Cemetery, the narrator's fanciful end of the road (which may also refer to a long-vanished Jewish cemetery); another is Pagudė, "by the border of Belarus," where Tūla is exiled, which I have translated as Bibelarus. A different exception is made for locations that are well-known tourist destinations, such as *Aušros vartai,* which commonly goes by its translation, the Gates of Dawn. You'll find it easier that way.

Ellipses are used a great deal in literary Lithuanian to express what might be called a mental pause. Because the English reader would find these ellipses intrusive in a way the Lithuanian reader would not, they were mercilessly pruned in translation. But then... the narrator's flights of literary fancy begged a poet's liberty, and mercy was granted: some of those naughty, non-standard things remain.

As always, this translation owes many, many thanks to those who read over early drafts and patiently pointed out at least some of the inevitable problems, missed subtleties, and typos in the text, most especially Violeta Kelertas and Loreta Mačianskaitė, but not forgetting Laimonas Briedis, Dalia Cidzikaitė, Rasa Kunčinienė, Aida Novickas, and Aurelia Tamosiūnaitė.